THE
KOREAN
WOMAN

JOHN ALTMAN

THE KOREAN WOMAN

BLACK
STONE
PUBLISHING

Printed in the United States of America

First edition: 2019
ISBN 978-1-4708-2697-0
Fiction / Thrillers / Suspense

1 3 5 7 9 10 8 6 4 2

CIP data for this book is available
from the Library of Congress

Blackstone Publishing
31 Mistletoe Rd.
Ashland, OR 97520

www.BlackstonePublishing.com

For Danny

Only after having acknowledged sins and reflected deeply upon them can a prisoner begin anew.

—Ninth law of the *kwan-li-so*,
North Korean prison camp system

PROLOGUE

The river was a smooth black mirror. She gathered her courage and stepped off the bank, rippling the surface. Icy water filled her sneakers. She moved forward. The water soaked the cuffs of her dungarees and rose up her calves. She paused to look back. She could just make out the low white retaining wall on the embankment. Beyond it lay a cornfield, a dirt road, a mountain.

She advanced again. Each step sent undulating circles through the faint reflections of stars. Freezing water climbed to her knees, her thighs, her sex. Her waist, her solar plexus. For a moment, halfway across, she felt herself floating. Her toes quested, found the bottom again.

She pushed ahead. Water reached her breastbone. She drew a deep breath and kept going.

Abruptly, the water level began to drop. To waist, knees, ankles …

And she was across.

She slogged onto the bank, hugging her elbows, shivering violently.

After a few seconds she shucked off the backpack. Inside, the *yukpo,* the beef jerky, tightly wrapped in plastic film, was fine. The phone and documents were safe and dry in their cases. But the carton of Jangbaeksan cigarettes had gotten damp. She could only hope the tobacco …

Her ears registered a soft sound in the long grass, not far away.

In a heartbeat, she was crouched. Flooded with bad *nunji,* bad intuition.

Something whisked closer. She could not distinguish where the sound was coming from. Silently she drew the knife. Her eyes raked the night. No moon—only stars. Tall grass bowing in a weak breeze. A guard tower rose in stark silhouette a hundred yards up the bank. Another rose a hundred yards down. She had chosen the point midway between to cross.

Her entire body was tingling. She had killed before, but never with a knife. Never like butchering an animal. She breathed. *Cha-ma.* Calm down. Lose her nerve now, and she would lose everything.

The man appeared from nowhere. He seemed five feet wide and ten feet tall. She sensed more than saw the automatic rifle in his hands.

But he had not yet found her in the darkness. He was looking past her, toward the sound of moving water, his chin slightly raised.

She rose smoothly out of the crouch, closing the distance between them in a single loping step, and angled the blade into the costal cartilage of the second rib—perfect.

She twisted the knife.

A suspended moment; then he fell heavily, jerking the haft from her grip.

She knelt beside him. He was about her age. He had a broad forehead and a thick jaw. He smelled of *soju,* rice liquor. His eyes were half open, mottled with broken blood vessels. Somebody's son. Maybe a husband, a father.

Though he was already dead, she held two fingers against the hollow of his throat to make sure.

It had not been so bad. No worse, really, than killing with VX.

For a moment more, she regarded the man dully. Then she stood, and her knees gave two flat pops. She found the backpack.

She moved away swiftly, without looking back, deeper into the moonless night.

SEVEN YEARS LATER

PART ONE

CHAPTER ONE

PRINCETON, NJ

Dalia Artzi gripped the lectern with both hands, scanning the faces inside the amphitheater.

Last day of May, last minutes of the last lecture of the semester. The *shayffellah,* little sheep, looked dreamy and distant. Mellow sunshine fell across laptops and smartphones and, spread open before one die-hard Luddite, an old-fashioned college-ruled paper notebook.

"If you take just one thing from my class, let it be this." Her accented English rang decisively off the hall's coffered ceiling. "We study war only to better enable ourselves to prevent it. As the incomparable Margaret Atwood said, 'War is what happens when language fails.'"

A young woman in the front row—curly dark hair, sleepy brown eyes—yawned.

Dalia rapped the lectern hard enough to make the gooseneck microphone whine. "Hear what I say. After today, we part ways. But it is people like you—young, American, educated, connected—who will determine the future. Not only your own futures, but those of your children and grandchildren. And of mine in Tel Aviv. And of others yet to be born, in Berlin and Beijing, in Seoul and São Paulo and Saint Petersburg. All our fates are entwined. But looking across this auditorium today, I must report, I do not feel optimistic."

Blank stares. Their complacency was impenetrable. After an entire semester, she was still just an old lady with a funny accent and a cane.

She uncapped a bottle of water, sipped, and tried again. "During the past months, we've discussed the battles of Agincourt, Waterloo, and the Somme. All involved British soldiers. All took place on roughly the same patch of land. But in 1415 at Agincourt, ten thousand men perished. Four centuries later at Waterloo, casualties numbered sixty-five thousand. And at the Somme, just a century after that, over a million were killed or wounded. Since then, Oppenheimer has invented his deadly toy, and Teller and Ulam have perfected it. What might the next war bring?"

Outside, a distant church bell clanged the hour. Students spilled from nearby lecture halls, laughing and chatting. But for a last moment, Dalia held the students with her gaze, loath to relinquish them.

Abruptly, the tension left her stance and she sagged over the podium. *Mit shnei ken men nit makhn gomolkhes,* her mother had said. You can't make cheesecakes out of snow.

"Exams next week. Contact your precept leader with any questions." She dismissed them with a wave, then added as an afterthought, "Enjoy your summers."

Amid the shuffling of backpacks and clearing of throats she pushed her notes into her shoulder bag and grabbed the cane she had propped against the lectern. Making a fast escape through the side door took some doing, but she managed, even with the bad knee.

A few heartbeats later, she was circling behind the ivied walls of the lecture hall. Moving with a staccato rhythm, cane and bad leg in unison, she hastened toward her teatime appointment. Past ramparts and Gothic towers, ribbed vaults and flying buttresses, all lit by soft gilt sun. Sparrows chirped and squabbled alongside chattering undergrads. The good green beauty of the campus surrounded her; nevertheless, Dalia thought wistfully of home, of sweetly mingled desert sage and *za'atar,* honeysuckle and terebinth and flowering campion.

Nearing FitzRandolph Gate, she turned onto a wooded byway. A Tudor arch sheltered an oak door. Inside, wall sconces lit a cool, dim stone passage. A dozen cane thumps later she stood in a parlor featuring mounted heads of kudu and elk and aoudad, a faded Anatolian carpet, and a half circle of burgundy club chairs before a fireplace.

Jim McConnell was reading something on his phone. At Dalia's entrance he held up one index finger. She took a seat opposite him, leaning her cane against an armrest. Somewhere outside, two students snickered. Through a mullioned window she glimpsed a Frisbee arcing above a stone rampart.

McConnell took his time reading the message then slipped the phone deliberately into a pocket. At last he looked up, offering a mild half smile. He wore smudged bifocals and a sweater vest—a Beltway insider's idea of academic attire. "Tea?" he asked.

"Actually," she said, "I'm in a bit of a rush."

His brow lifted. "Last day of classes, isn't it?"

"Which means the real work can begin. I'm writing a monograph this summer on the Battle of Issus."

Opening her bag, she burrowed past crumpled lecture notes and took out a lined tablet. "Don't shoot the messenger." On an inlaid loo table between them, she riffled through to the map she had worked up last night. "We knew our Russian forces would reach Estonia and Latvia quickly, but I didn't realize *how* quickly. In my reckoning, the drive to the NATO capitals takes just thirty-six hours. We've got five hundred T-14 Armatas fighting against essentially unarmored foot soldiers with peashooters. We're looking at more fatalities in one and a half days than in nearly two decades of Iraq and Afghanistan engagements combined. More aircraft lost than in every US engagement since Vietnam put together. But there's good news. Such a rapid advance leaves the Kremlin fatally overextended. A mobile force roaming the front, coupled with surgical strikes on supply lines, will quickly drive this point home."

McConnell leaned close over the map, scowling through his bifocals. Dalia could guess his thoughts. Bharadwaj, looking at the same scenario, had no doubt advised frontal resistance. As a rule, Bharadwaj preferred brute force. The man would play a dulcimer with a sledgehammer. Yet CENTCOM loved him, because he justified their juicy budget.

McConnell stroked his second chin pensively. "I'll send it up the chain." He leaned back. She knew that brooding look. "Something else I'd like you to take a look at, Dalia. Not a simulation. A developing situation. Of course, I appreciate how busy you are, but once you see what's going on, I have a feeling you'll want to help out."

"I hate to disappoint you. But Issus awaits."

"Issus has waited two millennia. Surely it can wait another day or two while you help us put out some sparks in the greatest geopolitical tinderbox of our time."

Finding the cane, she stood. "Enjoy your summer, Jim."

"Think it over, Dalia." Behind the smudged lenses, his green eyes flashed. "You know how you're always talking about all our fates being entwined? Well, it's true. You know how to reach me."

MANHATTAN, NY

Song was rereading the message when the baby cried.

Shaken, she started back at the beginning. The message was in Munhwaŏ, the DPRK standard version of the Korean language. It identified a man named William Walsh, and his wont to seek female company on weekend nights in downtown Manhattan. Also, his type: pretty young Asian women. And his usual haunts: a downtown bar called Six Degrees and another called Attaboy. Then the address of a storage facility on Thirty-Seventh Street, the number and combination of a locker, and detailed directions on how to use the equipment inside. She was to gain access to Walsh's

Liberty Plaza apartment, find his NYMEX pass card, and clone the data thereon. Then await further instructions, which would detail delivery to a yet-unnamed contact.

A photograph was attached. She opened it. Her brow crimped as she absorbed William Walsh's angular face. Judging from the graininess, the image had been captured with a telephoto lens.

The baby cried again. Song's lips pressed into a line. She turned off the phone and took out the battery. She returned both to the drawer, burying them beneath miscellaneous clutter—paper clips, lip balm, ibuprofen, travel lotion, sticky notes.

A framed photograph atop the desk caught her eye. The picture was from three summers ago, at Martha's Vineyard. She looked young and fresh and innocent, her yellow sundress belling in a breeze. Mark stood beside her, tall and suntanned and grinning, one arm hooked proprietarily around her shoulders. Shards of hard sunlight glinted off the water behind them.

The baby's cry took on an edge. Song turned away from the picture and left the study.

Baby Jia was standing in her crib, ringlets of dark hair in a wild pouf. "Hel-lo ba-by," Song chanted as she entered the nursery. "Good dreams?"

"Good dreams," the little girl echoed.

Song sniffed. "Poopy diaper?"

"Poopy," Baby Jia affirmed.

In the kitchen, Jia, freshly changed and strapped into her high chair, tracked her mother's movements with a philosophical gaze. She had Song's big, dark eyes, Mark's aristocratic nose, and a tiny Cupid's-bow mouth uniquely her own. Their son, Dexter, had it reversed: Mark's small bright eyes, Song's pert nose, and his own wide, expressive lips.

Song put grapes, crackers, and string cheese on a plastic plate. "Cheese," Jia said approvingly and had at it.

Song watched with her forearms crossed, hands cupping elbows. Her eyes closed. A buried memory stirred for the first time in years. The man she had killed by the river: broad forehead, mottled red eyes. Her twisting the blade. The suspended moment before he fell.

"Mommy sad," Jia observed around a mouthful of cheese.

Song opened her eyes. She found a smile. "Mommy's fine."

*　　*　　*

Dishes, another diaper change, a load of laundry started, straps on the car seat, crosstown traffic, and she reached the pickup line at her son's kindergarten only five minutes late.

Dexter piled in, throwing his backpack onto the Volvo's floor. "Can Dylan come over for a playdate?"

"I'll ask his mom."

"Dexter," Jia said happily.

Dexter ignored his sister and put on his seat belt. Song waved to a teacher she recognized, glanced in the rearview, and pulled out from the line. "How was school, Dex?"

"We had cupcakes," he said absently. "It was Ethan's birthday."

"Yummy?"

"Super yummy. Can Dylan come over for a playdate?"

"I said I'll ask his mom."

"When?"

"How about when I'm not driving?"

"When can I have a phone?" The question came at least once a day.

"When you're fourteen, we'll discuss it."—the standard answer.

She looped around the block, heading back toward the park. Jia babbled contentedly: "Dexter, Hexter, Bexter, Lexter, Fexter, Dexter. Good!"

Back home, Song set Jia on the living room floor in front of a screen, then ran water and got her son settled in his bath. She answered two emails from Jackie McNamara, head of the PTA, about a food drive she had agreed to help organize. She texted Dylan's mother about a playdate, transferred laundry to the dryer, cubed three chicken breasts and started them marinating in organic teriyaki sauce.

She toweled Dexter off and helped him dress. She filled a diaper bag with water, wipes, and snacks. She went into the master bathroom. Her period was almost over. She unwrapped a new Tampax Radiant, just to be safe. As she did, she found another buried memory. Evidently, the message from home had dislodged them. During her girlhood in Chongjin, there had been no sanitary napkins and no heat. She had known when her mother was menstruating, because bloody frozen rags hung from the shower rod in the bathroom.

In the front hall she put the diaper bag in one end of a plastic wagon and strapped baby Jia in the other. She slathered sunscreen onto both kids, using the extra on her own forearms. She took Dexter's hand, and they trundled to the elevator. They rode down with Mrs. Jackson and her toy poodle, Murray. "Doggy!" Jia said breathlessly. "Doggy! Doggy! Doggy! Doggy!"

At the playground, Dexter and Jia made for the swings at a full run. Song spied Nina Brooks sitting on a bench, doing something on her phone, and fell down heavily beside her.

"Fucking Jackie McNamara," Nina said by way of greeting, and pressed SEND.

"Food drive?"

"Penny social next fall." Nina wore a vintage powder-blue top and a silk scarf tied over her light-blond hair. In a former life, she had studied fashion at Pratt. "I'm going to Southampton on Monday, but Jackie's got me running all over town to look at venues this weekend. How are *you*, sunshine?"

"Lollipops and rainbows. Every day and every night."

Dexter and Jia were screaming.

"MOMMY! JIA'S NOT LETTING ME PLAY WITH MY ROCK!"

"THEN FIND A DIFFERENT ROCK!" Song shouted back.

"BUT IT WAS *MY* ROCK!"

"THERE ARE ROCKS EVERYWHERE, DEXTER!"

"BUT IT WAS MY ROCK!"

Jia, rock in hand, moved off toward a different bench. Dexter started crying. When his mother didn't react he sniffled, wiped his eyes, and went back to the swings.

The breeze was soft and fragrant with flowers. Jia climbed up a slide the wrong way. Nina's daughter skinned a knee and accepted a kiss from her mother. Louise Antrobas, who looked after Barb Goldman's kids, joined them and told a story about a local real estate agent who poached clients by crashing showings and claiming she smelled mold. Song gave her kids a five-minute warning.

Back home, she started preheating the broiler. Both kids went before the TV screen. The PAW Patrol helped a nest of baby sea turtles reach the ocean. Chase was on the case.

Song removed marinated chicken from the fridge. Threading the chunks of meat onto skewers, she found yet another unearthed memory. An old woman in Chongjin had proclaimed, with a certain dark glee, that the gray chunks of meat sold behind the railroad station were, in fact, the flesh of *kochebi,* orphaned children. You would never know, the woman insisted, that you were eating human flesh. It tasted just like pork. That glided into a memory of the *yukpo,* the beef jerky that Song had carried across the Tumen River. Two days after crossing, she had traded it to a farmer for a ride in his rickety K01 pickup truck.

She put water on to boil. As she was measuring rice, the latch on the front door worked. Jia burst out of the living room. "Daddy! Daddy! Daddy!"

Mark set down his calfskin bag and scooped up his daughter. He was lightly suntanned, as usual during warm weather, and glowing with good health, his tie jauntily askew. "Oof!" he said.

He came into the kitchen, holding Baby Jia. He kissed Song's lips, copping a squeeze of her left buttock with his free hand. Then Dexter came flying out of the living room. "Daddydaddydaddydaddydaddy!"

"Oof again!" Mark managed to heft the boy up beside the girl. "My poor back!"

"Oof again!" Jia mimicked joyfully. "Oof again!"

A sizzling came from the stove, and Song rushed to take the frothing pot off the burner.

PRINCETON, NJ

The rearmost guard of dense Macedonian ranks could not, standing shoulder-to-shoulder behind eight armored men—a ringtone made Dalia pause for a beat; then she finished typing the sentence—*have actively attacked as spearmen.*

She answered the call. "*Ma nishma?*"

"Say 'happy birthday'!"

Small voices chorused, "Happy birthday, Grandma!"

"We love you, Savta Dalia!"

Dalia smiled. "I love you, too, my little *kätzchen.*"

In the background, a cartoon blasted in Hebrew: "*I earned the Iron Fist! I use it to the best of my ability. I honor that power through my actions …*" The sound faded as Dalia's son moved into a quieter room. "You're home? Thought maybe you'd be out celebrating."

She looked at the mug of Moroccan chamomile beside her laptop. "No, a quiet night in."

"Did you get the scarf we sent? Udi picked it out himself."

"Give him a big kiss for me. Tell him he has good taste."

"Raya's on the night shift, but she sends her love."

"Send mine back, please."

"She's worked every night this week. She keeps saying the schedule will change, but it never does." He paused. "We miss you, Mom."

"I miss you too, *neshama.*"

"I hope your birthday wasn't all work."

"I … met with a friend."

A brief silence ensued. Birds convened noisily outside Dalia's study window, then fell quiet.

"Mom, I hate to run, but I kept the kids up late so they could talk to you. It's way past their bedtime. I just wanted to say happy birthday."

"Thank you for calling, Zvi."

"Enjoy your evening. Talk soon."

"Talk soon."

Dalia set the phone down slowly. She checked to make sure she had not missed a call from her daughter. Well, a few hours of birthday still remained.

After a moment, giving her head a small shake, she bent again to her work.

The primary role of the rear guard in phalanx warfare was to keep its fellows from fleeing. Such has been the true purpose of all rear guards throughout history: bolstering the will to combat, smothering the instinct for self-preservation, driving yet another generation into the breach.

As Jim McConnell was always trying to do with her. He fought to keep her in the present, in the fray, despite her natural inclination to flee into books, into the past. But the terms of their deal had been satisfied. The Kremlin-NATO scenario had been her last.

Once you see what's going on, I have a feeling you'll want to help out …

A coxswain counted strokes right outside her window—the lake's surface carried the sound with eerie clarity.

All our fates are entwined, she taught her students.

It was truer today than ever before. And Dalia Artzi—a *sabra,* one of the first generation born in Israel—knew better than anyone the price of isolationism.

But she had done her part. She had earned her books and her solitude. The military-industrial meat grinder would grind along just fine without her.

She focused. *Champing at the bit to engage Darius, Alexander made a rare miscalculation. Moving southward, he left his lines vulnerable. Coming up behind, Darius sat across those lines.*

Thus, the Macedonians were given a simple choice: turn and fight, or starve. But the young king brilliantly regained the initiative, snatching victory from a force more than twice the size of his own. He countermarched, engaging Darius on a narrow coastal plain where the Persians could not make use of their superior numbers. Alexander then mounted his horse and, with a brazen direct charge, drove Darius from the battlefield in panicked disarray.

The lesson of Issus, she told her classes: timing and maneuverability trumped brute force. This, too, was truer today than ever before. It was the small mobile squad—the OPSEC team, the lone wolf—that had enabled 9/11. And that would likely enable, in the not-too-distant future, nuclear, radiological, chemical, and biological catastrophes. Against a small, resolute, and unpredictable rogue player with nuclear or biological capability, all the bombers and land assault vehicles in the world made little difference. Fortress America was, in reality, a house of cards.

And Israel, home to Dalia's children and grandchildren, was even more vulnerable.

She rubbed at the loose skin around her eyes. The rowing crew was gone. The birds were gone. The study was silent.

She picked up her tea. It had gone cold.

She sighed, then set down the mug and reached for the phone.

CHAPTER TWO

NEW CIA HEADQUARTERS BUILDING, LANGLEY, VA

Beyond the double-paned windows, daylight was quickly failing.

A more observant Jew would now be lighting candles, honoring the Sabbath by abstaining from work. Dalia Artzi, however, was getting down to business.

The officer in charge—fortyish, fair, poised, in a blue twill suit that offset somber blue-gray eyes—had introduced himself as Benjamin Bach. "I'll be honest, Professor. You're here because Jim felt you should be here." Bach's voice was pitched low, inviting attention instead of commanding it. "He considers you the greatest strategic thinker since John Boyd. And I admit, he can be convincing. But left to my own devices, I would not choose to include a foreign national, whatever her security clearance."

The four other men seated around the table made no comment. One was Jim McConnell. To his left was Shyam Radha—"call me Sam"—from the CIA's Computer Ops Division (COD), known to one and all as "Codpieces." Third was Sonny Romano, from Science and Technology, the gadget shop. Fleshy and sensual, he wore his blond hair cut just long enough to lie flat against his scalp. The last, seated between Bach and McConnell, was Charlie

DeArmond, broad-shouldered with a chevron mustache, from the FBI's Directorate of Intelligence.

Bach swiveled around in his chair to face a wall-mounted monitor. That was Sonny's cue to draw the shades on the secure room and Sam's to chew on one thumb and bend over his laptop. The official CIA seal, eagle astride a compass rose, appeared on-screen, followed by "TOP SECRET, CLASSIFICATION K." Author attribution had been redacted.

The name file concerned one Song Sun Young. Affiliation was RGB, Reconnaissance General Bureau, the North Korean foreign intelligence apparatus.

A surveillance photograph showed a crowded subway platform. A woman with the brim of a baseball cap pulled low had been circled in red. She was East Asian, in her early twenties, with fine, ardent features and shoulder-length black hair. A *shana maidel,* Dalia's mother would have said. Pretty girl.

"Meet Song Sun Young, a.k.a. Park Ha-Soo, a.k.a. Mi-Hi Pyung, a.k.a. Mi-Hi Abrahams. This photo, coming to us courtesy of South Korea's National Intelligence Service, is eight years old." Bach gestured to Sam without turning. "If you want to see what she looks like today …"

Another window opened, time coded just five hours ago. In buttery late afternoon sunlight, a woman on a city street corner had been photographed from above. She held a small boy's hand and towed a toddler in a plastic wagon. Sam zoomed and enhanced. The black hair was cut shorter, the fine features carved in sharper relief. Enough of her T-shirt's legend was visible to suggest the rest: "California Dreaming."

Sam's mouse clicked. The first window scrolled to the cover of an official DPRK Workers' Party Politburo folder: blue sleeve, red tab, slightly lopsided and blurry from a hasty scan. "The woman's *songbun* file," Bach said.

Dalia blinked. She had never seen an actual *songbun* file before. According to Pyongyang, the dossiers did not exist. But according to defectors and moles, every citizen of the DPRK was born with a rating that determined where they could live, and thus the quality of soil they were given to work; access to food, education, employment, and membership in the Party—their *songbun.* The highest rating, "core," included the ruling elite, called *yangban,* and their peers. "Wavering," or neutral, citizens made up fully half the population. "Hostile" citizens included criminals, prostitutes, foreign collaborators, citizens of mixed blood, landlords, merchants, Christian ministers, fortune-tellers, shamans, and descendants thereof.

"Where did you get this?" Dalia asked.

"Straight from the horse's mouth. We hacked the primary RGB server almost two years ago."

The text was in Munhwaŏ. Translation and editorial remarks had been added by the CIA. Sam clicked through slowly enough that Dalia could keep up.

Song Sun Young had been born with a *songbun* rating of "hostile." The poor score was a result of her father, Song Jun Ran, getting into trouble with the Public Standards Police. A remark in the margins explained that *beulsun,* tainted blood, was a common enough albatross inside the DPRK. *Enemies of class,* Kim Il Sung had decreed in 1972, *whoever they are, their seed must be eliminated through three generations.* The policy rewarded good behavior; troublemakers saw not only themselves but also their parents, children, grandparents, and grandchildren suffer the regime's wrath. Officially, the elder Song's crime had been failure to properly maintain his portraits of Kim Il Sung and Kim Jong Il. In reality, the nameless analyst suggested, he had probably gotten on the wrong side of some government apparatchik or someone in his *inminban,* the neighborhood watchdog group.

Song Jun Ran had died two years after his daughter's birth. The official cause of death had been a heart attack. But the death had come during the most severe period of the 1994–98 famine known as the Arduous March. During this period, the analyst observed, DPRK hospitals had been forbidden to report starvation as a causal agency.

Song Sun Young and a younger brother had then been raised by their mother, a kindergarten teacher in the factory town of Chongjin. When Song was eight years old, the mother was arrested by the Electric Wave Inspection Bureau. Apparently, she had used a sewing needle to bypass preset government-approved stations on her TV.

In the Hermit Kingdom, guilt by association was not only legal but mandatory. The younger Songs had been sent with their mother to Camp 15, a.k.a. Yodok, the so-called family prison.

The next year, the mother had died. Again the official cause of death was heart attack. But diphtheria and whooping cough, the analyst noted, had sent thousands into Yodok's mass grave.

At age ten, Song and her brother had escaped the camp. An accomplice's corpse had been found wedged in the electric fence. The weight of the body had sagged the lowest strand of wire down to the frozen ground, conducting enough current into the earth that Song and her brother could scamper to freedom using the corpse as a bridge. By the time the body was found, it had burned to a crisp, preventing authorities from determining whether the incident was premeditated—the accomplice betrayed and murdered—or altruistic suicide, or simply opportunistic.

The guard deemed responsible had been executed. Song and her brother had been arrested again in Chongjin the following year. The punishment for prison escape was death. But for whatever reason—their tender ages, the whims of a capricious system—they had been spared. Back into the *kwan-li-so* system they went, this time to Camp 14.

And again they escaped, just two months later, climbing into the bottom of a coal train, burying themselves beneath the cargo, risking suffocation but ultimately surviving.

At this point, the CIA analyst speculated, the Party bosses in Pyongyang realized they had a couple of extraordinary specimens on their hands. Song Sun Young and her brother, Song Man Soo, had escaped two high-security prisons while still children. *Juche,* the official state ideology of North Korea, expressed that the individual was "master of his destiny." The closest English translation was "self-reliance." Clearly, Song Sun Young and Song Man Soo had *juche* in spades.

Thus, the siblings managed that most difficult of tricks, increasing their *songbun* rating from the lowest, "hostile," to the highest, "core." That they managed it while still fugitives, via the criminal conduct of repeated prison escapes, was an irony, the analyst noted dryly, truly worthy of North Korea.

Three years after the second escape, they had been recaptured again in Chongjin.

Here the *songbun* file ended. The girl's story was picked up by an RGB dossier, similarly translated and annotated.

"Interviews"—Dalia wondered at the euphemism—had determined that Song Sun Young was the leader between the two. She had been sent to a training camp on Paektu Mountain, considered by Korean mythology to be the place of ancestral origin. Here, on the banks of Heaven Lake, she had joined an operation code-named (after the roaming police units that patrolled the streets), Kyuch'Aldae. Her younger brother had gone to Pyongyang as a guest of the regime. Dalia read between the lines. In the event that Song Sun Young betrayed her masters once she got beyond their reach in the field, she did so knowing who would bear the cost of her insubordination.

For five years, Song had been trained, reeducated, refitted from the inside out. Details had been dutifully recorded. The RGB agent doing the reporting used a tone of awed admiration as he was pleasurably stunned again and again by the intelligence and thoroughness of his own great agency.

Song had grown out her hair, putting flesh onto her bones with rice and meat—slowly, shrewdly, so that her stomach would not reject the nourishment to which it was so profoundly unaccustomed. She had undergone extensive dental work. She had received double eyelid surgery, a common gift for high school graduates in the ROK, from which she would pretend to hail. She had learned English and the Gyeonggi dialect of Seoul, and Konglish, the commonly spoken pidgin that was a hybrid of the two.

She had watched Hollywood movies and South Korean TV, listened to K-pop and American top forty, read *Cosmopolitan* and *Wink* magazines, and browsed the internet, venturing well beyond the usual restrictions imposed by Pyongyang. She had learned from kidnapped South Korean tutors the finer points of manners: to clap in the South Korean style, hands vertical, instead of with one hand atop the other, as they did in the north. She had learned to sing with South Korean vibrato, wearing a South Korean facial expression—considerably less dramatic than that of the north. She had learned to dance with less grace, with more boldness and energy. She had learned to accept a man's proffered hand without flinching. In South Korea, couplehood was highly prized and dating was everywhere. In the north, no dating culture existed, and marriages were usually arranged, often by Party secretaries. Public displays of affection, including hand-holding, were scandalous. Not so in the south.

And at the end of every month, for five years, she had taken a polygraph test to gauge her developing loyalty. Usually, only people personally connected to the Kim family were trusted to undertake overseas missions. But the girl's exceptional *juche* had made her a rare exception. Still, the powers that be were taking no chances.

She had come to see, according to the report, how Chosun's brave leaders had stood alone in the world against American imperialism, tyranny, and hypocrisy. She now realized that she and her mother had, through their disobedience, done their great nation no worthy service. She had been grateful and flattered to learn that thanks to her exceptional *juche,* she would be given a rare chance to redeem herself.

She had undertaken nightly sessions of *chonghwa,* "total harmony," during which she was compelled to criticize her own mistakes and failings of that same day. She had been shown rap sheets of her family's offenses, beginning with her father's lack of care of his portraits, extending to her mother's theft of television signals, and then continuing to cousins she had never met, guilty of "brutality" and "disruption of public peace" and, in the case of one distant uncle on her father's side, suicide—strictly forbidden. She had signed oaths of fealty, first with an inked thumb and then, as she learned to read and write, in Munhwaŏ, Gyeonggi, and English.

As she was being reeducated politically, she had studied tradecraft: self-defense, cryptography, covert entry, surveillance and countersurveillance, steganography and eavesdropping, dead drops and brush passes, interrogation and counterinterrogation and assassination.

Her debut as an RGB operative had come eight years ago. In the Bundang district of Seongnam she had contrived to accompany a high-ranking North Korean defector back to his hotel room, where she used VX nerve agent to stop his heart. The NIS surveillance photograph that had opened the file, Dalia gathered, had been captured from a subway platform near the hotel.

After her adventure in *areh dongae,* "the village below," Song had been deemed ready for the main event. She had passed a final battery of loyalty tests and had been allowed, via telecom, to say a final goodbye to her little brother. Then she had come to the United States as a South Korean named Park Ha-Soo, with a B-1 domestic employment visa.

The RGB file ended. A marriage certificate followed: the State of New York Department of Health recognizing the union, six years ago, between Mark Abrahams, of Manhattan, and Mi-Hi Pyung, of Seoul.

Then a slim dossier on Mark Abrahams. Born and raised in Manhattan, graduated from Horace Mann, NYU, and Columbia Law. Degrees in public policy and international law, an internship with the United Nations Office of Legal Affairs, and then a career with the legal section of the US Mission to the United Nations, where he had been instrumental in the levying of sanctions against North Korea by the Security Council.

A long-lens photograph showed the newly minted Mrs.

Abrahams, standing at a magazine kiosk and looking at her phone. Facial recognition software had matched the photo against the picture from the subway platform. Twenty-nine common nodal points had resulted—nine above the threshold deemed actionable.

"She's been here for seven years." A muscle twitched in Bach's jaw. "Married for six. We've been watching for two—ever since we cracked the RGB server. All that time, she's had no contact with Pyongyang."

He swiveled to face Dalia again. "Until six hours ago."

MANHATTAN, NY

"Monkeys," Baby Jia observed brightly, pointing to the frolicking creatures on her pink nightgown.

"Monkeys," Song agreed. She joggled her daughter on her lap, opened the book, and started reading. "In the great green room there was a telephone. And a red balloon. And a picture of …"

"Monkeys!"

"No, honey. A cow jumping over a moon."

"Moo." Jia wriggled around, tiny Cupid's-bow mouth pursed, to look her mother in the face.

"Moo, indeed."

"Mommy?"

"Yes?"

"Monkeys."

"Monkeys. And cows and elephants and giraffes and lions and tigers, oh my."

Jia giggled. They rubbed noses, finished the book, and read another.

After three books, Song carried her daughter to the crib. She laid a blanket over her, leaned over, and rubbed the girl's back. "Sleep well, honey."

"Love 'oo, Mommy."

"Love you, too, sweetie."

"Monkeys," said Jia gravely, already drifting off.

Song switched on a Disney princess night-light and flicked off the overhead. Leaving the nursery door ajar, she went into her son's room. A trace of toothpaste on his cheek attested to at least cursory toothbrushing. She sat on the edge of the bed and stroked the hair back from a smooth temple. "What did Daddy read you?"

"The robot book."

"Sweet dreams, Dex. Love you."

"Leave the door open, Mommy."

"I will."

"*Wide* open."

She kissed him. He hugged for a moment, then let go. "Sweet dreams," she said again.

He repeated, "*Wide* open."

In the master bedroom, Mark lay in his boxers, reading the latest Jack Reacher thriller. Song went into the bathroom and closed the door. She showered, lotioned, and brushed her teeth. In the bedroom, she put on a nightgown. When she slid into bed, Mark grunted acknowledgment. He reached over absently and squeezed her hand. She picked up her Kindle.

Five minutes passed. Her eyes moved across Murakami's prose without taking the meaning. Mark yawned. "Beat," he murmured. He rolled over, switched off his lamp. "Night," he said.

"Night."

She skimmed a few more pages and then switched off her lamp.

The crooked trapezoid of light on the ceiling changed color rhythmically. Yellow, red … green. Yellow, red … green.

She considered her options.

One: follow orders. It would be only business. She understood the difference between sex and love. It would not be a true betrayal.

Two: run away. Start over somewhere fresh. Abandon everything. Cut the cord.

The idea held a certain brutal appeal. It was not the first time she had considered it. In fact, she had the necessary equipment ready to go, hidden in a Kate Spade bag in the back of her bedroom closet. The bag also contained just shy of ten thousand dollars in cash. Pyongyang maintained a devoted cadre of counterfeiters. After arriving in America, Song had accessed a safe-deposit box overflowing with crisp new bills. For her first three years here, she had patiently swapped them out for genuine currency. Now she could finance a run, and the start of a new life, without leaving any sort of trail.

But she had a husband. She had wonderful kids. This was her *life*.

And, of course, there was her brother to consider.

Three: do nothing. Ignore the message. Pretend she had never received it.

But that only delayed the inevitable. At best, her operators at Kyuch'Aldae would give her the benefit of the doubt and resend the message. At worst, they would fetch Man Soo from whatever gilded cage they kept him in. Bring him to some dank cellar. Beat him until he vomited. Then the stress positions, the hot tongs, the open wounds …

She must not delay. She must be ready before the next message arrived, detailing delivery of the data.

She closed her eyes. She saw a dead man by a river. Frozen bloody menstrual rags hanging from a shower rod. She opened her eyes and left them open, watching the changing colors on the ceiling. Shadows stretched out. Treacherous, shifting dark rivers.

Yellow, red … green.

Slow, stop …

Go.

LANGLEY, VA

Inside the conference room the close air smelled vaguely of body odor and stress.

A chime sounded, and six pairs of eyes turned to the wall-mounted monitor.

On a real-time map, red crosshairs tracked a figure as it stepped from beneath an awning.

The image came from an encrypted satellite link to a drone parked twenty thousand feet above Manhattan. ARGUS—Autonomous Real-Time Ground Ubiquitous Surveillance—let operators scan a thirty-six-square-mile overview. Sixty-five target-acquisition windows, each with a resolution of ten centimeters, could be opened at once.

Song Sun Young's face had been scanned into software called Persistics, making her a searchable value. Anytime she presented herself within the drone's area of control, automatic object-tracking would alert the operators and lock on. Hence the chime, and the crosshairs.

Shyam Radha turned to his keyboard. The view, tinted night-vision green, moved closer. The "California Dreaming" T-shirt had been exchanged for a belted trench coat. Song wore tasteful makeup, minimalist jewelry, a leather handbag with a double-chain shoulder strap. She displayed a premeditated hint of décolletage. She walked a few steps, turned a corner onto Lexington Avenue, and hailed a passing cab.

The time code on the screen read *00:04:06+15*. June had begun, Dalia realized abruptly, and with it, her eighth decade on earth.

She sneaked a look at her phone. Her daughter had officially missed her birthday.

She looked back at Shyam Radha and found herself wondering, where did he go when he left this place? He was intelligent and ambitious, or he wouldn't be sitting in this particular conference room. Not bad-looking, either. But he wore no wedding band, and his personal hygiene was somewhat lackadaisical. He had no family to miss him, she decided—not even a dog that needed walking. And in ten years or twenty, he would be right where he was today, sitting behind a computer, inside this or another US intelligence agency headquarters, tracking this or another agent, with no one to grieve his absence.

Her gaze returned to the screen. Persistics had transferred its lock from figure to vehicle. The red crosshairs followed the taxi down Lexington Avenue. Three distinct green crosshairs deployed behind it: three windowless vans, each carrying a four-man FBI team and Stingray antennas with a twenty-mile range.

Two windows beside the ARGUS feed streamed audio and video. The Stingray antennas had tricked the woman's phone into identifying them as cell towers, giving them access to her microphone and camera. Audio was the muffled whisk of tires against pavement. Video was darkness—probably the inside of the leather handbag. Another window used the phone's geolocation feature to reflect her progress on a second map.

In a window beneath the Stingray feeds, lines of code—green against a black background—shifted endlessly. Sam had explained that the message sent to the woman from the RGB used a different encryption from that of the hacked server. The algorithm was new to the CIA. His only recourse was to attack the cipher with brute-force statistical analysis. He had told them not to hold their breath waiting for the plain text.

Dalia looked back to the ARGUS feed. At a few minutes past midnight, traffic was light. The taxi cruised to Forty-Second Street as fast as it could catch lights, then cut across town.

At Thirty-Seventh and Sixth, Song left the cab. She disappeared through a door. A new target acquisition window found a better angle on the storefront. SCHWARTZ LUGGAGE STORAGE, NYC. MANHATTAN'S TOP-RATED LUGGAGE STORAGE SERVICE SINCE 2004! OPEN 8 A.M.–1 A.M. WALK-INS WELCOME.

Tense glances were exchanged. Bach gave a slight shake of his head. They could take her anytime, which meant they could afford to play out more rope.

Stingray's audio feed channeled canned background music. Three minutes passed. At 00:12:41+31, Song emerged onto the street again. From the way she shouldered her leather handbag, it seemed to have grown heavier. She hailed another taxi and continued downtown.

In Union Square, traffic thickened abruptly. The cab slowed to a crawl. At Broadway and Eighth, Song left the taxi and continued east on foot.

One surveillance van discharged two agents to follow. The remaining two vans, guided by DeArmond via encrypted cell phone, assumed a standard floating box formation, trading command and backing roles as they maneuvered through crowded streets, trying to keep up.

Dalia watched the screen. Her pulse had quickened. Despite her insistence otherwise, something inside her still craved the thrill of the hunt.

MANHATTAN, NY

Belting her white trench coat more tightly, she melted into the throng like water finding its level.

The crowd was largely bridge-and-tunnel: hipsters, students, junkies, tourists, and maybe even a friend or two from her Upper East Side neighborhood, downtown for a thrill on a Friday night to pick up a sex toy or a new drug.

She had thought her surveillance detection skills would be rusty. But she had spent so much time looking over her shoulder, once upon a time, that now they came back effortlessly, reflexively. Look without seeming to look. Scan the crowd; take the rhythm; seek anomalies. The city was alive. Streets were veins, pedestrians blood. Look for clots. Look for nonfunctioning brake lights, which avoided attracting the target's attention when the driver of a surveillance vehicle slowed to keep pace. Quarter the street. Use shop windows, sideview mirrors of parked cars, or any other reflective surface. Use everything. Most of all, use your *nunji*. *Feel* the street.

She found no sign of watchers. But in this crowd, they might easily avoid detection. She quartered the street, firing a glance into the windshield of a passing car. There. A man who didn't quite fit in. Watchful eyes, sport coat, thick shoulders.

As soon as she saw him, he was gone.

She kept walking. A boy urinated without modesty in a doorway. Two girls kissed passionately. A single sandaled foot extended mysteriously from a shadowed alleyway. She looked over her shoulder, found no sign of the man with the watchful eyes.

When she had first arrived in America she had felt like an actress putting on a show. If she could turn around quickly enough, she might catch the audience watching from beyond the footlights. As the years wore on, the sense of performing had diminished. But now it was back. In spades. *All the world's a stage.*

She reached the address she was seeking, sandwiched between lowered metal shutters. Stenciled red letters on the window read SIX DEGREES. The door was propped open, body heat inside outstripping the slight chill of the night. Industrial music throbbed.

Checking her reflection in her compact, she used the mirror to scan the crowd behind her. No sign of the man she had glimpsed earlier.

But the feeling was there: she was being watched.

Nerves. She had been out of the game for too long.

Clinically she took her own emotional temperature. A shiver of fear wormed down her backbone. But there was also, undeniably, excitement.

A last moment of hesitation.

She steeled herself and went inside.

CHAPTER THREE

It had been a long time since she stood alone at a bar waiting for a drink. Her lemon drop arrived. She handed the bartender a bill and then scanned the crowd. People were young and very thin. Apparently, heroin chic never went out of style.

Before coming downtown she had studied the photograph again, memorizing the target's angular features. But maybe the picture was not recent. Maybe …

He was standing near the end of the bar, half leaning against a stool. Lucky. First bar, first try.

He was a few years her elder, wearing a dark blazer over a white T-shirt. He had a long, rawboned face, slightly asymmetrical, with the beginnings of loose skin below the chin. He looked, in that first instant, like an expensive breed of dog.

He noticed her. She looked away.

She consulted her phone, then glanced up. He was still watching her. Of course he was. She was very much his type.

She let the eye contact linger for a moment, then looked down again, touching her hair.

The music changed to something even louder, more assaultive. He pushed off the stool and closed the distance between them with two long steps. He said something into her ear.

She leaned closer. "What?"

"I said, I can't hear myself think in here!"

She smiled.

"I know a better place!" he shouted.

"I bet you do!"

"Just on the next block! Quieter! Who are you with?"

She didn't answer.

"Come on!" Brazenly he took her hand.

She pulled the hand away. "I'm meeting my friend!"

She went back to her phone. He loitered.

She let two minutes pass, then pretended to read a text. She rolled her eyes. This brought a satisfied smile from her target. "You've been ditched!" he shouted. "Right?"

She sighed, nodded. He took her hand again. "Come on! I know a place!"

"At least let me finish my drink!"

He waited, holding her hand loosely, as she sipped. When she had finished, he led her outside, barely giving her time to leave the glass on the bar.

"Bill," he said on the street.

"Edie."

He was still holding her hand. She was still letting him. Her left hand. Her wedding ring was back in her night-table drawer.

They went down the sidewalk, crossing First Avenue. An unmarked door, a coded knock, a mascaraed eye behind a Judas hole. Bolts worked; chains chittered. The door swung inward. They faced an attractive young person of perhaps twenty-one, heavily made-up, wearing a *seifuku* uniform: navy blouse, sailor-style white collar, short pleated black skirt, tall white knee socks, powder-blue neckerchief, black penny loafers. Big smile, glittering dark eyes, dilated pupils. "Did you have an appointment?"

"No," Bill said, "but we'd like to see the blue room."

Song followed him into a dim, low-ceilinged hallway. A disquieting aroma—beef marinated in Lysol?—made her nose wrinkle. They passed a rocking horse tucked into a corner. They moved from the dim corridor into a small, crowded room with recessed lighting and a sleek young clientele.

A host in suspenders and two-tone brogues straight out of the 1920s waved them into a booth.

"What did I tell you?" Bill slipped into his seat without releasing her hand. "Quieter."

And indeed, it was. There was no music and very little street noise. Conversation murmured secretively. The man in suspenders took their drink order. Bill changed his grip on her hand, entwining fingers. No ring, she noticed.

"Last month," he remarked, "this place was in the back of a bookstore in Tribeca. Month before that, you went down a staircase inside an old phone booth."

Watching his lips move, she felt a faint, dreamlike sense of distance. She remembered crossing the Tumen River many years before, floating briefly in the current. She was floating again now, toes questing for bottom.

Their drinks arrived: two old-fashioneds. She sipped. It was quite strong.

He was studying her. "You okay?"

"I … should go."

"I knew you were going to say that."

"I really should."

He nodded grimly, then leaned forward and kissed her.

The kiss extended. She broke away and excused herself, bringing her bag. The bathroom was stainless steel. She hadn't drunk much, but it made her feel sloppy, not as sharp. Yet her face in the mirror remained impassive.

The first man she had kissed, besides Mark, in over six years.

It *was* a betrayal.

She had no other choice.

She went back and slid into the booth. "Hungry?" he asked.

She shook her head.

"I live downtown," he said. "Not far."

She nodded.

*   *   *

Quiet, except for the constrained hiss of high-end climate control.

He pushed into a sitting position, found a watery whiskey on the nightstand, and drained it. Apparently exhausted by the effort, he fell heavily back into the pillow. Song nestled into the hollow of his shoulder, which was slick with perspiration.

After a minute, he moved again, reaching into the nightstand drawer and withdrawing a battered Sucrets tin. Inside was a wobbly, stale-smelling joint. He lit it with a plastic lighter and inhaled deeply before exploding in deep, dry coughs. When he offered her the joint, she demurred.

He traced an idle finger across her collarbone. "You're staying?"

"For a little bit."

"And then what?"

She shrugged.

"Woman of mystery." His smile flickered. "I like it." He drew again and this time managed not to cough. Smoke coiled up beneath the darkened track lighting in the high ceiling.

She sank into a fugue. She had betrayed her husband, her children. Most of all, herself. The thought held no power. None of this was real.

She surfaced. He had stabbed out the joint in the Sucrets tin. He had closed his eyes. She examined him. He had a nice face—that expensive-dog look.

He breathed evenly. She climbed out of bed and dressed quietly. He didn't stir.

She wandered around the apartment. The master bath was done in pink and gray marble. A single toothbrush hung beside the sink. Inside the medicine cabinet, she found deodorant and razors and shaving cream. Tylenol PM, baby aspirin, and Pravastatin for high cholesterol. The toilet seat was up.

In the kitchen, houseplants hung in macramé harnesses. Did that indicate a woman's touch? Not necessarily. A Mets magnet on the refrigerator, a toaster that looked as if it had never been used. A killer view: glimmering baubles of traffic, a few lighted windows, deserted rooftops and construction sites. His phone sat on the counter beside keys and wallet.

She shut her eyes and listened to her intuition. A pricey, lonely apartment. No wife, no children. No unusual odor except the stale marijuana, already mostly whisked away by the climate control. More absence than presence. This was the apartment of a man who worked a lot—a man with few personal ties.

Down a hallway. Past another bathroom, clean and anonymous. Toilet seat up again. Into a study. She felt as if she was trespassing. She *was* trespassing.

Diplomas hung on the walls. BA in computer science from Carnegie Mellon. MBA from Harvard Business School. A CODiE Award, a Stevens Award. She saw programming books and business books. In the half-light, she examined framed photographs. Family, friends, fishing trips. A cut-out *New Yorker* cartoon pictured two business-suited men looking at clouds: *"That one, too. They all look like big bags of money."* A small wicker bowl on a bookshelf was empty. What it had contained? She sniffed. Maybe peppermints.

On the desk, a computer slumbered. She sat in the desk chair and nudged the mouse. The screen brightened, asking for a password.

She searched drawers and found pens, checkbook, postage stamps, blank envelopes, matchbook, stapler.

And in a bottom drawer: a plastic pass card on a pocket clip.

She turned it over in her hands. A smiling photograph. *William Walsh.* An ID number and a company name: NYMEX.

She retrieved her handbag from the front hall. In the study again, she spread the equipment retrieved from the storage locker on the desktop. The message had given specific instructions. She checked connections between the high-frequency antenna, the reader-writer, and the cloner. She switched them on and held William Walsh's RFID over the reader-writer. The hexadecimal string associated with his badge was automatically captured. Now any blank card set atop the device would receive the data. Whoever brandished the new card would be allowed access to the NYMEX offices, and records would indicate that the person entering was Bill Walsh.

She returned the pass card to the desk, the equipment to her handbag. She let herself out, rode an elevator down, walked through a polished lobby without making eye contact with the doorman. Out on the sidewalk, she checked her phone. 3:35 a.m. Jia would be up in a few hours. And when Jia was up, everybody was up.

She hailed a cab, giving an address two blocks east of home. The streets were empty. The cab cruised north. It all felt more real now. They sailed through the meatpacking district. By a construction site, they bumped over rough planks, past mounds of upturned earth.

Just work. Just business. Not a betrayal.

She closed her eyes and drifted.

LANGLEY, VA

"Dalia."

She turned away from the voice, deeper into the dream. She was fifteen years old. She and a friend had sneaked off the kibbutz for an afternoon's mischief. They had met some soldiers on leave and drunk some cheap army wine. Now she lay on the grassy bank of a stream, trailing two fingers in the cool, babbling brook. Her head mizzed pleasant nonsense. Not a care in the world ...

"*Dalia.*"

She struggled up from shadowland, from youth into old age. Pain flared in her knee, her back, her shoulder, her neck. "What."

"She's moving," McConnell said.

Dalia had fallen asleep in a chair, head propped at a strange angle. Blinking gummily, she straightened. She detected no sign of dawn through the drawn shades.

She felt like *gedemtke fleisch,* like overcooked meat. She tried to find the point when she had fallen asleep. She had watched the woman enter a bar, then emerge with a man. After visiting another bar, the couple had taken an Uber to a high-rise in Liberty Plaza. That was around 2 a.m. Sometime shortly thereafter, Dalia had dozed off.

Now ARGUS was tracking a taxi heading north up Tenth Avenue. The time code read 03:43:12+39. Green crosshairs showed two of DeArmond's vans following, leaving plenty of room. The third van remained parked by Liberty Plaza.

McConnell was pressing a cup into her hands. Dalia smiled thanks and sipped. American coffee was dreck. But the caffeine burned away the fog in her mind.

The taxi reached midtown, then turned east along the bottom of the Park. "Heading home," Bach mused. "Sam … our mystery man?"

"Great minds," Sam said.

The live feed resized, and an ARGUS-captured image appeared in its place: the man Song had met in the bar. Slim face, hard angles, slightly asymmetrical, nodal points highlighted.

A New York State driver's license followed in another window. WALSH, WILLIAM. The Liberty Plaza address they had just watched Song Sun Young leave. Between the license and the ARGUS photo, the computer matched twenty-four nodal points.

More windows: a Stingray hack of Walsh's phone, run from the van parked by Liberty Plaza. Both audio and video feeds were blank. In a third window, alphanumerically labeled folders were stacked in columns and rows. "What are we looking at?" Bach asked.

"Extracted data." Sam clicked ahead. The phone's most recently run apps were from the Weather Channel and Stock TickerPicker. The last call, placed at 9:47 the night before, had been to a 212 number and lasted seven minutes. He skimmed pictures, text messages, websites, email. An automatic email signature identified the phone's owner as one William Walsh, senior systems engineer, New York Mercantile Exchange.

The keyboard rattled as Sam typed again. "And his geolocation records. Every weekday morning, he goes to the NYMEX offices in the World Financial Center."

Dalia caught an apprehensive glance between Bach and McConnell. She understood its meaning. The New York Mercantile Exchange was part of the Chicago Mercantile Exchange, trading fundamental commodities such as oil, gold, and wheat—the basis of the world economy.

Sam nibbled thoughtfully on a callused thumb. "Bureau One-Twenty-One"—Pyongyang's cyberwarfare unit—"has a section called Hidden Cobra, tasked with hacking American infrastructure. That includes media, aerospace, and finance. Someone in Walsh's position could do some major damage."

"Such as?" Dalia had set her coffee on the conference table, beside a bottle of Poland Spring, and was rolling her chair absently back and forth on its casters, leaving furrows in the nubby carpeting.

"Ideally, systems like CME are all in isolated pieces. There's no bleed between the piece that talks to the network to receive orders, the piece responsible for prices, the piece responsible for order routing, et cetera. But in real life, there are always cracks in the architecture. Walsh has access to the network. In theory, he could get anywhere. Everywhere. Picture oil companies that can't price their product, farmers who can't go to market."

"Arrest them." Nervous excitement baked off McConnell. "Arrest them both. Now."

Bach shook his head. "See where she leads us." He spoke abstractedly, watching the taxi turn north again. "We've waited two years. We can wait a little longer."

McConnell grimaced but held his tongue.

The cab pulled over two blocks east of Lexington Avenue.

The time code read 03:50:11+27.

CHAPTER FOUR

MANHATTAN, NY

She leaned against the front door, and the lock gave a tiny click as it found the hasp. Silently she hung her coat in the hall closet. She hid the leather handbag and its contents behind rain boots and a Thomas the Tank Engine umbrella. After six years in the apartment, the closet still struck her as huge. Everyone in New York complained about lack of closet space. But back home in Chosun, only the richest had closets at all.

She felt filthy, but a shower would wake her family. So she made do with baby wipes in the hall bathroom, not even running water or flushing the toilet. She buried the dirty wipes deep in the wastebasket, hiding them beneath crusty Kleenex.

In darkness, she glided into the bedroom. Stripping off her clothes, she mixed them into the hamper, put her jewelry in the box on the dresser, found her wedding ring in the drawer, and slipped it on. She crawled into bed. The red digits on the cable box glowed like wolves' eyes. Two hours and change before Jia started the day with a bang.

Every nerve was humming. She would not be able to sleep.

Beside her, Mark rolled over, burrowing deeper into his pillow.

She looked at the back of his head. She had gotten lucky with Mark. She married him because she was following orders, but she could have done much worse. He didn't flaunt a mistress or buy sports cars or get his ear pierced, like Matt Waters down the hall, who turned forty last month and did all three. Mark was steady, kind—a good father.

Her mind turned fitfully to the day ahead. At 10:30 a.m., Leigh Cohen's sixth birthday party. A dozen screaming hellions, revved up on cake and juice boxes. And Mark had a tennis game scheduled. Then, in the afternoon, Dex had a piano recital. In between, she had to figure something out for lunch.

And just that quickly, she realized, she had fallen back into the regular rhythm of life—meals, kids' activities, Mark's tennis—as if tonight had never happened.

She yawned. And then slid, as if down a greased chute, into a thin and haunted slumber. Men not her husband crushed her beneath their weight. At Yodok, a *jagubbanjang,* a crew manager, had fallen in love with her. Between rapes, he had plied her with gifts: food, clothes, blankets. He had pulled strings to get her easier work details. But he had not loved her enough to stop raping her. Each rape had put Song's life at risk. Women who gave birth inside the camps were killed along with their newborns.

The dream face changed. The Chinese farmer now. Her first time crossing the Tumen, en route to Bundang, she had found, as planned, the guide hired to escort her to Changjitu. But the second time, she had found only the border guard. After disposing of him, she had searched in vain for her guide. She had started to panic, then calmed herself. She was prepared for this eventuality. That was why she had the backpack.

She had traded her beef jerky to a farmer in exchange for a ride in his K01 pickup. But in the middle of the countryside, he had suddenly stopped. She could walk the rest of the way to Changjitu, he said. Or there was another option ... She offered the damp cigarettes as a supplementary bribe. He shook his head. She considered killing him. But the Chinese were fed up with the endless flow of defectors across the Sino-Korean border. They set up roadblocks and conducted random identity-card checks. Lacking the guide, her chances were better in the farmer's company. What was one more man crushing her beneath his weight, holding her still by the nape of her neck? One more indignity, one more degradation …

She woke to a robust cry. Her eyes felt grainy. Mark muttered something she didn't catch. She went into the nursery and took her daughter from the crib.

Breakfast was cold cereal and milk. While Song was in the kitchen measuring out coffee, Jia started screaming from the dining room. Song rushed back to the table. Dexter was looking at her innocently. "Dex," Song said, "what happened?"

"Nothing," the boy said.

"Spoon, spoon, spoon!" Jia shrieked from her booster.

"Did you take her spoon?"

Dexter let her see the pink Elmo spoon in his hand. "She dropped it on the floor."

"No drop!" Jia cried. "No drop! Spoon! Dex take!"

"Give her back the—"

Mark emerged from the bedroom, blinking owlishly. "What's all the racket?"

Song showered. She had first experienced hot water at Heaven Lake. She had fallen instantly in love. One of the few bones of contention between her and Mark concerned her long, frequent showers. She would spend all day beneath the hot spray if she could.

She took three Advil and drank two cups of coffee. As she stood by the kitchen counter, starting another pot, her phone chimed: Dylan's mother reporting that they were free for a playdate, morning or afternoon.

Song replied that they were booked today. She asked about tomorrow. She answered another email from Jackie McNamara about the food drive. After pressing SEND, she felt a moment's dissociation. Floating again, as she had when crossing that long-ago river. Toes questing for bottom. That dreamlike sense of distance. Dexter and Jia were playing together in the next room—little angels now, laughing sweetly. Mark was in the bedroom, changing into his tennis clothes. And suddenly, Song was slicked with cold sweat. Her muscles were freezing, and the kitchen was starting to tilt sickeningly, and all at once she realized she was not floating. She was fainting; she was falling.

She set her phone down and held on to the side of the counter. Darkness puddled around her, lapping like waves. Then slowly receded. The world was clearing again. The morning was still going. She was still here.

She was okay.

The kids laughed louder. "The police are pulling you over," Dexter said, "giving you a ticket," and Jia knew enough to insist, "No. No ticket. No ticket!"

"They're giving you—"

"NO TICKET!"

"Kids." Mark must have come out of the bedroom. "Take it down a notch. Two notches."

The front hall was striped with cheery bars of sunlight. Mark had his racket in one hand, a gym bag in the other. "Back in an hour and a half," he said. "Two hours, tops."

"We'll be at the birthday party." She drifted over and kissed his cheek. Was it her imagination, or was his reaction cool? "Thoughts about lunch?"

"Lunch," Jia said. "Lunch, lunch, lunch, lunch! Mommy, lunch!"

"Not yet, honey."

"Daddy, lunch! Lunch!"

"Surprise me." He slipped away. The door clicked shut behind him.

"Mommy!" Jia was tugging at the cuff of her jeans. "*Lunch, Mommy, lunch!*"

She gave each kid an applesauce squeeze as a postbreakfast snack. The usual rule that all eating was to be done at the dining room table went unenforced.

More coffee. More Advil. She folded laundry. On her phone, she found the invitation to the birthday party. Ten thirty at Chelsea

Piers. She would grab a present on the way down. The Barnes and Noble on Fifth and Forty-Sixth. Pick up something for lunch on the way back. At the same time, do shopping for dinner. When they got home, Jia could go down for a nap before Dexter's recital.

It was a plan. Keep moving and she would be okay.

She did the breakfast dishes, changed Jia's diaper, packed a go-bag, and filled a travel cup with more coffee.

LANGLEY, VA

At the end of the hallway, Bach's small office overlooked the arched roof of the cafeteria and the back side of the old HQ, where senior directors toiled on the fabled seventh floor to protect truth, justice, and the American Way.

Charlie DeArmond was snoring, curled into the fetal position on a bonded leather couch two heads too short for him. Bach shook the man's thick shoulder. "Nine a.m. wake-up call."

DeArmond blinked groggily, sat up, nodded, stood. As he retreated sleepily from the office he closed the door behind himself without being asked.

Bach sat at his desk. He checked messages and then composed an intel report to the DDO, the Deputy Director for Operations. The report had a good chance of making the Presidential Daily Brief, known as "the Book." It was not every day that a sleeping RGB agent in Manhattan was activated. And then the White House would authorize the heavy guns.

He took DeArmond's place on the couch. The leather was still warm. He closed his eyes. His throat itched. Every eight hours, he took pholcodine to suppress the coughing. But nothing could suppress that maddening itch. By now, he was almost used to it. As used to it as he would ever get.

These days, he could not miss a night's sleep with impunity. But he had kept it together. He had stayed in Do-mode. Nobody suspected his frailty.

Thud-a thud, his heart went. *Thud-a thud, thud-a thud.*

A poor bed. He exhaled raggedly, shifting his cramped legs. He was used to poor beds. He had lived out of suitcases for half his life. He had slept in far worse places than this. And he was beyond exhausted.

Soon, he slept. And remembered a day from almost two decades before.

* * *

"Let's go live right now and show you a picture of the World Trade Center. Do we have it? We don't have that ready? What should we …? We have a breaking story. Can we …?"

Someone changed the channel. Here was a live feed. Dark smoke plumed from a fiery hole in one of the Twin Towers. The crowd gathered in the hallway gasped.

"… limited information at this point. We don't know about injuries in the building, or people on the ground right now, but obviously, um, this has potential for, uh, for …" The anchorman trailed off helplessly.

Then a plane arrowed in from the left side of the screen. For an instant, it seemed the plane would pass behind the towers. Instead, a tremendous fireball bloomed, boiling up, dissolving into another mass of oily black smoke.

"Another one!" The anchor's voice went ragged with adrenaline and horror. "Oh, my God! That was a plane? Now it's obvious, I think, that … oh, my God! There's a second plane that just crashed into the World Trade Center. Oh, God! Oh, God. Breaking news. Breaking … a second plane …"

Benjamin Bach found his phone, tried a number. The connection clicked, nattered, echoed emptily. He hung up and headed for the elevators.

Convention-goers filled the hallway. Some were crying. He pushed past them and stabbed the elevator's call button. The door opened immediately. He rode up to his third-story room, jammed a few personal articles into a suitcase, closed the zipper with a single hard tug. Heading back down, he took the stairs two at a time. In the parking lot he found his car. Tossing his case onto the passenger seat, he turned the key.

Fifty minutes later, blasting down I-84 toward Manhattan, he heard on the radio that the South Tower had collapsed. He dialed to another station, where a second announcer confirmed the news. But surely, they had gotten everybody out. How could they not have gotten everybody out?

Right?

Anyway, Dad was in the North Tower. And the North Tower was still standing.

He felt something ominous building in the air, like the charge before a thunderbolt.

Dad had once given him a private tour of the restaurant. Neat rows of tables, white tablecloths, red chairs. The best view in the history of great views, he had said proudly. Dad had grown up sharing a row house in Queens with a widowed mother and five younger brothers. He had worked his way up from fry cook at the local greasy spoon to kitchen manager at this restaurant with the best view in history. Of course he was proud.

Twenty-nine minutes later, merging onto the Hutch, Benjamin Bach heard on the radio that the North Tower had fallen.

He tried his phone again. This time, he got only a malevolent whoosh of white noise.

He tuned up and down the band, seeking more news. Another plane had hit the Pentagon. Another had hit the White House. Another had hit the Eiffel Tower. Widespread looting was rampant in Chicago and DC. They had found bombs inside Buckingham Palace. They had found bombs inside the Taj Mahal. Forty jetliners had been hijacked. Animals in the Central Park Zoo were inexplicably dying. In case of nuclear attack, locate your nearest civil defense shelter. It was the end of the world.

Nearing Manhattan, he spotted a column of smoke. It looked thick, greasy, ugly. Like the world's biggest tire fire. He felt a movement of energy. Not quite panic. A focusing. *Do-mode,* his cross-country coach in high school had called it. You got into Do-mode and nothing else mattered. Fatigue, pain, victory, defeat—all receded. You refocused and you kept going.

Traffic heading downtown was thin. Traffic coming the other way was murder: snarling, honking, gridlocked. Reaching Chelsea Piers, he found a barricade of yellow and black cross-ties blocking the West Side Highway. He parked in the North River lot. Leaving the car, he turned in helpless circles. He saw firemen, cops, civilians, National Guard, Humvees, dump trucks, Jeeps. Nobody seemed to be in charge.

A guardsman was waving vehicles through another barricade. The man was wild-eyed with shock. His words made no sense. "We're at the meat case," he said, waving a sanitation sweeper ahead. "Hot food and a warm bed. Chocolate ice cream for dessert."

Bach showed his Columbia ID. He identified himself as a doctor. He left out that his still-unearned PhD would be in East Asian studies. The guardsman motioned him to join a police cruiser waiting at the barricade. The cops were silent. Beneath peaked caps, their eyes were glazed, floating.

The cruiser turned east onto Fourteenth Street, then south again onto Broadway. Ghosts wandered aimlessly, covered in ash and silt and dust. Bach saw a child soaked in blood, wearing a shroud of gray, crying in its mother's arms.

The road was blocked by a shattered hook and ladder. The driver pulled over. The cops abandoned the cruiser and continued downtown on foot. Bach followed. The wind bore a toxic, evil smell: smoke and melting steel and combusted jet fuel and pulverized concrete and scorched flesh. People were wounded, sobbing. Or blank, staring. Makeshift Red Cross stations had been set up behind sawhorse barriers. Dusty gray garbage bags had been lumped on curbsides. Ash grew deeper with each step. He had lost the cops. He reached a cordon set up by the National Guard. No one was paying him any attention. He slipped through.

Building facades had collapsed. Body parts lay strewn about. He climbed over rubble, through dust and smoke, past a ruined ambulance. *Surreal.* The word was so inadequate, it echoed hollowly, meaninglessly, in his skull. Even in his worst nightmares he had never imagined anything like this. The destruction was not of this civilized era. The destruction was medieval. Biblical. Pressing ahead, he understood that his father was almost certainly … He put the thought aside.

Morgue trucks moved back and forth, phantoms in the fog. A backhoe labored with engine revving. The smell became ever fouler. Melting fingernails and bone and hair, pulverized Formica and asbestos and polystyrene foam. He could see fire ahead, burning beneath a hulking pile of debris. But mostly, he saw smoke and dust.

People hauled wreckage in old-fashioned bucket brigades, like firemen in an old black-and-white movie. He got in the line, accepted a pair of heavy-duty work gloves and a five-gallon plastic bucket, and started lugging debris. From pile to flatbed truck. Repeat.

The sun sank lower. Eventually, huge floodlights switched on. Search dogs appeared, led by men wearing NYPD windbreakers.

At a Red Cross station, he smoked a cigarette for the first time since high school. He accepted a cup of bitter Starbucks coffee. Full dark now. His arms were numb. Resting, he watched anatomy, chunks on stretchers, coming off the pile. He watched a cherry picker floating, looking in vain for somewhere to be of use. He found the phone in his pocket. Dread churned in his belly as he dialed.

No signal.

He smoked another cigarette. His throat itched. He coughed, spat. The phlegm came out ash gray.

He hauled more debris. Around midnight, a member of the Office of Emergency Management took him aside and gave him a gold security badge with a medical snake in the middle. Someone fitted him for a mask. It was an old two-canister type that snugged against the curve of his jaw.

Not long after getting the mask, he heard that no one had escaped from Windows on the World, five stories above where the first plane hit.

Something tried to swim up inside his mind. He dropped a steel door, sealing it off. *Do-mode.*

He went back to work.

Sometime later, golden sunlight slanted across the Statue of Liberty.

*   *   *

Awake.

For a few moments, he had no idea where he was. He sat up slowly. Midmorning June sunshine made him wince.

He was in his office at CIA Headquarters. Walls covered with commendations and awards. Credenza cluttered with souvenirs from his travels. *Buchae* fans from Yanji, *soju* liquor from Seoul, *gzhel* ceramics from Vladivostok. A single photograph of himself and his father. Standing together on the Brooklyn docks, Benjamin Bach somewhere in his late teens, Dad somewhere in his late forties. The background was shades of gray: gray water, a gray tug, a gray garbage scow. But an unseen boat off to the right was throwing spray. Lashes of water refracted sunlight. The camera had caught a slender rainbow, a moment of color amid all the grayness, frozen in time.

He remembered: the operation unfolding in the conference room down the hall.

This was it. At last.

Do-mode.

He checked his phone. No authorization from the White House yet.

It would take some time. With these particular heavy guns, the powers that be erred on the side of caution.

He put his legs over the side of the couch and went back to work.

CHAPTER FIVE

MANHATTAN, NY

Mark was struggling with the buckles on the car seat when his phone rang. He straightened, perspiring freely in the humid confines of the parking garage. "Mark Abrahams."

Song watched his face. He had fallen immediately into his lawyer persona: calm, soothing, dispassionate. "Yes," he said tonelessly. Mark Abrahams, Attorney at Law. Beneath the competence was something almost insolent: a master gunslinger wearing his gun belts low. "Did you try …? Yes. And …?"

"DADDY!" Jia screamed, apropos of nothing. Her nap had been cut short. She was cranky. Join the club.

Song slung the diaper bag onto the passenger seat, then leaned over the gearshift to quiet her daughter. "Shh," she said, "Daddy's working."

Another car inside the garage turned sharply. Tires squealed, echoing. Mark covered his free ear, hunching over his phone. He listened. He spoke briefly and hung up. His eyes met Song's, and he gestured with his chin. She disentangled herself from the Volvo's interior and faced him, standing beside the car.

"I've got to go in," he said.

Seat-belted on the booster beside Jia's car seat, Dexter, wearing a navy blazer and clip-on tie, said, "Wah."

"Sorry, champ. I hate to miss it." He put a hand on his wife's shoulder. "Video it for me?"

She covered his hand with hers. "You have to go?"

"Got to put out a fire." Dex was listening. He left it at that.

"Call when you're done. Maybe we can meet up."

He kissed her cheek, then her lips. Any coldness she had sensed was gone, if it had ever been there at all. "I love you," he murmured.

"I love you, too."

He seemed about to add something else, changed his mind, and leaned down to speak through the open passenger-side door. "Break a leg, kid."

"Break *what*?"

"It means good luck. Knock 'em dead."

"Knock 'em what?"

The recital hall was a repurposed dance studio on Forty-Third Street. Old sweat smells, wall mirrors patched with electrical tape, folding bridge chairs assembled before a gleaming upright piano. Before his turn came, Dexter clowned around with his fellow students. Song bounced Jia on her knee and chatted with mothers whose names she didn't remember: about a new cat café downtown, about a new dramedy series on Netflix, about the wisdom of spouses keeping separate bank accounts. (Everyone agreed it was a good idea.)

A text arrived from Dylan's mother. A rain check was fine. She'd be in touch early next week. Song felt her spirits lift. She might just get through this.

Two kids performed before Dexter. Jia listened civilly from Song's lap: a small miracle. Walking to the piano, Dex in his miniature jacket and tie seemed preternaturally self-possessed. As he played, Song videoed with her phone.

The feeling returned: If she turned around quickly enough, she would catch the audience, just beyond the footlights, gazing hungrily. Watching her as she watched her son … videoing her even as she videoed him?

Her intuition stirred; her head cocked.

Before she could follow the thought, Dexter was playing his last note. He let it ring. He dropped his hands into his lap in a graceful arc. He took his time standing, then faced the audience and gave an exaggerated bow. Insolent in his competence. You could see his father in him.

She sent the video to Mark. After the performance, the stern Russian teacher took Song aside. Dexter had what it took to become a serious piano player if only he would apply himself. The reprimand, Song understood, applied mostly to her, for not cracking the whip harder.

For a reward, she bought Dex ice cream just down the block from the studio. Before handing over the wafer cone, she made him take off his blazer. Jia watched alertly. "Ice cream. Mommy, ice cream."

Song shared spoonfuls of vanilla bean with her daughter. She drank a double espresso. "You sounded really good up there," she told Dex. "Were you nervous?"

"Nope."

"Not even a little?"

"Those songs are easy. A baby could play them."

"Baby play them," Jia repeated with satisfaction.

They stopped at a playground. So far, coasting on adrenaline and sugar and caffeine, Song was staying ahead of things. But when she closed her eyes for a moment, fatigue tugged like a riptide, trying to drag her under.

Her phone was ringing. Mark. She answered. "Hey. Did you get the vid—"

"Bad news. I'm stuck here."

"Drat."

"How was it?"

"He killed it. Got it all on video. I sent it."

"Can I talk to him?"

"He's on the monkey bars. Should I get him?"

"No. Tell him I'm proud. I'll try to make it for dinner, but don't wait."

"Love you." She looked at their children playing in the bright sunshine. Suddenly, she felt like crying. Or maybe laughing. Gales of semihysterical, tear-streaked laughter.

"Love you, too."

She hung up, covered her eyes briefly with one hand. Then she hollered, "Kids! *Two minutes!*"

Back home, she got chicken in the oven. She chopped potatoes and covered them in Lipton onion soup mix. Mark hated the stuff, said it caused cancer. But the kids loved it. Mark would never know.

Another secret.

She got the kids bathed and changed into pj's. She installed them before their screens and went into the study. Listened for a moment to make sure Mark wasn't getting home. What would her story be if he caught her? She didn't need a story. It was her own study—half hers, anyway.

Nevertheless, she could explain that she had to write a solicitation for the food drive and needed quiet to concentrate. But no, that would be overexplaining. That was how liars got tripped up. *The lady doth protest too much, methinks.*

Move quickly, and she wouldn't be caught, anyway. She opened the desk drawer, sifted through junk, found the phone and the battery.

Before clicking them together, she paused. Bureau 121 had designed this device to be secure, immune to hacking. But seven years had since passed—in computer security time, an eon.

Nothing for it. She had to check the server. Without new instructions, she could not hand off the data to her contact and then move on with her life. And no matter how out-of-date, the RGB phone was surely more secure than her cell phone.

She plugged in the battery, thumbed the power button. She entered her password, logged on to the site. No new message awaited.

Her brow creased.

All she could do was try again later.

She dismantled the phone and hid it again in the drawer. Stripping off clothes, she went into the bathroom and showered. Needling hot spray gushed out hard enough to sting. She toweled off and checked on the kids. She cut up some fruit, gave them each a bowl to curb their appetites until dinner was ready, and asked if they needed the bathroom. Neither answered. Both stared at their screens, slack-jawed, folding strawberries mindlessly into their mouths. She felt a flicker of dark amusement. Her kids, for better or for worse—for better *and* for worse—were truly American.

She went back into her bedroom and sat on the edge of the bed, naked except for the towel. Goose bumps had sprung up on her forearms, the back of her neck.

She could send a message, pressing for information about where and when the handoff would occur.

During her first two years in America, she had sent several messages to Pyongyang, passing along as instructed anything she thought might be of interest. She had identified herself to her handlers using code phrases that indicated she had not been compromised and was sending the messages of her own free will. The phrases had come from the laws of the camps. As an inmate, she had been forced to memorize and recite them frequently. *Anyone caught trying to escape will be shot immediately. Any witness to an attempted escape who fails to report it will be shot immediately. Prisoners who neglect their work quota will be shot immediately. Should sexual contact occur without prior approval, the perpetrators will be shot immediately.*

At least once a week, she had searched her husband's calfskin bag, his paperwork, and his phone and his laptop. She had relayed a few items concerning the finer points of the legal justification behind sanctions against Pyongyang. Then her reports home had slowed and finally stopped. Her rationalization had been that every time she contacted the RGB, she risked discovery. She would wait until something top-priority presented itself. But she also recognized that she had grown complacent. Well fed, well loved, with access to plenty of hot water. And learning ever more, of course, from her late-night sessions surfing the web …

She could turn herself in.

An illicit thrill rolled up her spine. She had never allowed the thought into the daylight.

She could throw herself on the FBI's mercy. She had been sent here as a spy, yes. But she was American now, goddamn it. Lipton onion soup, slack-jawed TV-watching children, and all. She had seen the light. Surely, that counted for something. Surely, it counted for a lot.

But her brother would pay the price. She felt the guilt as a physical sensation, a twisting in her gut. The only times, back in the camps, that she had not been an animal were when she was when looking out for her brother. Sharing food and blankets, propping him up in front of the guards when he was too weak to stand. In saving him, she had saved her humanity—the only part of her *worth* saving. And now, fat and happy and spoiled in America, she considered throwing him to the wolves?

It might be for naught, anyway. If the prevailing winds in Washington demanded a blood sacrifice, her fate would be sealed. Imagine the fallout at school. *Your mom's a traitor. You half-breed slant, go back where you came from. We don't want your kind!* No matter that both kids had been born right here at Lenox Hill. Americans didn't care about things like that—not when their backs were to the wall.

No, she could not turn herself in.

Stay the course. Soon enough, she would receive further instruction. She would hand off the equipment. And then she would be finished.

But of course, she had indulged similar fantasies before. When the CIA director had visited her country as an emissary of peace, when the Panmunjom Declaration had formally ended the war after sixty years, when the thaw between nations had, briefly, seemed undeniable … She had dared let herself hope. Détente would be her salvation.

She had been naive. Every diplomatic thaw was followed by another freeze. She would never be set free.

For many minutes—at least, it seemed that long—she sat without moving. Wrapped in her 900-gram Egyptian cotton towel, dripping onto her Donna Karan silk quilt. These were the trappings of the life she had earned for herself.

Trappings. Trapped. The rock and the hard place.

A thought nosed up from the substrata of her mind. The flash of intuition she had while videoing her son's recital.

You are being watched.

More: *You are being videoed.*

She remembered walking to the bar to find Walsh. Her sixth sense insisting …

"Mom?"

She almost jumped. Almost screamed. But somehow, she managed not to react at all.

She turned slowly. Her son was standing in the bedroom doorway, in his *Star Wars* pajamas.

"Can I watch another episode before dinner?" he asked hopefully.

LANGLEY, VA

With the shades drawn tight, the light in the conference room never changed. Dalia covered a yawn. She checked the time code in a corner of the live ARGUS feed. Twenty-four hours had passed since she came to this place. During that time, she had slept, patchily, for less than three hours.

On-screen, Sam resized his windows, moving the ARGUS feed into a neat line on the left side of the screen. The row also contained the ongoing effort to decrypt the RGB's message, and two other windows, displaying Mi-Hi Abrahams' Facebook and Twitter accounts.

In her Facebook profile pic, the woman grinned broadly, arms around two kids in Halloween costumes. Both kids wore overalls and fake mustaches and hats: one red, one green. The Super Mario Brothers. Beneath the picture, a box offered personal information. Mi-Hi Abrahams identified herself as self-employed, profession unspecified. She had studied early childhood education at Ansang University in Gyeonggi Province, South Korea. She lived in New York City. She was married.

Beneath this were thumbnail photos. Mi-Hi standing with her husband—a tall, tanned, handsome man—before sun-kissed water. A smiling selfie of the whole family together, the toddler looking away with a comical frown. A black-tie charity event, Mi-Hi posing in elegant evening wear beside two similarly attired women.

Beneath the thumbnails were Mi-Hi's Facebook friends. She had 290. The list included some well-known New Yorkers: prominent lawyers, a Philharmonic performer, a bestselling author, and a justice of the New York Supreme Court. The common denominator was a private kindergarten on the Upper West Side, well represented on the Facebook wall via Back to School nights, PTA fund-raisers, and visits to upstate farms.

The Twitter profile handle was @mihiabrahams. *Harried and happy mother of two #momslife.* The tweets were all retweets. *One day, when my kids are grown with their own homes, I'll come over, grind food into all their keyboards, and lie about it. @MomOnFire. Someday, my son will have warm, loving memories of watching kids' movies while I looked at my phone. @TheRealDratch.*

On the right side of the screen another row of windows streamed live feeds from spoofed phones. Song's iPhone sat on a flat surface, faceup. The camera afforded only a view of a blank ceiling with a faint water stain. But the microphone, with signal boosted, provided a vivid window into the apartment nevertheless. She was putting her kids to bed in the next room, reading aloud.

"Do you choose to chew goo, too, sir? If, sir, you, sir, choose to chew, sir, with the Goo-Goose, chew, sir. Do, sir ..."

Song's affection for the children seemed genuine. Perhaps she and Dalia had more in common than one might think. Both had come of age with the stench of labor camps in their nostrils: Song firsthand, Dalia through her mother and father, who had survived, respectively, Auschwitz and Treblinka. Surely, survivors of camps valued family in a way that few others could ever grasp.

And yet, whatever they had in common, certain truths could not be ignored. The woman was an agent working for a regime that placed Dalia's own family, her children and grandchildren, in peril. Pyongyang saw Israel as an extension of American tyranny. Their gestures toward accommodation struck her as manipulative, opportunistic, untrustworthy.

Using an invisible hand, they empowered those who would destroy the Jewish homeland. The Simorgh launching platforms of Iran's Fateh-313 missiles bore more than a passing resemblance to DPRK technology. Pyongyang had advanced the Syrian and Iranian nuclear programs, shared with Hezbollah and Hamas its expertise in subterranean tunnels, and invited Hezbollah's Hassan Nasrallah to receive training personally in the late 1980s.

"... a tweetle beetle noodle poodle bottled paddled muddled duddled fuddled wuddled fox in socks!"

Two other windows streamed William Walsh's phone. After a day of movement—breakfast at South Street Seaport, a lunchtime meeting with a friend near Grand Central, where conversation had largely focused on the waitress' ass—the device had returned to Liberty Plaza. There it had remained since midafternoon, the video feed dark, the audio silent.

Sam was resizing and moving windows to no purpose. Nervous energy.

Bach paced. Dark divots underscored his eyes. He leaned against the beveled black edge of the conference table, scowling.

"I want to see what she's up to," Sonny Romano said suddenly.

Dalia could guess his thinking. The woman's cell phone, according to Sam, showed no evidence of having communicated with the RGB server that had sent the message. This suggested that she possessed a second device, still unknown to them. And this device might be receiving messages from a server they remained unaware of.

The man from Science and Technology brooded, his fleshy lower lip folding down. Among the densely packed skyscrapers of Manhattan's Upper East Side, satellites and drones could not achieve sight lines into a fifth-floor apartment. The Stingray spoof was limited by the location of the phone. But installing and servicing surveillance devices was risky enough when an apartment was empty.

"Thermals," Sonny suggested at last. "Get into a neighboring apartment. Or …"

"Or?" Bach said.

"Emergency sprinkler inspection. Feed them in from the hallway. Right above her head. Add some contact mikes while we're up there."

Dalia shook her head. "*Shwya, shwya.*" Easy, easy. "You'll tip her off."

But Sonny had made up his mind. "I want to see what she's up to," he said again.

MANHATTAN, NY

"You guys burn the midnight oil," Mark was saying as he came through the door. "The nine-thirty-on-a-Saturday-night oil."

He was talking to someone in the hallway. Song left the sofa, where she had been paging through the latest *InStyle,* to look past him. Two men with a ladder were doing something above the paneled ceiling. They wore blue jeans, name tags, and white shirts emblazoned with a triangular logo. *New York State Fire Marshals: Inspection, Investigation, Education.*

"Sprinkler system's on the fritz," one said.

"Don't work too hard." Mark was using his man-of-the-people voice. "It's bad for you."

He closed the door, then worked the locks quietly, not wanting to imply anything about the men in blue jeans. Song went to him, leaned up on tiptoe to peck him on the cheek. "Back from the salt mines," she said.

He nodded. "Long day."

"Did you eat?"

"I grabbed something. I need a shower."

"Go." She slapped his bottom playfully.

He went. She dallied for a moment in the front hall, head canted, listening for sounds of activity from the corridor outside.

Then she switched off the living-room lights and started the dishwasher. When she first moved in, she had been disconcerted by the Whirlpool's rhythmic churning. *Chum-chum-chum-chum-chum,* alternating with creepy sibilant hissing, like a wild animal. The only standard appliance in Chosun was *ondol,* a system using hot water under the floor to heat the home—silent except for the occasional gurgle or sigh.

She turned off more lights and went into their bedroom. The shower was already running. The bathroom door was cracked open, letting out billows of steam. She changed into sleep clothes, then lay down, closed her eyes, and breathed.

She could fall asleep right now and sleep the sleep of the dead.

Something skittered above the ceiling. Her eyes opened.

The sound came again.

The sprinkler system.

A steep downhill grade led into the next thought: *You are being watched.*

The thought encircled her.

Maybe paranoia. Or maybe not.

Maybe they had hacked into her smartphone. Maybe they had hacked the RGB device, despite Bureau 121's best efforts to prevent it. Maybe the very "sprinkler system" they were now fixing was, in fact, a network of microphones, sensors, X-ray scanners, thermal cameras …

The shower stopped. She reached quickly for her Kindle, not wanting to be caught staring into space.

Mark emerged naked from the bathroom, toweling his hair. He looked at her significantly. He must have noticed that the Tampax were back under the sink. Saturday night, kids in bed …

Turning him away would invite suspicion. Instead, she smiled. He came forward, tossing the towel aside. He was in excellent shape for a man his age: strongly built, toned from regular exercise, well nourished since early childhood. After all these years, she still desired him.

He put a hand behind her head. Her lips parted as he leaned in for a kiss. She wondered fleetingly if he might somehow smell another man on her. Ridiculous. She had showered twice since last night. Yet the fear, irrationally, remained.

He tasted of mint. She reached down and found his erection. She set the Kindle on the nightstand, then pulled down her panties and guided him inside her.

It was faster than usual. She was hungry for him. She gasped with pleasure and came quickly, digging her nails into his back.

Only when it was done, when the lights were off and the damp hair matted against her neck was drying, did it occur to her that they may have been watched.

LANGLEY, VA

"We're in business."

In six new windows, six thermal images portrayed Apartment 5D in shades of neon.

Three views were top-down, from cameras fed into the ceiling. Three were side-on, imaging through thin drywall. Metal—mostly piping and appliances—showed pink. Wood was dark orange.

Organic matter was a vibrant violet. Shower, dishwasher, and recently extinguished bedside lamps blazed vermilion.

"The five-year-old"—Sam pointed with the cursor at a motionless figure—"in his bedroom. The two-year-old in the nursery. And the main attraction ..."

Two figures lay still, limbs entwined, in the master bedroom. Sam expanded another window, running Stingray IMSI, now also hooked into Mark Abrahams' phone. From the dresser top, the phone conveyed the same quiet audio—slow, even breathing—as the contact microphones freshly installed in the ceiling.

As they watched, a thermally rendered figure stirred, stealthily extricated itself from the tangle of limbs, and got up from the bed.

MANHATTAN, NY

She connected the battery, logged on, and entered her password. Still nothing.

She ran her index fingers beneath her eyes, disassembled and hid the phone, and went back to bed.

The traffic light reflected off the ceiling. Yellow, red ... green.

Above the ceiling, wires hummed. She could feel them in her back teeth. She could feel eyes crawling over her like ants.

She needed sleep.

No. She needed to trust her intuition. And get the hell out of here, get away from the crawling eyes, before it was too late.

Sprinkler system's on the fritz.

Union workers—New York State employees—toiling at nine thirty on a Saturday night without the slightest whiff of woe-is-me? *My ass.*

She thought of courtrooms and prison cells. Needles and gurneys. She had envisioned the moment many times. The middle-of-the-night knock. Just like the knock before the Electric Wave Inspection Bureau arrested her mother and sent them all to Yodok. The sleep-addled family trying to make sense of it. *You are under arrest for espionage as an agent of a foreign power, in violation of USC Title 18. You have the right to remain silent. Anything you say may be used against you in a court of law. You have the right to consult an attorney.*

She had researched this. Espionage in America was punishable by death. The United States federal government offloaded responsibility for executions onto the state where the crime was committed. If that state had no death penalty—New York, for instance—the judge simply chose another state to do the deed. In some states, the prisoner had the right, if lethal injection did not suit her temperament, to request an alternative method. Electrocution, gas inhalation, firing squad, or hanging.

She would choose lethal injection. First an anesthetic, then a paralytic, then potassium chloride to stop the heart. Quick and painless.

She tumbled into a light, troubled sleep. In the dream, her tae kwon do instructor at Heaven Lake put her through her paces. His soft, musical voice belied his penchant for brutality. *Speed is more important than size.* Song was panting, bathed in sweat, hair in strings. *Bring as many muscles as possible to bear on a strike, but strike the smallest area possible.* The left side of her rib cage throbbed dully where he had kicked her. *Relax the body between blocks, kicks, and strikes. Present a soft underbelly, inviting attack. Master the* dwi chagi, *the subtlest of maneuvers, in which one turns one's back to the enemy, feigning weakness …*

Beside her, Mark gave a snuffling half snore and rolled over.

His breathing settled again.

Gingerly she left the bed.

Tiptoeing to the bedroom closet, she poked through shoes and slacks and dresses. The Kate Spade bag was undisturbed in a back corner. She took it out and cradled it to her chest. Enough cash in it to start a new life. But only as a worst-case scenario.

After a moment, she carried the bag and some clothes out of the bedroom. She gentled the door shut behind herself with one hip and dressed in the front hall. The dishwasher, in its last cycle, thrummed rhythmically from the kitchen.

Behind the Thomas the Tank Engine umbrella, she found the leather bag containing the NYMEX pass-card data.

She found her smartphone and, in a kitchen drawer, the phone case she never used. She used a screwdriver to loosen two screws by the phone's charging port so she could reach the battery quickly.

She went into the study and found the RGB device in the desk. She found her keys.

She listened by the bedroom door. Mark still slept.

She started toward her children's rooms. Then stopped. Why make this harder than necessary?

Because—get the thought out into the light—she might never come back.

She went to the nursery. Baby Jia's door was cracked open. A rind of light illuminated the tiny Cupid's-bow mouth.

Goodbye, Baby Jia. I love you.

She went to her son's room. He lay tangled in his blanket, mouth agape.

Goodbye, Dex. I love you.

She spent a last moment looking at her sleeping son, then went.

CHAPTER SIX

She waited in the lobby wearing an empty smile, hoping nobody she knew would come through.

A car passed outside, playing loud pop music. Everyone within earshot was implored to *"shake it off, shake it off."* Song's Volvo pulled up out front. "Thank you, Ted," she told the doorman.

"G'night, Miz Abrahams."

She left her bags in the passenger seat and set her phone, inside its camera-blocking case, in the cup holder.

She headed for the FDR. Turning onto a small feeder road, she saw no boats on the water. The east side unrolled around her like a string of luminescent pearls. Half a mile downtown, Roosevelt Island, straddled by the Queensboro Bridge, sparkled like a light-up toy surrounded by darkness.

Present a soft underbelly, inviting attack. Master the dwi chagi, *the subtlest of maneuvers, in which one turns one's back to the enemy.*

God willing, she was wrong and nobody was watching. And she would be back home in a few hours, awaiting instructions for the rendezvous. Soon enough, she would hand off the data and this would all be over.

But if they *were* watching, she would force them to show their hand.

She joined the flow of traffic heading south.

LANGLEY, VA

They watched the Volvo turn onto the FDR.

Red crosshairs tracked the car: past Gracie Mansion, past John Jay Park, past Sutton Place. The audio feed provided the dense white noise of tires against pavement, an occasional faint horn.

"Meeting Walsh again?" Bach sounded unsure. "Same bar?"

"Why didn't she set it up?" McConnell said. "Why take her own car this time?"

Sam quit gnawing his thumb long enough to say, "Maybe she *did* set it up. With the second device."

"Then why didn't we see it on *his* phone?"

"Maybe he's got another device, too."

They watched the red crosshairs pass the United Nations Building, the Queens Midtown Tunnel, Kips Bay, Bellevue. Two pairs of green crosshairs followed a hundred yards behind.

When the Volvo merged onto Houston heading west, the audio became more varied: music, street voices, blaring horns. The FBI vans merged behind it.

The red crosshairs reached Bowery. If Six Degrees had been her destination, she would have turned by now.

"His apartment," McConnell suggested.

Sam brought up the windows hooked to Walsh's phone. It had not been touched since arriving back at Liberty Plaza, six hours ago. Two emails delivered during that time shed no light. The first, from a Gmail account registered to a Karen Westwick: *"We like Ishare ETF for Basic Materials Sector, IYM. 4 cent premium over Net Asset Avenue. 8 Mil shares outstanding. Newmont, Alcoa, etc."* The second, from the Yahoo! account of one Jason Moorhead, read, *"Far be it from me to speak ill of GS.*😊 *JM."*

Sam nibbled the pad of his thumb again. McConnell pushed his glasses higher on his nose. Bach stared at nothing on the wall. Sonny drummed on the tabletop with his fingers. Dalia felt her gut tighten. *What's she up to?* She found her cane, levered herself up, and moved closer to the screen.

MANHATTAN, NY

On Sixth Avenue, traffic was bumper-to-bumper. Orange pylons split the avenue in half. Two lanes to the left were marked *Thru Traffic Lower Manhattan Only.* To the right, *Interstate 78. Holland Tunnel New Jersey. 12'6" Clear.*

Song eased to the right.

Her eyes made a steady circuit from rearview to sideview, to windshield, then back to rearview. A birdlike woman driving a Tesla behind her brandished a vape pen. A mustachioed man in a PT Cruiser to her right laughed into a Bluetooth headset. In the rearview mirror, her own eyes looked glassy.

As traffic inched forward, the undertow of exhaustion tried to drag her down. She pinched the tender flesh inside her left elbow and twisted hard. Awake again. Another yard forward.

Her gaze rested briefly on a line waiting to get into a late show at Film Forum. Knit caps, slim-fit pants, plaid sport jackets, horn-rimmed glasses, full bushy beards. When she had first arrived in America, every hipster affectation, every pair of skinny jeans and ironic display of plaid, had seemed to reinforce the lessons learned back home. Western capitalism was decadence, pure and simple. After she had married and moved uptown, the spectacle of Upper East Side housewives with their chemical peels and fifty-dollar bottles of Jimmy Choo lotion made her seethe with righteous fury. Even as her own countrymen starved, thanks to criminal international sanctions, Americans competed to see who could waste the most money. It would be an honor to help destroy them from the inside out.

There had been no defining moment, no single shining epiphany, when her devotion began to flag. Rather, it had been a slow process of accretion and decay. Her defenses had eroded before the onslaught of creature comforts. New loyalties had developed to replace the old. And there had been the web. While Mark slept, she had surfed at length, finding things that made too much sense to ignore.

For example, the Massacre of Sinchon. During her reeducation at Heaven Lake, she had visited the Museum of American War Atrocities in South Hwanghae. She had learned that US troops tortured and murdered more than thirty-five thousand innocent Koreans during the occupation of Sinchon in 1950. But Americans taught a different version of the story. The butchery, they said, had been the work of right-wing Korean security police, abetted by youth gangs and Communists, albeit under American overseers who had chosen to look the other way. Thanks to the Kim dynasty's relentless propagandizing, the details of the tragedy had become shrouded in fog that would never be entirely cleared away.

Her first reaction had been skepticism. *The Kim dynasty's relentless propagandizing.* But of course, American propagandizing was the most shameless in all the world. *One nation under God, indivisible, with liberty and justice for all.* Ask Trayvon Martin about that last part. Ask the victims of the Tuskegee Study of Untreated Syphilis in the Negro Male. Ask Jacobo Árbenz. Ask her starving countrymen back home, who had suffered under sanctions only because they tried to defend themselves, to arm themselves with the same weapons America used to terrorize the world. What kind of bully picked up the biggest stick on the playground and then forbade everyone else to pick up a stick? The worst kind. The most transparent kind. The *American* kind.

And American citizens gave up, for their country, exactly nothing. They slathered themselves with Jimmy Choo as they blithely agreed to let Koreans starve. They sent their poorest and most desperate to fight their wars—or, even worse, they sent robot drones. They embraced hypocrisy, shallowness, violence, religion, imperialism, pornography. These people had no honor, no pride.

No *juche*. Even at her lowest, even going without food for days on end so that her little brother could eat, Song had always had her pride and her *juche*.

She remembered her mother at Yodok, struggling to breathe, throat swollen, flies buzzing. With each cough, Mother had hacked up another bloody bit of lung. In her last moment, face purple, eyes bulging, she had turned to her daughter and reached out one supplicating hand. All she had wanted was one final moment of human contact, human kindness. But Song had been too frozen by horror to take the hand. In fact—and she cringed at the memory— she had shrunk away.

She had blamed the *kwan-li-so* system for her mother's death. But after reeducation, she had seen the truth and put the blame where it belonged: on the Americans.

After her initial skeptical reaction to the American propaganda, however, had come other, more nuanced reactions. Not all at once, but slowly, on little cat feet, like the fog in Sandburg's poem.

She realized that her own kindergarten lessons had not been so different from the indoctrination shoved down the throats of American children. *Our enemies are the American bastards, who are trying to take over our beautiful fatherland. With guns that I make with my own hands, I will shoot them. BANG, BANG, BANG.* She had played her accordion and dutifully sung the lyrics along with the rest of her classmates.

And the entire "reeducation" had been still more propaganda— even worse, in its way, than American propaganda. Because American children never had to scour the countryside for silkworm larvae to quell their growling bellies. They never had to search through cow dung for undigested kernels of corn. They never used a garden hoe to chop frozen shit from a latrine, to use as fertilizer. They did not know how to spread a rat on the blade of a shovel to roast it. They did not fall to their knees, instinctively abasing themselves at the first sign of trouble. What was the primary duty of any country? To protect its own. And in that, Chosun had failed.

And perhaps, America was not entirely to blame for the Arduous March. On the internet, she learned new histories of the Korean Peninsula. She learned that until the collapse of the Berlin Wall, the Soviet Union had subsidized North Korea with fertilizer, fuel, and ready-made markets. She learned that before the partition, North Korea had supplied 90 percent of the peninsula's electricity, with hydropower from its many fast-moving rivers. But the Kim family had failed to leverage this tremendous resource. Instead, they had decreed *songun,* military first.

She found pictures of UN and US aid—food and supplies that had been sent to Korea but never reached the people. During 1995–2003, a billion dollars' worth of rice, wheat, powdered milk, fertilizer, blankets, medicine. And she found satellite photos of the Supreme Leader's yachts, his luxurious private islands, and his ranks of underage concubines. The family dynasty maintained no fewer than eight mansions, equipped with movie theaters and basketball courts and shooting ranges, horse-racing tracks and water parks and private railway stations. All while starving children considered themselves lucky for catching a rat to splay open and roast.

Her eyes repeated their restless circuit inside the Volvo: windshield, rearview, sideview. There, two blocks back, a windowless van. Traffic shifted, and she lost it.

She refocused. *The subtlest of maneuvers, in which one turns one's back to the enemy.*

If she was being watched, she had to know.

A space opened in front of her. She touched the gas, and the Volvo surged ahead.

LANGLEY, VA

"Where's she going?"

Bach's question was rhetorical; the short-term answer was clear enough. The car-jammed entrance ramp fed into the Holland Tunnel. She could not have turned around now if she wanted to.

Sam was typing again and talking at the same time. "ARGUS loses her inside the tunnel. Stingray, too, unless they're right on her bumper. But there's CCTV every tenth of a mile. If I can access the network, she won't be out of sight for a second ..."

His fingertips whickered across the keys. On-screen, the drone gave a bird's-eye view of the Volvo merging, inch by inch, into four lanes of crawling traffic. A massive Dodge Ram pickup truck nosed in front of it. Both of DeArmond's vans were stuck two blocks behind.

"What if she switches cars?" Dalia asked. "Inside the tunnel?"

"That would be a neat trick," Bach said. "We'll have her on CCTV the whole time, yes?"

"Working on it," Sam murmured.

Dalia considered Bach. Beneath the almost-convincing poise, she sensed something untrustworthy in the man. Some raw ambition that would not be checked. He, too, lacked a wedding band. He had given everything to his work. And he would continue to do so. In ten years he might be running the CIA. In twenty he might not be satisfied even with that. He might pivot into a political career. But he would have made enemies. And when he was not looking, some trusted friend might sink a knife into his back.

On-screen, a dozen new windows popped up. "CCTV!" Sam crowed. "Inside the tunnel."

Just in time—the Volvo was disappearing into the maw.

MANHATTAN, NY

Traffic proceeded herky-jerky: slowing to almost nothing, accelerating to ten miles per hour, then suddenly stopping dead.

A pickup truck blocked her view ahead. Oversize American truck. Ram tough. Not like the rickety Chinese K01 pickup that had picked her up after she crossed the Tumen. More like the Soviet Tsirs, called "crows" for their black canvas canopies.

When she and her brother were recaptured after their first

prison escape, they had been thrown beneath a black canopy, into the back of a crow. She remembered a heavy downpour. It had been the rainy season. Huge tires splashing through snaking streams on muddy roads. A handsome soldier on the running board held a Kalashnikov. She kept trying to make eye contact, but the handsome soldier knew better than to meet her eye. He avoided looking at her as the crow passed through checkpoint after checkpoint, then delivered them in chains to Camp 14.

At Yodok Prison, she had reluctantly agreed to throw in with a prisoner named Kang who had stolen a pair of garden shears, with which he planned to cut through the fence. Kang had already been inside Yodok for ten years. He had lost his teeth, and he walked hunched over, from malnutrition and from bones that mended badly after being broken during torture sessions. His last living relative, a daughter, had recently died. And so he had no reason not to risk escape. But the instant the shears touched the fence, he went rigid, trembling violently. Song smelled smoke. She did not hesitate. Grabbing her brother's hand, she climbed across Kang's vibrating body, feeling the current tingling through him, jabbing her like a thousand tiny needles.

Engines reverberated off yellow-tiled walls. Forward. Slow, fast, slow again. Stop. She wanted to reach for a phone. She wanted to call Mark, talk to the kids. But no.

In the back of the crow, she had been prepared to do whatever was necessary. Now, too, she must be ruthless.

With herself, most of all.

LANGLEY, VA

Dalia's gaze jumped from one CCTV feed to the next.

Between Homeland's and Port Authority's cameras, all nine thousand feet of the Holland Tunnel were covered. But to the untrained eye, headlights in night-vision gloom all looked the same. She lost the Volvo immediately.

She gave her head a shake. They'd had the woman cornered. They could have taken her at any time. But, smug with their upper hand, they had sat back. Played out rope. Pushed their luck with the "sprinkler inspectors." And let their quarry slip through their fingers.

McConnell, standing now on Dalia's other side, kept a bracing hand ready in case her knee gave out. Bach's intense stare raked the screen. His finger stabbed at the monitor. "There."

Almost halfway through the tunnel. But as soon as Dalia found it, the Volvo moved on to the next window and she lost it again.

Her phone was vibrating. Her daughter, calling from Tel Aviv at last. Bad timing. She let it go to voice mail.

They watched via ARGUS as the Volvo left the tunnel on the New Jersey side. Persistics kicked on, stamping the car with red crosshairs that bore northwest, forsaking Route 78 for Route 9. No more tunnels in that direction. Wherever the woman went next, the drone could follow.

Yet Dalia found herself thinking suddenly of the half-written monograph awaiting her attention back in Princeton. At Issus, Darius' overconfidence in superior technology and manpower had proved fatal. At Gaugamela, two years later, he had compounded his mistake and dealt the Achaemenid Empire a blow from which it never recovered.

Determined this time to fight on a field of his own choosing, the Persian general had lain in ambush near a large open plain. Alexander had appeared to blunder into the trap, letting his enemy confidently deploy his overwhelming force. But in fact, the young Macedonian king had held in reserve his most vicious mercenaries: a second line, a stockpiled force to encircle the enemy once they believed they had encircled *him*. Alexander had watched, biding his time, as the Persian army revealed its numbers, positions, and tactics. And then he had once again wrested victory from a force outnumbering his own by more than two to one.

"Be ready," Dalia said tightly.

DeArmond's two vans held position about fifty yards behind the Volvo.

"See where she leads us," Bach said, eyes pinned on the screen. "Hang back."

"Be ready," Dalia repeated. "She's up to something."

DeArmond raised his phone. "Checking Alpha."

"Roger Alpha," a thin voice answered. "Tango twelve o'clock."

"Checking Bravo."

"Roger Bravo."

"Alpha, move to Tango six o'clock."

On-screen, one pair of green crosshairs pulled into the passing lane.

Bach watched. Shadows pooled in deep hollows around his eyes.

The time code read 22:45:26+01.

NEWARK, NJ

Song merged onto the turnpike proper. Quarter of eleven now. Traffic flowing smoothly. Theatergoers returning from an evening in the city. Wetlands glistening with light pollution on her right. On her left, stacked boxcars and cranes. Ahead, smokestacks and factories, overpasses and billboards. All was right in New Jersey and the world.

Then a state trooper appeared in her rearview, and fear pushed up from her stomach, closing her throat.

Any second now, the siren would whoop. And then what? Would she, Mi-Hi Abrahams, mother of two, PTA volunteer extraordinaire and assistant chair to the food drive, jam her Volvo XC90's pedal to the floor and take off down the New Jersey Turnpike through Saturday-night traffic? This was one of the most accident-prone stretches of highway in the developed world. They called it the Black Dragon.

Her hands tightened on the wheel.

The prowler eased into the passing lane and glided by.

She released a hot, shaking breath.

Coming up behind the prowler: a windowless, anonymous van. Maybe the same van she had seen on Sixth Avenue, maybe not.

The van passed.

An off-ramp was coming up: *Exit 14-14A-14B-14C – 78-1-9-22 – Newark Airport – Holland Tunnel.* She could see aircraft queuing for landing beyond the sign, lights that seemed to hang motionless in the night sky.

Without haste, she reached for the phone in the cup holder. Holding the wheel with her knees, she put the phone in her lap, ready to shed the case.

The van had passed the exit ramp. She took the wheel in both hands and, traveling at exactly fifty-five miles per hour, bore right.

LANGLEY, VA

One pair of green crosshairs followed the red bull's-eye off the highway. The other, already committed to the Turnpike, was forced to continue south-southwest.

"Do we have backup?" Bach asked.

"That *was* our backup." DeArmond licked his lips and raised the phone. "Alpha, return to Interstate Seventy-Eight via Route Nine. ASAP. Bravo, maintain visual on Tango."

On the monitor, the audio feed of the spoofed phone was suddenly joined by a video feed. Images joggled crazily. The roof of the Volvo's interior: black panel, rearview mirror, sun visor, flush-mounted LEDs. A woman's hip clad in denim. A gearshift. A wheeling slice of highway outside a window. Then darkness again as the phone was set facedown.

"She took the cover off her phone," said Sam. "Why?"

Feeds died on-screen—first audio, then video.

"She took out the battery." He sounded unsurprised.

"She's onto us." Bach's voice was hollow. "Goddamn it! How?"

"You pushed your luck," Dalia said.

On the ARGUS feed, the Volvo approached a tollbooth. Taking an E-ZPass lane, it continued toward the airport.

"Newark International." Now Sam sounded weary. "Class B airspace. Technically, so is Manhattan. But unless we want to risk bringing down a passenger jet …"

ARGUS's thirty-six-square-mile overview had until now moved automatically to keep the red crosshairs center screen. But suddenly the crosshairs were edging off center—the drone's operator at NRO headquarters in Chantilly, Virginia, reluctant to proceed.

Dalia shook her head. In the space of ten seconds, they had lost a van, Stingray, and now ARGUS.

The woman had chosen the battlefield that best suited her. She had relied on her enemy's overconfidence. Dalia had seen it coming—and done nothing to prevent it. And suddenly, their vaunted technological dominance meant nothing.

"Take her," she said hoarsely.

DeArmond nodded.

"Bravo," he said into the phone, "apprehend."

CHAPTER SEVEN

NEWARK, NJ

A siren whooped behind her, then engaged fully for a moment, howling up, descending in a liquid glissando.

A strange coolness enveloped her. Somehow, she had not truly believed that this moment would come. But here it was.

She flicked on her turn signal and eased the Volvo onto the shoulder. Tires rolled to a stop, crunching gravel. An airplane passed almost directly overhead, making a terrific whoosh. To her right, beyond cyclone fencing, copper-colored runways spread like an alien landscape. To her left, traffic sped past. Just ahead, the highway split: NORTH 1-9 TO 78 and ALL TERMINALS.

In her rearview mirror, a red light spun on a dashboard—another windowless, anonymous van.

The Volvo's engine idled. Her hands rested in plain sight on the steering wheel. Nothing to see here, Officers. Just an ordinary housewife. A case of mistaken identity.

She could do this.

The van doors opened.

A few moments passed. Then two men left the vehicle. They wore the same unmemorable white shirts and blue jeans as the "sprinkler inspectors." She didn't see guns, but they were no doubt concealed within easy reach.

The two men were fanning out. One approached on the driver's side, one on the passenger's. She might throw the Volvo into reverse, slew backward, spin the wheel, and run down one or both of them.

Her right hand moved onto the gearshift. She could almost feel the dull thud of vibration that would travel through the chassis, up her arm, when she made contact.

She hesitated. This was not the kind of thing you could take back.

And like that, the chance was gone. One man came up beside her window, his carriage easy; not quite smiling, but open-faced, friendly, nonthreatening. She returned her right hand to the steering wheel.

The one outside the passenger window wasn't bothering to smile. He was using a high-powered flashlight to look inside the Volvo. Before the light blinded her, she glimpsed medium-length chestnut hair tossing in the wind from passing traffic.

The friendly one on her left gestured for her to bring the window down. After a second, she complied.

"Evening," he said. "Mind stepping out of the vehicle?"

He could see both her hands, but she could see only one of his.

"What's the problem?" she asked.

"Step out of the vehicle, please."

"Can I see some ID?"

"After you step out."

To her right, beyond the fencing, running lights moved. Thunder began to build as turbines roared up to speed.

She had two choices. She could slam down the gas. They would try to shoot out her tires. Or she could put them further off their guard by leaving the car.

She opened her door. "Was I speeding?"

"Step out of the car, ma'am."

With courage that felt like clothes she had just stepped into, she left the car.

She saw that indeed he held a gun, a compact SIG Sauer P229, in his right hand, slightly behind his hip.

Her body moved of its own accord. She feinted left, then used her own right hand to seize the weapon and twist it back, trapping his finger in the trigger guard. He grabbed her right elbow reflexively. She stepped away, jerking down hard on the weapon, dislocating his index finger, and then twisted savagely.

The other one was looking at her openmouthed. From the awkward fit of his white shirt, he must be wearing a vest underneath. That made it easier. She aimed the automatic straight-armed across the roof, shaking free the severed index finger. She found center body mass and fired. The trigger had a long, heavy pull. The recoil drove back the slide, feeding the next round and cocking the pistol automatically.

The man tumbled back. She snapped another shot—shorter, lighter pull—into the leg of the man writhing in agony at her feet. He jolted and cried out.

Back behind the wheel of the Volvo. Brake lights flared as drivers slowed, trying to process what they had just seen.

She felt very calm.

She slammed the door, found drive, and punched it, leaning down, minimizing the size of the target she would present in case of return fire. At the same time, she aimed the gun at the passenger-side window, ready to shoot if the chestnut-haired one got up again.

But both men stayed down. And nobody inside the passing cars found the courage to stop and engage her.

The engine revved as she gained speed. Her lips skinned back from her teeth. She bore right: ALL TERMINALS.

LANGLEY, VA

Dalia closed her eyes. Behind the lids, she was fifteen years old, lying on a grassy bank, trailing her fingers in cool water, without a care in the world.

She had been on her feet for too long. She opened her eyes and looked for the nearest chair. McConnell took her elbow helpfully.

On the wide view, the red crosshairs were traveling southwest at a good clip. They navigated a tangled double cloverleaf and then, nearing the edge of the window, accessed the wide loop circling the airport terminals.

In a target-acquisition window, two men on a gravel shoulder struggled to get their feet under them. DeArmond was on his phone again. Sam was typing, always typing. A police bandwidth opened. "Ten fifty-two," a woman was saying. "Eleven ninety-nine, ten fifty-three." A crackling response: "Dispatch, this is six-oh-six, I'm ten sixty-one …"

The red crosshairs reached the edge of the screen—and blipped off.

Dalia had to sit. She gestured sharply, and McConnell helped her back to the table and eased her down.

NEWARK, NJ

Short-term parking. She paused at the gate to take a ticket, then took the first space, between a Kia Sorento and a Mini Cooper.

A horn honked, echoing. Headlights splashed behind her. Her hand moved for the gun in the passenger seat, but the car glided on. Nothing to do with her.

Colors seemed too bright, sounds too loud. Her cheeks were damp. She wiped tears away and turned her attention to the Kate Spade bag. She pulled out a wig. As she straightened it in the rearview mirror, her face remained blank. Only the big dark eyes showed any feeling. Inside those eyes, thunderclouds stormed.

Latex and makeup thickened her jaw and lips. Contact lenses turned her eyes hazel. She gave her reflection one last check. She looked okay, considering.

Her coat was reversible. She reversed it. She unfolded a canvas gym bag and quickly repacked. She transferred equipment from the leather bag. She slid the magazine out of the SIG so it couldn't go off unexpectedly, racked the slide to clear the chambered round and reinserted that in the magazine, then zipped gun and magazine into the canvas bag.

She put her cell phone in one coat pocket, the battery in another, and tucked the two empty bags beneath the passenger seat. She left the car, chirping the alarm on with the key fob. Thinking only of the next minute. Then the one after that.

An opaque globe mounted in a corner concealed a camera. Approaching the globe, she didn't look at it, but she didn't look away. She did not rush, but she did not dawdle.

She crossed two lanes of traffic. The terminal concourse bustled with activity: skycaps tagging bags, children crying, smokers smoking, cops patrolling in full paramilitary riot gear. She walked past them all and entered the terminal. She passed more Port Authority cops, police dogs on chain leashes, parents trying to corral irritable children, and clerks wearing tired smiles like armor. Dunkin' Donuts, Starbucks, Cinnabon, Travelex ATM. Loudspeakers announced arrivals and departures, paged personnel, sometimes spat out meaningless bursts of static. None of it seemed real.

She rode an escalator down, then angled toward Ground Transportation.

LANGLEY, VA

"Got her," said Sam.

She was leaving the Volvo, walking fearlessly toward the camera. Sam froze the CCTV image. Dalia's eyes flicked to the time code: eight minutes ago.

The hair was shorter, the face blunter. The computer scanned the new face, locking in the new nodal pattern. New windows opened: a web of closed-circuit cameras around the airport. They picked her up threading through a crowd on the concourse of Terminal C.

On the feed, the woman vanished from the concourse. For a

floating moment, they had her exactly nowhere. Then another camera picked her up inside the terminal. Wearing a fixed expression, she breezed past canines. She rode an escalator to Ground Transportation. They watched as she considered choices: AirTrain, taxi, shuttle bus, Avis, Hertz, Budget, National, Alamo, Enterprise.

In other windows, live feeds ran. A private ambulance carrying DeArmond's wounded operatives was just leaving the shoulder near the tollbooths. The second windowless van was turning into short-term parking, where the abandoned Volvo waited.

Dalia looked back to the woman, eight minutes ago.

Song chose Hertz, which had no line, and then disappeared from the field of view. Sam was already typing. A new angle opened. She stood by the desk, wearing a small, polite smile.

Apparently, the clerk was offering her choices. Song nodded. She made a selection, passing over a driver's license and credit card. Sam froze and zoomed. The image was blurry and upside down. He flipped and enhanced. The photo on the license matched the new blunt face. The name was Min-Soo Park, the address in Glenwillow, Ohio.

Yet another window. A digital receipt appeared: *Hertz RR T 15256500,* followed by 1-800 numbers for roadside service and customer care. Sam had hacked into the Hertz network in the time it took most people to log on to their email. He scrolled down. Rental location was EWR. Rental time was 11:29 p.m.

Dalia found the cane and levered herself up again. She moved close to the monitor, scanning quickly. Rates, service charge, mileage, fuel tank, taxes …

Make and model: 2015 Chevrolet Trax LT.

DeArmond was dialing. "We've *got* her, goddamn it."

NEWARK, NJ

Song Sun Young climbed into a blue van with white wings painted beneath slanted letters. NEWARK SUPERSHUTTLE. NEED A LIFT?

She found an empty row halfway back on the left. The driver

was already closing the door. They pulled out onto the loop, heading toward AIRPORT EXIT—RENTAL CAR RETURNS.

Past Terminal C with its strange up-curving roof, as if the building were winged and straining to take flight. Past a road marked LOADING AND UNLOADING ONLY. Past the Hertz lot. She squinted, trying to make out the scene she imagined must be going down. Feds wearing blue jeans and bland white shirts, clustered around a 2015 Chevy Trax, talking on phones and radios, trying to figure out where she had gone. In a room somewhere not far away, they would be poring over surveillance feeds, CCTV, and satellites and drones and spoofed phones. But she had been out of any camera sight lines when she hooked into the ladies' room. She was 99 percent certain. Ninety-eight.

She found no strange activity in the parking lot. Maybe they were on the other side of the building.

Her shuttle was getting on a feeder road, moving faster. She leaned back into her seat.

They would figure out her bait and switch. And sooner rather than later—their surveillance cameras were legion.

Assume she made Port Authority. What next?

Every paranoid thought had been on target. She had indeed been under surveillance at home. In her car. Picking up her kids from school. Everywhere. They had seen her meeting with Walsh. They had seen everything.

She could not go anywhere she had ever been before.

She had the NYMEX pass-card data in her bag. Pyongyang might welcome her. They might fete her as a hero. They might lavish her and Man Soo with gifts procured through Office 39, which bought luxury goods from overseas to keep well-connected families supplied.

Or they might not. They might declare her an enemy of the state for leaving a job half-finished. They might throw her into a labor camp. They might tie her to a pole and shoot her.

Even if they praised her, welcomed her with open arms—what

did Office 39 have to offer? In Pyongyang, luxury meant electricity and warm blankets and fresh fruit. Maybe a DVD player. Nothing compared to the lifestyle she had been living.

The highway lights streaming past all blurred together.

One minute at a time. She would stay near New York City. It seemed reasonable to assume that her rendezvous with the contact would be nearby. Pyongyang would want the data delivered with all possible dispatch.

One minute at a time.

She looked out the window, and the minute passed. Then another, and then one more.

LANGLEY, VA

Two dozen windows crowded the monitor. The largest displayed the most recent image of the woman, at the Hertz desk: short hair, blunt face, hazel eyes, pale coat, canvas gym bag. Other windows showed baggage-claim carousels, taxi lines, AirTrain platforms. The computer scanned faces, counted nodal points, compared with earlier images, found fewer than twenty matches, and scanned again. And again.

Another window showed Stingray seeking the woman's phone. If the battery was returned while the baseband chip was in range, IMSI Catcher would find it.

Two other windows showed green code scrolling against black backgrounds. One was the ongoing effort to decrypt the original message from Pyongyang. The other was a direct interface with the RGB server. Anyone connecting to the server would doubtless use a fabricated IP address. But the computer behind the falsified address would have no reason to distrust the server, and so that computer would receive a virus of Sam's design, switching on any geolocation function and relaying coordinates directly to this room.

Other windows conveyed video feeds from state trooper dashcams and NYPD bodycams, and highway tollbooths and airport checkpoints, and surveillance CCTV from the Port Authority—all scanned incessantly by facial-recognition software. Another window scrolled voice-to-text transcriptions from New Jersey, Connecticut, and New York police radio scanners. Every department in the tristate area had received a be-on-the-lookout from the FBI. Upon apprehension, the woman would be held for DeArmond.

Another window ran ARGUS, sweeping endlessly with Persistics.

The last two windows showed the work Sam was currently engaged in: following cybertrails left by Bill Walsh and Mark and Mi-Hi Abrahams, seeking red flags, any faint whiff of espionage or criminal conduct, improper or unexplained relationships, debts or addictions. He was also hunting for undiscovered traces of Song Sun Young, at Ansang University or in the files of Interpol or RIPR, the secure coalition network used to convey classified information between the Republic of Korea and the United States, under the name Mi-Hi Pyung, or Park Ha-Soo, or Min-Soo Park.

For the moment, there was nothing more that Bach could do here.

Fatigue was a black horse thundering up on him. He could either surrender or be trampled.

He turned away without calling attention to himself. They would find him if necessary.

In his office, he composed and sent a new report to the DDO. There was a bright side to the woman's flight. The development would cut through red tape, speed along permission to bring in the heavy guns.

He dry-swallowed a dose of pholcodine and lay down on the couch. He shut his eyes, listening to his shallow heartbeat against the armrest.

Soon, he slept. And again remembered.

CHAPTER EIGHT

On October 14, 2001, he buried an empty casket.

Mom had died sixteen years earlier. Dad's closest friends had all been inside the North Tower. The service was attended only by Benjamin Bach, a priest, a registrar, and two gravediggers.

That night he went for a walk. Through the main gates of Columbia and then west to Riverside Park. He sat on a bench. A hundred-odd blocks south, fire still smoldered beneath the pile. When the wind turned, the breeze still bore a hint of that toxic, evil smell.

He was underdressed in a windbreaker and blue jeans. He shivered, hugging his elbows. He watched F-15s sail in tight circles over the Hudson. He watched Apache helicopters hover before the sinking sun. He closed his eyes and saw bandaged hands, melted badges, the remnants of a firefighter's helmet. An empty jacket glued to a stretcher by tacky blood. People taking pictures. Why did they take pictures? Did they really think they could ever forget?

He kept his eyes closed. He heard the hollow raking of his own breath in the canisters of the gas mask, his heart pulsing in his ears.

He opened his eyes and spat out a gob of yellow-gray phlegm.

One month after the fact, he was still in Do-mode. Feelings were still locked behind that steel door. Airtight, negative pressure. He rose from the bench and strolled back to campus. Exams soon. Dad was gone, but life went on.

*   *   *

Two years later, walking past a restaurant in Columbus Circle, he saw two women eating lunch behind a plate-glass window, and suddenly boiled with fury.

Like normal? he wanted to scream. *You're eating lunch like everything is fucking normal?*

He wanted to grab a trash can and shatter the window. He wanted to seize the women, frighten them, shake them, hurt them, rape them. One was laughing so exaggeratedly that he could see gold and silver fillings glinting in her molars. The other was striking a pose of skeptical amusement, her depilated eyebrows delicately raised.

He closed his eyes. He saw smoky flame eddying above the towers. Blood-soaked children, ruined ambulances, melted badges.

If this was a breakdown—if the sealed door inside his mind was finally giving way—the timing could not have been worse. In six days, he would fly to McLean, Virginia, to run the final gauntlet before entering on duty as a case officer with the CIA.

The Company had first extended feelers last year, inviting him to an informational meeting in DC. He must have caught their eye after writing and, unusually, publishing an undergraduate thesis on *kamun sosŏl,* the vernacular Korean lineage novels. He had gone on to earn a PhD in East Asian Studies from Columbia, which had undoubtedly compounded their interest. Losing his father at the World Trade Center had surely put him over the top. They had figured, rightly, that Benjamin Bach would do anything to help prevent the Twin Towers, Part Two.

So far, he had passed everything they threw at him. Polygraphs, background checks, questions about drug use and relationships with foreign nationals. Psych profiles: men and women making frank eye contact while asking probing questions. *What problem would you fix if you had unlimited resources? What would you most like to be remembered for? What are you proudest of? Least proud of? Are you self-reliant, self-confident, and adaptable? Are you open to critical feedback?* He had answered honestly—after checking to make sure that the steel door still held.

Standing outside the Columbus Circle restaurant, he released a long, shuddering breath. He was okay.

Heartbeat slowing. Door lowering again. Airtight, negative pressure.

He opened his eyes. The women behind the window were just women. Two Upper West Side housewives squeezing in slices of avocado toast between Pilates classes. They posed no threat to him.

He coughed. Then again, a percussive series raking his torso.

He spat a plug of phlegm the color and consistency of tar onto the sidewalk.

He focused. *Do-mode.*

He walked on.

*   *   *

He made sure, on 9/11 anniversaries, to keep busy, to avoid dredging something up.

In March 2010, he found himself back in the States, after almost seven years overseas, to attend an emergency cybersecurity conference at the Pentagon. Seven years of fleabag hotels in Yanji Province and Vladivostok made the extended stay Marriott in Arlington feel like the Plaza.

Each morning, he would take his free continental breakfast in the Marriott's lobby. Then he would be picked up at 8 a.m. sharp by Command Chief Master Sergeant Woodrow "Woody" Whitlock, US Air Force. According to the grapevine, Whitlock was on track to become chief master sergeant, maybe even someday director for operations of J3, the Joint Chiefs' Command System Division. Despite a résumé bristling with commendations and command tours, the man proved strikingly down-to-earth: soft-spoken, polite, and unmistakably intelligent. Whitlock played loud classic rock on the radio of his Toyota Highlander. A photograph of a four-year-old daughter in a frilly pink tutu dangled from the rearview mirror.

Each morning, they would park in a reserved spot near the river entrance of the Pentagon's sixty-seven-acre lot, so close to Ronald Reagan International that the Toyota's windows rattled when planes took off. They would swipe their badges over a sensor at a guard podium. Whitlock's red-striped laminate included a small number 3 beside the square-jawed photo, indicating that he was of sufficient value to merit evacuation to Site R, the alternate command center in Pennsylvania, in case of crisis. Bach himself, with no number beside his laminated face, was evidently expendable.

But Bach determinedly did not think of crises as he followed Woody Whitlock past E-ring offices populated by senior military leadership. Even in this distinguished company, Whitlock inspired grins and handshakes on every side. When Bach's gaze brushed a plaque commemorating forty-two Navy personnel lost inside the Pentagon on September 11, the steel door in his mind remained flush, hermetically sealed.

Each morning, they walked the polished halls alongside people in business attire, dress blues, full flight suits. An elevator carried them down to the subbasement labyrinth of offices, cubicles, and conference rooms that constituted the National Military Command Center. Seated around a twenty-five-foot boat-shaped table, they joined representatives from the DIA, CIA, FBI, NSA, NSF, NIST, DARPA, IARPA, DHS, NASA, and J3.

Some of the faces were familiar to Bach; he had hosted them at Seoul Station. Publicly, US efforts to curtail Pyongyang's ballistic-missile program focused on saber rattling and missile interception schemes such as THAAD. But behind the scenes, high-tech sabotage got the real work done. Because preemptive policies were officially verboten, such work unfolded in a zone purposely kept gray.

Operation Nimble Fire took a page from the Israelis' playbook.

Unit 8200 of the IDF had pioneered modern cyberwarfare, in 2005 creating Stuxnet, the worm that made Iran's fast-spinning centrifuges tear themselves apart. And in 2007, during Operation Orchard, the IDF had deactivated Syrian air defenses by feeding them a false sky picture. Applied to North Korea, cyberwarfare had already yielded several successes after sanctions and threats failed. DPRK ballistic tests had been derailed via malware, laser, and signal blocking; missiles had blown up on their launchpads and gone careening into the sea.

Now a snafu in Wyoming had driven home just how vulnerable US missile systems remained to the kind of attack Bach directed regularly against America's enemies. Fifty nuclear-armed Minutemen in underground silos had vanished, without warning, from the monitors of their launch crew. As operators scrambled to make sense of the disappearance, the Pentagon had gone into emergency mode. They knew that hackers continually bombarded the firewalls of US nuclear networks. If attackers had found an electronic back door, this was what it might look like. Until the situation was resolved, the fifty missiles could not be launched by CENTCOM, and—worse—the crew had no way to interrupt a launch triggered by an enemy.

After an hour, a faulty circuit card in an underground computer had been discovered and replaced. But spooked investigators had kept probing the system. Cheyenne was the gold standard of Global Strike Command. Something like this might conceivably happen at Minot, even Malmstrom. But not Cheyenne.

They had found, to their great dismay, that flight guidance systems were accessible via the internet. Digging deeper, they discovered that critical firewalls had been breached. Much of the software and hardware used in vital networks had come from off-the-shelf commercial sources. A top-to-bottom reevaluation had been ordered.

The first week of Pentagon meetings dealt with that reevaluation, and new measures that would be implemented as a result. The second week, top brass widened the scope to encompass larger cybersecurity issues, including policy.

A woman from NIST, the National Institute of Standards and Technology, fired the opening shot across the bow. "I have a question for the architects of Nimble Fire." She pinned Bach with small, hostile eyes, a smirk on her overlipsticked mouth. "By indulging a policy of preemptive maneuvers, do we not invite retaliation in kind? Have we fully considered the political and strategic consequences of our actions?"

Before answering, Bach checked to make sure the steel door remained tightly sealed. You couldn't just tell the woman from NIST that in the real world, people who clung to the moral high ground ended up with blood-soaked children and melted badges and dead fathers. You couldn't scream in her face, throw her onto the floor, rape her, kill her, show her what the world was really about. No, you had to tiptoe around the issue. Here at the Pentagon, surrounded by ribbon-studded brass and bureaucrats in two-thousand-dollar suits and professional Boy Scouts like Woodrow "Woody" Whitlock, you had to finesse the truth.

He cleared his throat. Softly but firmly, he answered. "Nonkinetic technologies implemented by my team in Seoul target electronic radar signals and embed Trojan horses with a higher success rate than any existing missile interception system. When coupled with HUMINT to ensure strategic target selection, we're looking at the single most promising strategy to counter ballistic—"

"The question on the table, sir"—the paunchy director of US-CERT, the United States Computer Emergency Readiness Team of Homeland Security—"is not whether we can use left-of-launch against the bad guys. It's whether, by doing so, we lose any grounds on which to protest their using it against *us*."

Bach nodded somberly. The Sony hack was still four years in the future. But he already had plenty of firsthand experience with Bureau 121. "And the question that naturally follows: does *not* engaging in preemptive strikes do anything to guarantee our security?"

He could see already how this would end. They would bicker. Nothing would be resolved. But everyone would get what they needed. Bach would continue electronically sabotaging North Korean missile systems. The woman from NIST and the man from CERT could honestly claim that they had protested a preemptive doctrine. The White House, turning away without looking too closely, would maintain plausible deniability.

On the meeting's second-to-last day, a very young man from the NSA and a very young woman from IARPA gave an update on a program called Luna Moth. So named, the young man reminded them—a very eager young man with shoulder-length hair, a bad mustache, and flecks of spittle that flew from chapped lips when he got excited—because it would bring light to the darkness, on gossamer wings. In fact, it would provide the answer to *all* the problems under discussion today—at least, until America's enemies caught up.

Weary skepticism traveled around the table. It seemed they all had heard the wunderkind's promises before. Bach vaguely remembered hearing some tell of it himself, from the Codpieces in Seoul. Quantum computing would revolutionize cryptography and cybersecurity. It would represent nothing less than a (yawn) total paradigm shift. He who achieved quantum computing would achieve complete cybersecurity dominance. Lofty promises notwithstanding, Bach had yet to hear of any actual advances being made.

But the young man spoke with the conviction of the true believer: "Last week, Luna realized Critical Achievement One." He paused expectantly. The response was evidently less than he'd hoped for. He traded an uncertain glance with the young woman before continuing. "The first solid-state quantum processor. A two-qubit superconducting chip. Maintained for almost nine-tenths of a second. Early days yet, early days. But this is the Turing machine all over again. And this time, we get to witness it. We get to be a part of it."

The chubby little CERT director was shaking his head and

scowling. But Bach wanted to hear more. Bureau 121 was proving far more resourceful than the Codpieces had expected. He was a people person—knew how to gauge when an asset was approachable, when it needed time and when it needed a push. He relied on others to handle the technological heavy lifting, but *complete cybersecurity dominance* was language he could understand. "Refresh us," he said, "about what's under the hood here."

The young man looked at him gratefully. "We take an entangled system of subatomic particles—that is, a group of subatomic particles whose qualities cannot be described separately but must be described as a whole. We can create such a system in a variety of ways: a fiber coupler, atomic cascades, the Hong-Ou-Mandel effect …"

His friend from IARPA nodded. She was pretty, slender, and comfortably in command of her audience. "How we get there doesn't matter. What matters is that the system is entangled. If we've got two electrons with opposing spins, whenever one spins up, the other will always spin down."

"Remember that subatomic particles exist in multiple states corresponding to different possible outcomes." The young man had warmed to his subject now, and the flecks of spit were flying under the gimbal lighting. "Schrödinger famously illustrated this idea with his theoretical cat. He meant it to be absurd—a criticism of the Copenhagen Interpretation. But it remains a good way to visualize what we call quantum superposition. The cat, both alive and dead at the same time, represents an atom or a photon, existing in multiple states that correspond to multiple potential outcomes—until you observe it. When you open the box, the particle—and the cat—falls into a single outcome, a single state."

"Back to our entangled electrons," the young woman said, smiling pleasantly at the scowling director of CERT. "Until they're observed, they exist in superposition. But once you look at one particle and see that it's spinning one way, you know that the other is now spinning the other way. This holds true even with measurements made light-years apart. Measure one electron, and its entangled partner immediately assumes the opposite spin. This, by the way, is why Einstein thought quantum mechanical theory must be incomplete. Entanglement violates general relativity's speed limit on the universe. '*Spukhafte Fernwirkung*,' he called it—'spooky action at a distance.'"

"But in 1964, John Stewart Bell proved that the principle of locality—the idea that something can be affected only by something else close enough to travel at the speed of light to reach it—is mathematically inconsistent with quantum theory. His proof is called Bell's Inequality. And it's experimentally testable. In fact, it's been validated many times. We don't understand this property of the quantum universe, but we do observe it."

"Then ... we can send information faster than light?" Bach asked.

The smile turned to him. "Unfortunately not. But entangled particles do appear to *communicate* with each other faster than light."

"Now," the young man said, "apply this to computers. A digital computer uses binary digits, called 'bits,' that are always in a state of either zero or one. Just like the first computers, the punch cards, which had either a presence or an absence of holes in predefined positions."

"Of course, you can build some big numbers using just zero and one." The young woman's eyes looked animated, alert. "Take a matrix with columns in ascending powers of two. In the rows, plug in zeros and ones. With six bits, you get sixty-four possible combinations. With eight bits—that's one byte—you get two to the eighth power possible combinations. That's two hundred and fifty-six. Encryption schemes today use two hundred and fifty-six bits. The number of possible different combinations is bigger than one with seventy-seven zeros after it. That's about the same as the number of ordinary particles in the known universe. And to solve a two-hundred-fifty-six-bit encryption with brute force would take a digital computer longer than the *age* of the universe since the big bang. Public-key encryptions assume that factoring large numbers is computationally intractable."

"But Luna Moth could shred a two-hundred-fifty-six-bit encryption in a few minutes." The young man's enthusiasm was proving contagious. Bach felt the old juices beginning to flow. "Because a quantum computer doesn't use bits, which are either zero or one. It uses *qubits,* which are in superpositions. Not just zero and one, but also all places in between.

"Imagine trying to find the key for a lock," the woman said. "Using a digital computer is like testing each tumbler to find its position. With a quantum computer, you run an equation that sees what position the first tumbler is in, then uses entanglement to move other tumblers into the necessary position to turn the key."

The director of CERT was underwhelmed. "But it's a pipe dream."

Eyes turned in his direction.

"There's no way to keep the particles isolated for any significant time. And *any* interaction disrupts the entanglement."

"Moscow and Beijing don't think it's a pipe dream," the young man said pointedly.

"Until 1934," his associate added, "splitting atoms was entirely theoretical. Give the best minds in the world unlimited resources to attack a problem, and who knows what they might accomplish? And we've got the very best: Yale, MIT, Google, Apple, Microsoft, Raytheon, Georgia Tech …"

"All the king's men," said the director.

But Bach was intrigued.

Complete cybersecurity dominance.

*   *   *

A hand on his shoulder: Dalia Artzi.

For an instant, he felt something maternal in her: a mother gently waking a child. Then it was gone, and she was back, harsh as ever and blunt as a blackjack.

He followed her down the corridor, knuckling one eye. Inside the conference room, McConnell and DeArmond faced the monitor expectantly. Sonny Romano inspected his cuticles. Shyam Radha was typing—always typing. "Followed a hunch." His voice was soft, his eyes bloodshot.

On-screen, the doorway of an airport ladies' room. The feed played. Passengers zipped. Red crosshairs appeared. The image froze again.

"Been scanning every feed around her last known location and coming up blank. So I started to expand the perimeter. But then I thought, no. She's not made of smoke. She didn't vanish. Somehow, she's fooled the software. The truth is, you can trick billion-dollar object-tracking with a fifty-cent dollop of putty that changes the shape of the face. So I went back over the footage. But this time, I scanned *gaits*. Software breaks down the body into parts—knee, foot, shoulder, and so on—then builds a composite signature. And …"

The feed rolled forward again. Crosshairs followed from the ladies' room a woman of indeterminate ethnicity, wearing heavy-rimmed eyeglasses and no coat, with a scarf covering her hair.

Pause again, and zoom. White pancake makeup, thick lenses, a canvas gym bag. Sam enlarged the bag and compared it with the image from the Hertz desk.

"God knows how many disguises she's got in that thing." He upended a can of Red Bull, found it empty, and shook it to double-check. "So." Fast-forward. "She took a shuttle. Left Newark at eleven fifty-five. Reached Port Authority at quarter past twelve. I took the liberty of hacking into PABT CCTV, *et voilà!*"

Tired-looking people shuffled off a bus in shadow. The woman in the scarf was among them. Head lowered, she moved through a door.

Another angle. She stepped onto an escalator. Another feed picked her up stepping off.

Even past midnight, Port Authority bus terminal was packed. People bunched up by doors leading to the street. People swirled, elbowing, circling. In the confusion, the crosshairs flickered … and vanished.

Sam leaned away from the keyboard. "This was thirty-eight minutes ago. No sign of her since—gait or face, street cameras or ARGUS."

Bach frowned. "Underground passages connect Port Authority with Times Square. Not to mention with the subway: the A, C, E, N, Q, R, W, one, two, three, and seven. It's the biggest transit hub in the city."

"Don't forget the shuttle to Grand Central," McConnell said. "And from there, the entire lower forty-eight."

The only response was silence.

The time code read 01:34:17+53.

PART TWO

CHAPTER NINE

MANHATTAN, NY

Song woke with sweat-spiders crawling over her chest and neck. A man sleeping on the next bench gave a thick snore. She saw no sign of trouble, but her instinct said, *keep moving.*

She pushed off the bench and walked on.

The view of the Statue of Liberty was postcard perfect. Rowdy laughter drifted from a booze cruise trolling by. The river licked desultorily at dark pilings. A cool, fresh breeze coming off the water dried the perspiration in the hollow of her throat.

A young couple sat canoodling on the grass. A teenager strummed sad minor chords on an acoustic guitar. Gazes lingered for a moment of evaluation as she passed. What did they see?

She walked.

"Hey, Mami," called a voice from a bench just ahead.

The man wore Carhartts, work boots, and a muscle shirt that showed off biceps sleeved with ink. "Hey, Mami." *Kissy-kissy-kissy.* "How much?"

She paused. Letting yourself get picked up in a Manhattan park at 2 a.m. was a risk, of course. On the other hand, getting off the street would be priceless. She had fallen asleep after just sitting down for a moment to rest her legs. Hotels were not safe. In a day or two, she might risk another subway, or car rental, or bus station, or airport. But not yet.

Kissy-kissy-kissy. "How m—"

"Fifty bucks," she said.

*   *   *

As soon as they stepped through the door, he grabbed her. His tongue was hot and insistent. His hands moved over her breasts. He stroked her hair, dislodging the wig she had donned in the subway, and then started taking off her top.

"Too rough," she breathed. "Slow down."

His fingers paused, then resumed.

Her top was off. He peeled away his sleeveless T-shirt. His chest was a slab of muscle. He smelled sweaty.

He went to rummage through a drawer. She had a moment to absorb the apartment: a tiny studio with freestanding claw-footed bathtub, bonsai tree on window ledge, pallet bed, kitchenette with dishes piled in the sink, yellow crescent moon hanging outside a fire escape.

He returned, picked her up as if she weighed nothing, and threw her onto the bed. She banged her hip against the frame, hard. When she cried out, he grinned.

He worked her zipper and tugged away her jeans. Her sneakers came off. He unbuttoned his Carhartts and fumbled with the condom.

"Hold on," she said.

She slipped into the bathroom, fast.

Wearing only panties and socks. Fine hairs standing up on her arms, on the back of her neck. Hip throbbing where it had struck the bed frame.

The SIG Sauer was in her bag.

Which would be worse: fucking him or killing him?

She held her own gaze in the mirror for a moment, weighing.

She went back to the studio.

*   *   *

A phone was ringing.

She blinked into the weak light of dawn. In her dream, a loudspeaker had blared. *"Comrades! Gather 'round and hear of our latest brilliant victory! We have infiltrated the highest social ranks of the American hyenas! Our brave and heroic emissary has outmaneuvered the decadent capitalist imperialists at their own game."*

The phone rang again. The man climbed out of bed with a groan. He walked naked into the kitchenette as it rang again.

He found the phone and answered in curt Russian. He listened for a long time to the party on the other end. At last, with an air of conciliation, he said, *"Pravilno, batya."* He set the phone down on a counter, then rubbed his face wearily.

He came back to bed. In the light of dawn, she could see his tattoos clearly for the first time. A skeleton laughed. An angel wore a crooked halo. A wandering scrawl of Cyrillic circled one biceps. Batman's logo was centered between his collarbones.

His penis hung limply from the dark thatch of hair. But it was stirring, coming to life. He kissed her, mouth open, tongue searching. She rolled on top of him, to retain some control. He found another condom in the drawer without leaving the bed. Her hips quickened. Then slowed. Then quickened. His fingers dug into her upper thighs hard enough to leave bruises.

After, she stared blankly at the ceiling.

"So that's a hundred?" he asked.

A moment passed, and she nodded. She stood, slowly gathering her clothes and bag. She went into the bathroom, limping slightly from the bruised hip. Her heart was thudding hard.

She used the toilet, washed her hands. What now?

A headache throbbed. She found Tylenol in the medicine cabinet, took three, and gulped down water from her cupped palm. She was about to close the mirrored door when another vial caught her eye. Adderall: twenty-milligram tablets. She swallowed two and palmed the vial.

She inspected the mottled purple-and-black flesh on her thighs where he had mauled her. The left hip, where he had thrown her against the bed frame, was swelling.

She took off the wig and splashed water across her face. Pancake makeup peeled off like sloughing snakeskin.

She showered, dialing the water as hot as she could stand and then a little hotter. A curtain of wet hair hung before her eyes. Steam billowed. She breathed deep, braced for his knock on the door. No knock came.

She stayed in the shower as long as she could bear it, and then for a minute longer. Superheated air scalded her lungs. She twisted off the spigots with a gasp.

Better.

The only towel on the rack reeked of mildew. She dressed, still wet. Voluptuous fatigue enveloped her. She felt like a vessel that had been emptied and awaited refilling. But the amphetamine would be kicking in soon.

Sunday morning. In her former life, she would be getting breakfast on the table.

It was the first time she had thought of it as her *former* life.

She left the bathroom. The man was asleep again.

In her bag, she found a wide-brimmed sun hat to cover her face, and let herself out.

LANGLEY, VA

Reading the message, Bach allowed himself a tight smile. He found an already composed dispatch in his drafts folder. No text; subject line: *Alas Babylon.* He clicked SEND.

He went to sit beside Sam. Nodding at the on-screen window that held scrolling lines of code, he said in a low voice, "Send it over to Fort Meade."

Sam's eyes flashed. NSA and USCYBERCOM HQ. He nodded. They had their reply in two minutes. With a keystroke, Sam stopped the shifting lines of data.

Dalia, McConnell, Sonny, and DeArmond blinked awake, as if they all could sense something happening. Bach watched them regain their bearings. Warm sunlight glowed outside the shaded window. On a tray at one end of the table sat coffee and orange juice and bagels from the cafeteria. But attention turned reflexively to the wall-mounted monitor.

"The message sent by the RGB on Friday." Sam tapped another key with satisfaction.

The plaintext was in Munhwaŏ. Bach translated aloud. The message named William Walsh. It described the man's habit of taking home attractive young Asian women. Following the addresses of his stalking grounds were the location of the storage facility, and instructions for retrieving and using the data-cloning equipment inside. Once Walsh's NYMEX pass card was accessed, the data should be secured until further instructions detailed delivery to an unnamed contact. Attached was a grainy photograph of the angular face, taken with a long lens.

"A contact." McConnell stroked his chins. "A sleeper we haven't found."

"Which means a server we don't know about," Sam said, "sending them orders."

"Walsh is no collaborator." Bach faced the screen with a scowl. "He's a mark. Notify NYMEX of the data breach. Tell them to detain anyone trying to use Walsh's personal information. Then invite Walsh into Homeland's New York Field Office for debriefing."

"O captain, my captain." DeArmond already had his phone out.

"Song's our ticket to the other sleeper," Bach said, still looking at the screen. "When she logs on again for rendezvous information, we'll see it—yes?"

"Assuming she uses the same server she used before," Sam

said, "yes. But we still won't be able to geolocate her … unless she's switched to a vulnerable device."

Two dozen other windows on-screen gave no promising leads. The Volvo abandoned in short-term parking had offered up nothing. IMSI Catcher had not found the woman's phone again. ARGUS and Persistics scanned in vain.

Facial-recognition software continued to pore over CCTV recorded in subway stations overnight. Bach knew that the MTA wanted to put cameras on the trains themselves, but civil libertarians had cried foul. One or two more terrorist "events," though, and the Transit Authority would win out. Until then, they could scan only video of platforms, and follow arriving and departing trains, using Public Address Customer Information Screens.

All through the small hours of the morning, Manhattan had seethed with life. A man coming out onto a platform lost his hat. A girl pushed past him onto the train without looking up from her book. A frat boy vomited into a garbage can. A rat scurried across tracks. A game of three-card monte went into a bag as a policeman approached. A woman in gypsy garb told fortunes from behind a folding bridge table. Another woman, dressed in a flowing ball gown, played a pedal harp. A boy who looked about eight years old used a MetroCard to swipe multiple friends through a turnstile. A woman carrying a huge fern that blocked her line of sight lost her wallet to a pickpocket. A man in a wheelchair wore an overcoat with no shirt underneath. Another man was inexplicably dressed for rain, in oilskin and wading boots. Teenage girls held hands. Workmen carried lanterns. Laughing friends posed for selfies. Bach saw piercings, shavings, Halloween costumes, bare skin, muscles, cuffed jeans, black-tie evening wear, parakeets perched on shoulders, elaborate facial hair. Even through the mute security feeds came a crackling frisson: young, excited, sexy, naughty.

He looked from the monitor to his team. Except for Sam, who was gratified at having broken the encryption at last, they all looked frustrated and weary.

"We're trying too hard." Dalia Artzi tilted her head back, considering the monitor down the line of her nose. "*A kats vos m'yavket ken kain meiz nit chapen.* A meowing cat can't catch mice."

A long moment passed.

"You've got something in mind?" McConnell asked.

MANHATTAN, NY

The sunlight felt like daggers. Song pulled her hat brim lower and oriented herself. Across the street to the south, marble steps climbed to shuttered government buildings. To the east, a small park bustled with early risers, running, dog-walking, doing their morning tai chi. Beyond it, brightly colored signs ascended in lopsided ranks, advertising in English and Cantonese grocery stores, restaurants, beauty salons, liquor stores, massage parlors, pharmacies. Distant church bells clanged off-key.

East, she figured. In Chinatown, she would stand out less.

A man was coming around the corner, speaking into a phone or radio. She froze. Too slow. He was on her already.

Then he was past. Just a man.

A car idled by the curb. A teenager sat behind the wheel. Slender, stylishly unshaven, nose ring. He looked at her. She looked away and struck off, favoring her right leg.

Engines revved, idled, passed. People laughed, argued, held hands. Tourists, homeless, children, elderly. Churchgoers in their ill-fitting Sunday best.

She crossed a street, limping slightly, throwing a look into the sideview mirror of an idling car. No sign of pursuit. She entered the park. Old women played xiangqi and mah-jongg. Children nibbled too-hot dumplings. Vendors wielded their zongzi carts like battering rams.

She moved quickly, gait ragged, head down, past a playground and a basketball court. Then out of the park, crossing Mulberry. The morning was sunny and warm. Garbage bins overflowed with feathers and chicken guts and rotting fruit. Signs implored in English and Chinese, NO SMOKING OR SPITTING. Smells were thick: fish, fermentation, smoke, sewage, and, incongruously, blossoms.

She worked her way along crowded sidewalks. Even in her current state, gazes appraised her appreciatively. *Nam-nam-buk-nyeo* was the saying in Korea—literally, "south men, north women." Southern men were the handsomest, and northern women the comeliest. To East Asian eyes, she fulfilled a particular standard of beauty. She tugged the sun hat's brim yet lower and hastened on.

Early Sunday morning, but vehicular traffic was thick. Windows down, elbows cocked jauntily. She might jack a car. Force the driver at gunpoint to bring her out through the tunnel, or over a bridge into a different borough. It was an option, but a desperate one.

She threw another glance over her shoulder. A sea of faces shifted, rose, fell.

Her family would be waking up, finding her gone and the car missing. The doorman would tell them she had left in the middle of the night, with luggage. Mark would surely come up with some story for the kids. But inside he would be reeling, blindsided.

Or maybe not. On some level, he must have known that she kept secrets. He wasn't stupid.

Surely, he kept secrets of his own. Sometimes, there was an unaccounted-for half hour in his schedule, around work or tennis. So what? This city. Traffic, MTA failures. So she told herself and didn't let her mind dwell on it. People were only human; life was complicated; marriage was difficult. Don't ask, don't tell. Thus did a marriage survive.

Everyone kept secrets. Not on the level of hers, of course, but the difference was of degree, not of kind.

Or was she rationalizing?

Vendors thrust their wares in her face. Lychee, wasabi peanuts, rock salt plum. Swords, fans, umbrellas, live baby turtles. Watches, knockoff handbags, Blu-rays and DVDs, sunglasses and phones, golden Buddhas and cats and monkeys. She passed a restaurant, a salon, another salon. A tiny tea shop, invitingly empty and cool beneath a narrow awning. Without conscious thought, she stepped inside.

Calm air smelled of chrysanthemum, jasmine, honey, and peach. An old woman sat motionless in shadow. A cat lay on a shelf, tail flicking. A younger woman emerged from a back room and gestured encouragingly at teas arranged in faded boxes.

Song gave a meaningless smile and puttered among the shelves. Maybe the Chinatown bus, she thought. Maybe not. She couldn't think straight. Her head buzzed from fatigue, fear, amphetamines.

She went back onto the street. Past liquefied offal, chicken parts, fish heads, eggshells. Not quite gagging, she walked faster.

Two police, a man and a woman, turned the corner in front of her.

Their gazes were searching. Prodding into storefronts, beneath awnings. The woman consulted something held in a cupped palm.

A knot of tourists blocked the way back into the tea shop. She was trapped.

Parked by the curb, a Ford Crown Victoria idled with the trunk gaping open. A driver had just taken out a suitcase. He stood filibustering, waiting for a tip before relinquishing the luggage. She could not get around him to the driver's seat.

But the trunk was spacious—empty except for an ice scraper and jumper cables and a ragged old blanket.

Someone would see her.

The cops were yards away.

Even if she made it into the trunk, she might end up trapped. She might suffocate, or starve.

She climbed inside smoothly, before she could second-guess herself. No one called out. She curled into a fetal position and pulled the ragged blanket over her knees, her body, her head.

Seconds later, the trunk slammed shut.

Her breath felt hot. The air was close. She clumsily adjusted her position, maneuvering her lips as close as possible to the keyhole.

Still no one called out.

A car door opened and thunked shut, making the Ford vibrate. It began to move, then turned sharply.

She slid about like poorly stowed luggage. The ice scraper dug into her back. Her canvas bag was still looped around her neck. The shoulder strap drew tight, choking her. She braced herself against the left wall to relieve the pressure against her throat. Trying to stay oriented, to track the direction they were going. South?

They turned again. Her head bumped. Just outside the car, surprisingly close to her ear, someone shrieked with laughter.

Hard to breathe in here. A memory wormed up. The coal train at Camp 14. She pushed it from her mind. *Stay focused.* Turning again. West? She was lost already.

She was sweating. Her hair clung in strings to her temple.

The car bumped over a ramp. She heard echoes, squealing tires, and distant voices. A garage.

They came to a stop. The engine died. She had not been aware of its thrumming beneath her, all around her, until it quit.

She shucked the blanket aside and disentangled herself as best she could from the bag's choking strap. Made herself breathe quietly, evenly, readying herself. When the trunk opened, she would lead with a palm heel under the chin.

Seconds passed. The trunk didn't open.

A minute passed. Then another.

A bell rang somewhere, not far away.

She managed to get one hand around, up from under her body, close to the mechanism beneath the keyhole. Then against the mechanism. She pushed.

No give.

She pressed. Changed angle, tried again. But it was an older Crown Vic, and the trunk was not designed to open from the inside.

Force it, then. She drew her hand back as far as possible and hammered up again.

No give.

Gently, with a lover's touch, she tried to find the tongue and slide it from its lock.

Nothing.

She pressed her forearm against the trunk's lid and pushed. And for an instant, the flimsy sheet metal seemed to bend.

But it held.

She tried again, to no avail.

She adjusted her position, a centimeter at a time, trying to get her right elbow against the felt-covered floor for leverage. But the trunk was too deep, her forearm too short.

She hammered again. And then again. But the lid held. Maybe if she had been at her best, and positioned well, she could have forced it open. But maybe not even then.

It would be a stupid way to die.

Locked inside a stuffy car trunk, into which she had delivered herself. Maybe it was all she deserved. Maybe it was a metaphor. She had delivered herself into this entire situation. Not at first, of course. At first, she had been born into a country, into a system, that devoured its best and rewarded its worst. But she had never accepted her lot in life. She had struggled. She had escaped—repeatedly. And then, through a stroke of extraordinary luck, she had been delivered to America. Completely beyond the walls of the Hermit Kingdom.

And she had found love. And she had started a family. And when the order came from the RGB, she should have gone immediately to the American government and thrown herself on its mercy. At least, there would have been a chance.

But after a lifetime of keeping secrets, of trusting no one but herself, she had not been able to change course.

And now here she was.

She still might call for help. Capture was better than death.

Her brother would pay the price. Her children.

She closed her eyes. Concentrated on breathing shallowly. Make the oxygen last.

Her legs were beginning to cramp. She willed them to relax. *Cha-ma.* Mind over matter.

Some switch inside her clicked. She ceased struggling, exhaled lightly, and gave herself over to the hot, stuffy darkness.

She counted breaths. Up to ten, then again from one.

And waited.

CHAPTER TEN

Her mind replayed obsessively the moment of climbing into the trunk.

Moving quickly, without overthinking it. A fleeting thought that she might starve, might suffocate. She had climbed in anyway. It had seemed a risk worth taking. She had curled up and pulled the blanket over herself, and then the trunk had closed, the sturdy mechanism snapping shut with deceptive quiet.

Now she was back on the coal train. Her brother curled into the hollow of her body. Tons of coal above them, pressing down. Lungs itching. Breath like hot liquid. They would get away with this, she had told herself. They had dug deep enough that the guards would miss them. Yet she could feel the unbearable tickle coming. One cough was all it would take. *Anyone caught trying to escape will be shot immediately.* This was the way it ended. Her heartbeat accelerating with panic …

Cha-ma. Calm.

But beneath the smothering coal, she had not been able to regain her calm. She had tried in vain to find her breath. But it had come ragged and too fast. At last, she had pulled her brother close. Pressed her ear against his chest. And used *his* breath to find her own. Focusing on the *tick-tock* of his respiration. Slowing her mind. Drinking deep his calm and taking it for herself.

One, two, three. A dry, hard lump sat in the middle of her throat. It was hard to swallow. *Four, five, six.* What was her family doing right now? Sunday morning. Mark had probably dumped them in front of a screen. Chase was on the case.

Seven, eight, nine. Her brow was dewed with sweat along the hairline. Her mind turned to the Lipton onion soup mix. She had put the pan into the dishwasher and run it. But that caramelized chemical powder left a residue, even after a pots-and-pans cycle. When Mark emptied the dishwasher, he would notice. He would know what she had done. *It is the beating of his hideous heart!*

She had lost count. *Damn it.*

She swallowed the lump in her throat and tried to move her right hand. The hand paid no attention. It had fallen asleep. The entire arm was numb.

With her other arm, she managed to shift her position slightly, taking pressure off her right side. Her face ended up pressed into the tangle of jumper cables. The sharp metal clips threatened to abrade her cheek.

For a terrible timeless stretch, she couldn't change position. Then her feet kicked out in a spasm, pushing her into a new configuration. Her face disengaged from the jumper cables without losing any skin or getting any acid burn. She racked in a breath of hot, stale air.

She lay still, aspirating weakly. Fighting panic. Panic meant hyperventilation, and unconsciousness would soon follow.

How long would the Crown Victoria sit in this garage?

She tried to reconstruct her glimpse of the car's interior, to find a hint of the owner's identity. A parking pass inside the windshield, a tag hanging from the rearview mirror, an Uber decal on the window. Was it a gypsy cab? A limo? A private car? If she knew, she might hazard a guess how long it could sit here unattended. But she remembered only that feeling of having nowhere to go, no other option. The cops coming down the street. Thinking she would never get away with it. Moving before she could second-guess herself.

She might be trapped here overnight. Or all week. Or all month. By the time someone found her, she might be a desiccated skeleton. A fun-house Halloween prop. A mummy. Mommy. Mummy.

She remembered the free-floating anxiety of the first pregnancy. Puttering endlessly; checking stocks of diapers and formula; checking emergency contact numbers, thermometers, night nurse availability. Babyproofing cabinets, drawers, corners, closets, toilet seats, for a child who wouldn't even be able to crawl for another half a year. Packing her hospital bag and adding outfits for this creature who did not yet exist outside her body. She remembered the night before her water broke. Standing in the doorway of the nursery, which was ready to receive its charge. She had felt as if she were peering in at some exotic foreign terrain: a desert, a tundra, a moonscape. In that instant, the feeling of an audience watching from beyond footlights had returned with more force than ever before. And she had wanted nothing more than to flee. This was more than she had bargained for. She had gotten in over her head. She had not signed up for this. Every man for himself. Her brother would survive, or not, on his own.

And then her water had burst. And Dex was born. Placed in her arms. Cooing and burbling, looking up at his mommy with wise, ageless eyes. And all at once, she had felt more comfortable, more at home inside her own skin, more truly *herself* than ever before.

Watching Mark feed their baby—*Good job, Dexy! Mmm! Nummy! Open up again for Daddy! Here comes the choo-choo train! Choo, choo, open up! Chug-chug-chug-chug choo choo!*— she had felt deep, profound bodily peace.

By the time Jia came along, Song had rolled with it. She knew now how she would get through: one day at a time. It would work itself out. On some level, she was *meant* to be a mother.

All in the past now.

She moaned softly, low in her throat.

On top of everything else, she needed to pee.

She tried again to move her right hand and was rewarded by tingling starbursts of nerves.

She struggled to think straight, despite the stifling heat and the encroaching panic and the stifling air—was the air really thinning, or was it just her imagination?

Her earlier efforts to escape the trunk—trying to force the latch, trying to bend the body metal—had been driven by emotion. She must stay calm. She must approach the problem rationally.

She had not searched thoroughly enough for an interior release mechanism. Once her arm was awake, she would methodically check the entire seam where the trunk lid met the body.

She counted to ten.

Then ten again.

And again.

When she tried to move her right arm again, it obeyed.

So.

She maneuvered, running her fingers along the nearest part of the seam. Searching for a toggle, a button, a handle, a cord. She readjusted. The ice scraper poked rudely into her thigh.

Her palms were sweating. So, too, her brow, armpits, chest, soles, crotch.

She checked the farther part of the seam to the best of her ability. She found nothing.

Okay.

She might still force her way out, but not using her bare hands. Using tools.

The ice scraper. The jumper cables. What other tools were back here?

Her bag. The gun inside. But then she might as well scream her lungs out. She might as well shoot up a signal flare. Here I am! Come and get me!

Maybe the spare tire was hidden just beneath her.

She felt stupid for not having thought of it earlier. That was where her Volvo stored its spare, under a felt-topped false bottom.

And not just the spare but also a jack, a lug wrench. Either of which she could use to force the lock.

But she could not get out of her own way enough to find the false bottom, if there was one. She could not even get her fingers around to the edges of the trunk's interior, to feel for a lip.

Her sweaty hair stuck to her cheek, irritating her eye. She hissed in frustration. Pulse accelerating again. *It is the beating of his hideous heart!*

Calm. Think. Calm.

Outside the trunk, keys jangled.

She froze.

The trunk wasn't opening.

The jangling moved away. Someone walking past.

Call for help. Her hands balled into fists. *Do it.*

But her brother. Her children. And she herself. She would spend the rest of her life inside another prison.

She'd rather die.

The sound of a key pushed into a lock seemed only feet away. She seemed to hear each individual tumbler falling into place as it turned. A door opened and clunked shut.

An engine turned over. A car moved. The sound receded.

She let out a ragged breath.

So.

Think rationally.

Maybe the ice scraper could force the lock. Or maybe the clips on the ends of the jumper cables.

Again she shifted position. She touched the handle of the scraper. It slipped away from sweat-slick fingers. She tried again and succeeded only in pushing it farther from her grip. Wriggling, she tried again. The hellish irony of it was that she could extend herself in *this* direction; she could push her legs against the rear of the backseat and exert leverage …

In her Volvo, the backseat folded down to increase cargo space.

Yes.

She repositioned again, not daring to hope. She placed her feet against what must be the rear of the back seat. Not in the center; that would be solid. But on one side, either side.

She set her legs. Grunting, she pushed as hard as she could.

Solid resistance.

The pungent smell of her own fearful sweat filled her nose. She folded her legs at the knees and then pistoned them out, not pushing now but kicking. Again. The backseat held. Again. Again. Anyone walking by would hear. Fuck it. Again. A sound erupted from her throat—an animal cry of aggression mingled with despair. Again, again, again …

Fresh air flooded the trunk.

She gasped, thrusting her feet all the way into the interior of the car. Following them with her hands, she pulled herself forward.

To freedom.

She climbed into the front seat, bag still looped around one shoulder.

She was inside a parking garage. No one in sight. But she could hear people, not far off. A child whined. Someone replied sharply.

Her eyes moved to the juncture of wheel and steering column. Beneath that seam, she would find the starter solenoid. She could hot-wire the car. But the theft might be reported immediately.

She wanted to be out of this goddamned car, anyway.

She unlocked the door and stepped out into cool shadow.

Light drew her. She moved past ramps and rubber-lined railings, past fat arrows painted on concrete floors. An office glowed. A short queue of people held tickets, waiting for their cars. Here was the child who had whined. Wearing a *PAW Patrol* shirt. Her heart caught. She kept moving. Past a rack of keys. Past a sign reading STOP HERE, HONK HORN, LEAVE KEYS IN VEHICLE, WAIT FOR ATTENDANT.

Out into sunshine: brilliant, warm against her skin, prickling her dilated eyes. She had the sensation of coming out of a long sleep only to discover, bafflingly, that it was still daytime.

She chose a direction at random. Cantonese restaurants quickly ceded to pizza places, small traditional pharmacies to chain drugstores, packed sidewalks to wide, clean avenues and expensive stonework. In Manhattan, a single block could make a universe of difference. She came to a stop. Sluggishly aware, despite her disorientation, that she was exposed. *Too* exposed. She had been safer back in Chinatown. She turned ...

"Mi!"

A woman was waving exaggeratedly. Standing with a man, by the next storefront. Song had almost walked into them. "Earth to Mi! Come in, Mi!"

The man was a stranger.

The woman was Nina Brooks.

LANGLEY, VA

"Again," Dalia said.

On-screen, the footage restarted. Dalia watched, frowning critically.

"Is it the angle?" Sam clicked, clicked, and clicked again. "Better?"

She shook her head. "Something about the shadows ..."

He grimaced and hunkered back down to his work.

McConnell circled the conference table. For a moment, he watched Sam tinker with the images on-screen. His skepticism was palpable. "Run me through this again," he said.

"She loves those kids more than anything," Dalia said. "A meowing cat can't catch mice. But the right piece of cheese, the right mousetrap ..."

"You give her too much credit," McConnell said.

"We'll see."

Sam ran the video again. A Volvo Cross Country pulled over on a nighttime city street corner. The license plate, the same as Song's, was clearly visible in center screen. Song Sun Young herself sat behind the wheel, looking strained and tense. A heavily bearded young man in black fleece and a watch cap emerged from a doorway and slid into the passenger seat, then turned to inspect the back seat of the car. For an instant, the gun in the young man's hand was clearly visible. The car pulled away. The video ended.

The young man was an agency whiteboard jockey named Dafiq Farid. He had been videoed inside the Langley parking garage, entering a Volvo of the same make, model, and color as Song's. Sam had combined the footage with video of another Volvo, driven by one of DeArmond's agents on the streets of New York, and with ARGUS-captured images of the woman and her license plate. After considerable digital smoothing of edges, the illusion was seamless.

"Yes?" Sam asked hopefully.

Dalia nodded, satisfied. She turned to McConnell. "Shall we?"

On their way out, McConnell snagged a poppy-seed bagel from the tray. Bach and DeArmond were doing something on Bach's phone. When Bach realized they were leaving, he couldn't keep the disapproval from his face. But he had agreed to let Dalia try. He said only, "Stay in touch."

They took McConnell's Range Rover. Out of the parking lot, past Langley's children's center, onto Dolley Madison Boulevard and then George Washington Memorial Highway. Seas of windblown trees caught the morning sun like sparkling waves. Dalia never ceased to marvel at America's vastness. In Israel, they had the untamed Galilee and the immense Negev. And yet, the entire Jewish homeland was barely larger than New Jersey—the fifth-smallest US state.

The trees glimmered. Her eyes closed.

She dreamed of forest. Thundering hoofbeats, a frantic retreat. Snowy tangled roots tripping up men and horses. On every side they fell, slipping, grunting, cursing, whinnying.

Leaving the frozen forest, gaining a frozen pond. Fleeing in wild disarray. Rolling white eyes, laid-back ears, curling upper lips. Cuirassiers mixed with skirmishers, artillery with dragoons. They abandoned cannon as they went, dropping swords and muskets and carbines, leaving trails of gore. Dalia slipped on bloody ice. She regained her feet, slithering and sliding, and stumbled on.

A man had lost a leg. Still he pressed on, half crawling, half dragging himself. Passing him, Dalia turned her head to look back. The man was James McConnell. His sweater vest was streaked with wine-dark blood. Bifocals hung crooked from his left ear, one lens shattered. He reached toward her imploringly ...

She ran faster, but she could not outrun the feeling of dread. She was missing something dangerous. Something right underfoot, something all around. The horses, the thundering hooves.

The ice.

Distant thunder. More hoofbeats ...

No. Artillery now.

And she realized too late that she was running with five thousand desperate men and a thousand fear-maddened horses across a frozen pond. And their enemy was loosing heavy cannon on them. The enemy needn't find any target smaller than the vast pond itself. The barrage would shatter the ice, and they all would drop like weighted stones into black, frigid depths.

Awake.

They were inside a tunnel. McConnell glanced over. "Close your eyes," he said softly. "Get some sleep."

Dalia blinked, then sat awake, staring at rows of fluorescent lights, waiting for an exit from the tunnel into daylight that never seemed to come.

MANHATTAN, NY

"Personally," Nina said, "I'd do it at the Y."

A pair of policemen were coming down the sidewalk. One looked at Song and Nina—two uptown ladies waiting patiently for an attendant by a downtown parking lot—and smiled pleasantly. Song smiled back.

"You don't need a five-thousand-dollar space for an elementary school fund-raiser." Nina's slate-gray Lexus pulled up, and the attendant stepped out. Nina handed him a folded-up bill. With her white linen sundress and a hank of red ribbon in her blond hair, she looked very young. "But Jackie has her heart set on this place," she prattled on. "Prada and Phillip Lim both rented it, she said. She must have said it a thousand times. Prada and Phillip Lim, Prada and Phillip Lim."

Her sunglasses were Oliver Goldsmith, like Audrey Hepburn's. Before climbing into the Lexus, she tipped them down onto the bridge of her nose. Above the lenses, her eyes looked sad, vaguely dreamy. "Want a ride?"

Song had been expecting the offer. She moved her shoulders easily, then nodded.

Heavy lumps sagged inside the canvas bag as she slipped into the passenger seat. A standard SIG Sauer magazine held ten rounds. Assuming the agent had kept his weapon fully loaded, seven remained.

She must be ruthless.

Nina took a long time readjusting her seat and all three mirrors. Pigeons cooed on a windowsill high above. Up the block, a car honked. The air held the smell of encroaching midday, of sunbaked tar heating up. Song fidgeted. She wanted to do it before she lost her nerve. She would force Nina to cross the Queensboro Bridge, then find some back lot in Long Island City. A dumpster or a loading dock, somewhere off the beaten path. The body would not be found for a few days at least.

"Ready ready," Nina said, and latched her seat belt.

They turned east. Song, donning a blank half-smile, gazed out her window. They passed trees, construction scaffolding, a double-parked FedEx truck. The same sights, give or take, that she had seen every day for the past six years. Suffused now with new layers of meaning. These were ghosts from a life already finished.

Nina switched on the radio. *"Current traffic conditions for*

Manhattan including all local bridges and tunnels, weather, and more. That's next. Now here's Ten-Ten Wins *news anchor Roger Young."* An orchestra swelled. *"All news, all the time. This is* Ten-Ten Wins. *You give us twenty-two minutes; we'll give you the world. Good morning. Seventy-one degrees at one o'clock, Sunday, June second. And here's what's happening. A stabbing spree in Lond—"*

Nina turned the sound down. "Traffic's every ten minutes on these ones, right?"

Song shrugged absently.

"Call me crazy. But I think something like this should be old-fashioned." It took Song a minute to realize that her friend was back on the penny social. "Poodle skirts and letter sweaters. Not chrome and black. Not fucking *Miami Vice.*"

Nina had barely listened to Song's murmured excuse (early Father's Day shopping) for being downtown. She was far more interested in venting about Jackie McNamara. "And why *today?* I've got my hands full getting ready to go get the house in shape. It couldn't wait a week?"

The house in Southampton, she meant. The memory clicked into place like a key slipping into a lock. "You're going out tomorrow?" Song asked.

"Yup. First time each year you always find some nasty little surprise. Last year it was bats in the attic. The year before, a squirrel nest in the chimney. That's why Tristan sends me up early. I'm the canary in the coal mine. Three years ago, there was a beehive in the wall. It was like something from *The Exorcist,* I swear to God. Ten thousand bees. The exterminator said he'd never seen anything like it. He said he's never been scared on the job like that before."

They turned north onto East River Drive. Song considered her friend from the corner of her eye. Nina expected to return to her clean, safe apartment, to her waiting husband and child. She would take a catnap to sleep off the mimosas she'd had that morning—you could smell it on her breath—while Yasmin, the hired help, kept an eye on Morgan. In the morning, she would go to Southampton.

She would spend the next week sleeping late, eating well, relaxing, "getting the house in shape."

Southampton would be far enough away for Song to lie low, but close enough to get back to the city on short notice when the rendezvous instructions came. But Nina was a problem. In this scenario, Nina was nothing but a potential liability.

The thought made her chest contract. She closed her eyes. Black rings spread in ripples behind the lids. She remembered stepping into the black waters of the Tumen. She had moved forward, sending ripples through faint reflections of stars.

Two nights without good sleep. Her mind flickered like a nickelodeon movie. From the Tumen to the Chinese farmer in his pickup. Then the man in Carhartts, bruising her thighs with his jabbing fingers. *So that's a hundred?* Then to the anonymous van, the blinding flashlight, the building thunder of jet turbines. None of it had been real. Firing the gun across the roof of the Volvo. Snapping another shot into the man at her feet ...

How had they found her?

They must have been watching Walsh. They had followed her home after she made contact.

Or maybe they had been watching Song herself, for God knew how long.

Maybe they had hacked the RGB server. Maybe every time she had accessed it, she was shining a spotlight on herself.

Did it matter? The result was the same.

Nina droned on: "... skinny ties and those scarves you see them selling in the garment district, with the beaded ..."

Song dreamed of an apartment. Her own but not her own. Wallpaper of blue moiré, furniture of antique walnut. Behind a dressing table, she found a secret door. As she pushed the dressing table aside, she heard Mark laughing somewhere nearby. Behind the door, a cramped hallway led to another apartment. The second apartment was filled with rat droppings and cobwebs. Unbeknownst to her, it had been there all along.

She tried to rouse herself. She must wake up. She must act. She must be ruthless.

Instead, she sank again, into black on black.

"Mi."

The voice came from the far end of a dark corridor. Echoing. "*Mi.*"

Usually when someone woke her, it was a child, Dex or Jia. But this was an adult voice. A woman.

A hand touched her arm. Her eyes popped open.

They were parked outside her building. She recognized the green awning. Phil, the weekend doorman, was standing just inside the lobby, peering truculently at the *Times* Sunday crossword.

"You passed out." Nina looked concerned. "You must be really exhausted."

"I guess I am."

"Well … so here we are."

The engine idled. Song took a moment to come more fully awake. She wiped the heel of her hand beneath one eye. "Nina," she said, "this is going to sound crazy."

Nina waited.

"I need you to take me to Southampton."

Nina smiled apologetically. "We're so booked until August, it's crazy. But we'd love to have you guys as soon as—"

"Now."

Song unzipped the bag. She wrapped her hand around the grip of the gun inside.

Nina watched. Still smiling, but tentatively now.

Song took out the gun and held it loosely atop the bag on her lap, pointing not directly at her friend, but toward the dashboard. She curled her finger through the trigger guard.

"I'm sorry," she said.

Neither noticed the Range Rover double-parking just ahead, emergency blinkers flashing on as two people, one using a cane, stepped out and walked toward the green awning.

CHAPTER ELEVEN

McConnell knocked on the apartment door. Shuffling feet, a turning lock, a rattling chain, and the door opened. A tall man in rumpled clothes filled the doorway. A pretty two-year-old girl with a halo of dark hair peeked out from behind one leg.

McConnell held out his ID. "James McConnell. JCS, with the Pentagon."

The red-rimmed eyes looked at the identification, then at Dalia. "Mark Abrahams?" she asked.

He nodded.

"May we come in?"

Another moment. Then he nodded again and moved out of the doorway.

"Daddy?" the two-year-old said.

"It's okay, honey." He picked her up. A five-year-old boy wearing *Star Wars* pajamas emerged from an adjoining room and looked at the visitors with naked curiosity.

The apartment was in disarray: scattered toys and books, socks, DVDs. Bowls of soggy cereal shared the dining room table with broken crayons. Dalia's nose twitched. The little girl needed a diaper change.

"Dex," said the man, "why don't you guys watch TV for a few minutes so I can talk to our guests?"

"Who are they?" the boy asked.

"Go watch TV with your sister." Abrahams set the girl on the floor and pointed her toward the living room. "Watch TV, Jia."

"Watch TV!" She ran ahead, and her brother followed.

Mark Abrahams led them past the kitchen, master bedroom, nursery, boy's room, and into a study. Dalia felt strange seeing it all in person, in real colors.

In the study, diplomas from NYU and Columbia Law hung on walls. A frame on a desk displayed the same picture they had found on the woman's Facebook page: a happy pose before sun-flecked water. There was only one chair. The men left it for Dalia, who remained standing with her cane.

A cartoon theme song started in the other room. Mark Abrahams listened for a moment, then turned to face his visitors. His body language was complex, both aggressive and defeated.

McConnell took out his phone. "Surveillance footage from Lex and Eighty-Fifth, about eleven last night."

Abrahams accepted the device warily. For a long moment, he looked at McConnell. Then he pressed PLAY on the screen.

Dalia had watched the video again in the car. Shyam Radha had done an expert job. The final product would be the envy of any Hollywood 3-D animator or visual-effects artist.

After the video had played, McConnell took the phone back. He replayed the footage, freezing on the clearest image of the young man's bearded face, and reverse-pinched the frame to enlarge it. "Know him?"

Abrahams looked pale. He shook his head.

"His name is Yusuf Bashara. He drives a cab in Jersey City. He's been on Homeland watchlists for the past two years. Ever since a new imam took over his mosque—a Wahhabi Saudi named Muhammad ash-Sheik."

"I don't understand."

"Neither do we," Dalia said. "That's why we're here."

"Was that my wife? With this Yoosif character?"

McConnell nodded.

Abrahams closed his eyes. He pinched the bridge of his nose and opened his eyes again. "This is surreal."

"When's the last time you saw her?" McConnell asked.

"Last night."

"Here?"

"Yes."

"What time?"

"I was at my office until around … I got back here around nine thirty. I remember because there were some men working in the hallway. I made a joke about working late."

"And then …"

"I took a shower. We went to bed."

"Anything seem unusual?"

"No." Abrahams rubbed one hand across a day's growth of stubble.

"And then …" Again McConnell trailed off encouragingly.

"This morning, she was gone."

"Gone."

"Gone. I asked the doorman when she left. He said she asked for the car around ten thirty."

Dalia frowned. "You were already asleep?"

"I was exhausted." A defensive note. "It was a stressful day."

"Did you hear a phone ring, or a text come in?"

"No. But I don't see who might've called or texted that would make her leave like that … without telling me."

A tactful pause. "She never mentioned a Yusuf Bashara?" Dalia asked.

"No."

"Did she ever go to Jersey City?"

"Not as far as I know."

From the next room, a small child's gleeful laughter.

"Forgive me, McConnell said, "but I have to ask. Have there been problems in your marriage lately?"

"There have not."

"Has your wife been behaving strangely?"

"No. I ... no."

"You hesitated."

"The answer is no."

Dalia asked, "Is it possible that your wife met Yusuf Bashara somewhere, without your knowing?"

"Of course it's possible. She has her own life."

"How long have you been married?"

"Six years."

Dalia's knee flared. After another moment's hesitation, she lowered herself into the chair. "How did you meet?"

"Through a mutual friend."

"Named?"

"Eliza Crystal, a paralegal I used to work with."

"Has your wife ever expressed sympathy for Islamist causes?" McConnell asked.

Abrahams snorted.

"I'll take that as a no."

"She's apolitical."

"Korean?" Dalia said.

"She was born in Seoul. She's American now."

"Family back home?"

"No. Both her parents have passed. She's an only child."

"Mr. Abrahams," McConnell said, "two federal agents are in critical condition as a result of Yusuf Bashara's actions last night. And your wife appears to be an accomplice. We've got a BOLO across the tristate area. You can imagine how cops deal with someone who's hurt one of their own."

Abrahams looked at him heavily.

"But she's got no history," McConnell continued. "No priors, no motive, no red flags. Maybe she's been abducted. Or extorted.

But we can't figure out how, exactly, Bashara got to her or why she's helping him."

"If she turns herself in, things will go better." Dalia paused artfully. "For everyone."

She held her breath. If the man refused to play along, the entire visit would be for nothing. But Abrahams frowned, blinked slowly, and nodded.

SOUTHAMPTON, NY

Nina's phone was ringing. Song went through her friend's bag and found the phone. Rummaging a bit more, she found a nail file and used it to pry apart the casing. She removed the battery. Throughout, the gun remained on the seat, near her right thigh.

Nina stared at the road. Scrubby trees lined three eastbound lanes and three westbound. Song smelled the first hint of seashore coming in through the air-conditioner vents.

When they left the highway, traffic thinned to a trickle. They went through the outskirts of a small town, then into a residential neighborhood. Before long, slices of water glinted through trees between the houses. The road grew rougher, the houses less frequent, the glimpses of water longer.

As they pulled up to a gate, Song spied a stretch of private beach through a screen of trees. In all the times Nina had described the house—usually during funny rants about the snooty neighbors—she had neglected to mention that it was right on the beach.

They left the car together. Gulls wheeled and cawed. Song held the gun pointed loosely at the sandy ground as Nina programmed a code into a keypad.

Small purple flowers speckled the unpaved driveway. It was rutted and potholed, but that was part of the rustic charm. So were the big, mossy oak tree that had fallen alongside the drive, and the crumbling rocky seawall.

The house, wood frame with a fieldstone base, had a two-car

garage, a small covered swimming pool, and a dock and boathouse. Parking outside the garage, Nina seemed oddly embarrassed. "We got such a deal on it, you wouldn't believe. One of Tristan's cousins had to unload it fast."

As they left the car again, Song put weight on her left leg and winced. Nina asked too quickly, "You okay?"

"Fine." Song's tone closed the subject. "What kind of security system?"

"Alarm."

"No cameras?"

"No cameras."

"Nina, don't try anything." She heard the beseeching note in her own voice. It betrayed weakness. Too late to take it back. But her friend said nothing.

Outside the front door, they paused while Nina searched on her ring for the key. Inside the foyer, she programmed another code into a box. Song tensed. Maybe Nina could send a signal with the code. Maybe she had lied about cameras.

Inside, everything was in its place: flip-flops lining a mat, ranks of cubbyholes filled with neatly rolled beach towels. From a sunken living room, a baby grand piano and antique grandfather clock gleamed. Song gestured with the gun, and Nina went in ahead of her. They walked a circuit of the first floor's lustrous hardwood floors. A jar of seashells made a stylish centerpiece in the dining room. Dried starfish and seahorses had been mounted under glass on the walls. Song could feel Nina's hand in the design.

They climbed a half-spiral staircase. Shafts of late afternoon sunlight lanced through skylights. They passed a kid's room, a bed piled with stuffed animals. Then a bathroom of brushed nickel and Calacatta marble. Song could put off the need to pee no longer. She made Nina stand just outside the open door as she used the toilet.

A guest room. Then the master bedroom. Hepplewhite armchairs, chestnut night tables, cream love seat and matching wall-to-wall carpeting. The view of mint-green sea through the bay windows was pristine.

Song absorbed the vista. Two gulls hovered like flat white M's sketched on the sky. An American flag fluttered softly at the end of the dock. Dappled light moved on the water. Farther out was a floating lighthouse. Not really floating, of course. Affixed underwater, somehow, to a foundation. But some distance from the nearest shoreline. A line of buoys bobbed before the lighthouse. Orange diamonds indicated a hazard. She saw no other houses, no other boats, no other sign of life.

The gun in her hand was pointed down at the carpeted floor. She could do it now. No one but the gulls would hear. But it would leave one hell of a mess. Maybe better to do it outside, on the beach. Spray the mess into the water and then …

A flickering movement behind her. She turned. Nina had edged a few inches toward the near nightstand. There was a gun in the drawer, no doubt. *Home protection,* Tristan Brooks would call it.

For a bottomless instant, their eyes met. There was accusation in Nina's gaze, alongside wounded self-pity. Song felt a gust of anger. Nina had no right to pity herself. She had never splayed open a rat on a shovel to roast it. She was a wealthy New Yorker, born and bred. She had attended Covenant of the Sacred Heart, where she won the lead role of Abigail Williams in the junior-year production of *The Crucible.* After a good experience onstage, she had decided to pursue the arts. At the same age, Song had been undergoing the surgeon's knife and enduring nightly *chonghwa* sessions, tearing herself apart for the benefit of her trainers.

Nina had gone to Pratt. She had married a successful doctor. Song had gone to Bundang and murdered a defector. Nina had her fancy apartment, her hired help, her vacation home with its boathouse and stretch of perfect white private beach. She had so much more than her fair share that she felt embarrassed of her good fortune. And yet, she dared resent Song, who was only struggling to survive.

Raise the gun; shoot her dead. Fuck the mess. And still Nina would not appreciate how good she had it in the big scheme of things. There were far worse things than a quick, painless death. Consider Song's own mother, fighting to force one last husky, choking breath down a swollen throat as flies buzzed and her own daughter turned away …

Nina edged closer toward the nightstand.

Song reached into her bag, and her fingers found the SIG.

Nina dived for the night table. Song fired instinctively, and a little spray of blood and brain and bone poofed outward from the back of Nina's head.

The body continued its dive toward the nightstand, banged against it, and sprawled onto the floor. Blood welled from the hole in the forehead, turning the bib of the linen sundress a deep crimson.

Song vomited onto the cream-colored love seat. Nothing but bile came up.

She fell to one knee, steadied herself, then looked back over one shoulder to make sure Nina wasn't moving.

The woman was as dead as yesterday.

Song looked away before her stomach could heave again. The shot had not been loud, she thought. Not loud enough for anyone to hear. No neighbors lived within sight. She was okay.

But in fact, she couldn't attest to how loud it had been, because somehow she had not heard the gunshot at all.

She straightened. Her gaze dragged back to Nina. Her best friend. A bloody mess.

Nina's own fault. If she had behaved herself, things might have turned out differently.

Probably not, but maybe.

Over now. Spilt milk.

The headache was coming back.

Carpet and bedspread were spattered like a Jackson Pollock canvas. Song might hide the body, but plenty would remain. *It is the beating of his hideous heart!*

She had hoped for a brief sanctuary, but it was not to be. Nina would be missed. The car was in the driveway. Song had to keep moving.

For a few moments, she indulged a fantasy. She stuffed the body into the car and lit it on fire. The FBI found the charred Lexus, and inside it the body of a woman about Song's age, with about Song's build, with Song's phone still clutched in one hand. Of course, this woman would have smashed her mouth against the steering wheel during the crash, preventing any useful application of dental records. They didn't even bother to test DNA.

But she couldn't figure out how to make the fantasy reality. Prop the body behind the wheel, sure; that was easy enough. And say, just for the sake of argument, that she could clean the bedroom. Then what? Would she get the car up to speed somewhere and then jump out? Even if she tucked and rolled, she would break a leg in the process. Maybe prop the accelerator down with a broomstick, like in the movies. But even if that worked—admittedly a long shot—a car was not likely to burst into flames upon colliding with something. She might help it along with a gas can and a match. But that would leave evidence.

Her eyes turned to the window, the lovely view outside. The boathouse, the lighthouse, the hazard buoys ...

The plan rose fully formed into her mind. When it was done, she would move from one anonymous motel to another, paying cash, leaving no trail. She would not try to cross an international border. She would not try to rendezvous with her contact. From this moment on, Song Sun Young was a free agent.

An excellent plan. It would not only end pursuit by the FBI, it would also spare her brother. Pyongyang could not punish her for dying in the line of duty.

Eventually, she would settle in another city, far away, where she could blend in. She would live the rest of her life keeping to herself, never daring to grow close to anyone. Intimacy invited unnecessary risk. She would find a modest job: low profile, anonymous. She wouldn't need much to get by.

Thus would she grow old and die, free but alone. Queen of her own private hermit kingdom.

The rock and the hard place, but here was the way out. All she had to give up was everything she held dear.

And that was already gone.

She looked at her friend's body with distaste.

LANGLEY, VA

Night was falling when they turned into the parking lot. As Dalia got out of the Range Rover, her bad knee folded beneath her, and she just managed to catch herself against the mirror.

McConnell hovered, ready to help, but she waved him off. She moved under her own steam through security, onto an elevator, and into the conference room. Little had changed during their absence. More cans of Red Bull littered the table near Sam, and a platter of tired-looking sandwiches had replaced the bagels and coffee. Benjamin Bach was on his feet, still or again, looking at his phone. Sonny was seated, resting his eyes. DeArmond watched the wall-mounted monitor, rolling a pencil idly on the tabletop.

On-screen, windows had been rearranged. A long row of minimized tabs ran along the bottom. Only six windows remained open: the interface with the RGB server; the ARGUS live feed; IMSI Catcher seeking the woman's phone; Stingray monitoring Mark Abrahams' phone; the voice-to-text of police feeds; and a new window relaying updates from agents dispatched from the FBI's Intelligence Branch to start knocking on doors, interviewing people who knew Mi-Hi Abrahams.

"The miracle worker," Bach said dryly as they entered. "See yourself on TV?"

Dalia sat down carefully, shaking her head.

Sam fortified himself with a sip of Red Bull before reaching for his keyboard. "Twenty outlets picked it up in the past ninety minutes. And counting. Everything from majors to locals. CNN's pretty typical. Gives you the flavor …"

An anchorwoman with big hair and an electric-blue blazer appeared. DEVELOPING STORY, read the chyron beneath her. TERROR SUSPECT INJURES FBI AGENTS.

"The FBI has announced that the attempted apprehension of a terror suspect went horribly wrong on Saturday night when the suspect brutally gunned down two federal agents near Newark International Airport, wounding both, one seriously."

The screen changed to two placards of agents posing before American flag backgrounds.

"The confrontation occurred around 11 p.m. According to a spokesperson, Special Agent Craig Elwell remains in critical condition at Newark Beth Israel Hospital. Special Agent Angel Alfaro's condition is fair, with favorable indicators. Identified as a suspect: Yusuf Bashara of Jersey City …"

A blurry screen capture appeared: the man in a watch cap, with a heavy black beard. Then a somber taxi-medallion photograph of the same face. *"Authorities caution that Yusuf Bashara is armed and dangerous. He may have a hostage, Mi-Hi Abrahams of Manhattan. Anyone with information on his whereabouts is requested to call the dedicated FBI twenty-four-hour tip line."* An 877 number appeared at the bottom of the screen. Dalia felt a moment's sympathy for the whiteboard jockey who had lent his visage. He would have a hard few days, insisting it was a case of mistaken identity. But they all made their sacrifices.

Now came the photograph from Martha's Vineyard. Song Sun Young looking young and innocent in a yellow sundress, Mark Abrahams with an arm around her shoulders. *Desperate appeal from kidnap victim's family.*

"A dramatic appeal tonight from the family of Mi-Hi Abrahams, the Manhattan woman abducted by Yusuf Bashara before a brutal attack that left two federal agents in the hospital, one in critical condition."

The scene changed to the living room of the Lexington Avenue apartment. Mark Abrahams sat on the couch. His children sat on either side, the boy looking shell-shocked, the girl gazing offscreen at something distracting her.

"*Mi-Hi.*" Abrahams' voice was steady and calm. "*If you can see me or hear me, please know we are looking for you. We will find you. You will be okay. And to Yusuf Bashara ...*" His voice took on an edge. "*Turn yourself in. If you don't, there's no telling what might happen. The authorities promise me that every effort to be fair will be made if you turn yourself in. We are going to get you one way or another.*"

The anchorman again. "*In Washington today, the GOP made a last-ditch attempt to push through—*"

Sam stopped the video. The sudden silence felt empty and dead. "Good work." Bach sounded grudging.

Dalia said nothing. She had baited the trap. Now they would learn whether she had read the woman correctly.

SOUTHAMPTON, NY

Beneath emerging stars, Song approached the boathouse.

The flag at the end of the dock fluttered softly. Smells of saltwater and fish veiled an undertone of something rotten.

She held a key ring she had found in a kitchen drawer. Shaped like a life preserver, the ring held two keys. One unlocked the boathouse.

She stood in the doorway without turning on a light, letting her eyes adjust to the gloom. The craft was big, almost thirty feet long, covered with a heavy-duty vinyl casing and winched up out of the water.

After a few seconds, Song moved forward. She found the winch controls. A motor hummed, and the boat lowered with a creaking groan.

She unhooked the boat's cover. Stenciled letters on the stern read *Windsong*. The boat was white with blue trim, with seats in the bow and more seating wrapping around the transom and port side.

Under a rear seat, she found the battery. Before starting the ventilation fan, she paused, listening. Nothing except the quiet lapping of water, and the squeak of the hull against the cushioned slip. She turned on the blower and let it run, clearing out gas fumes before starting the engine.

She dropped into the driver's seat. The second key fit the ignition. For the moment, she left it unturned. A worm of uneasiness wriggled inside her. Eight years had passed since she last drove a boat. In the darkness, distance would be hard to judge. She had seen no other lights on the water. Even the lighthouse was dark.

After two minutes, she turned off the blower. By the winch controls, she found the button for the boathouse's roll-up door. She pressed it, climbed back into the driver's seat, and fired the engine. Shifting into forward, she cautiously leaned the throttle up. A powerful engine growled in response, and she was out in the bay. Confident again now that she was moving. This would work.

She looked at the rolling boil of froth behind the boat. Dissipating, vanishing. This would work.

The boat rose high on the waves, then fell. The night breeze was stiff. She opened the throttle wide, leaving all lights off. No other boats out here—no birds, no people, no drones, no moon, no lights. Nothing except her and the stars and the dark water. This would work.

She pounded over swells, hair whipping in the wind. The sensation of streaking across empty water was thrilling. The headache was gone.

She slowed, seeking the floating lighthouse. It had vanished. Using the compass to keep her bearings, she peered into the blackness.

She found it: a hulking silhouette empty of stars. Why was the lamp dark? All the better for her story, whatever the reason. She eased the throttle back to neutral and let the boat drift. The wind, the waves, seemed to be gaining force. But let her drift. This wouldn't take long.

First, she found a life vest in a compartment beneath her seat. She buckled it in three places, then tested the fit. Snug.

Next she went aft and opened a lockbox near a downrigger. She lifted out three vinyl-coated ball-and-fin weights: six pounds, eight pounds, ten pounds. She turned to her canvas bag and took out credit cards and passports and cash, Adderall and rations and rolled-up sun hat and compact SIG Sauer P229. She left behind clothes, disguises, her own two phones and Nina's, and the cloner, antenna, and reader/writer.

She zipped her supplies into two freezer bags she had taken from Nina's kitchen, then fitted the bags inside two waterproof Tupperware containers. She stuffed the Tupperware inside an embroidered Etsy fanny pack she had found in a hall closet. Zipping the pack shut, she buckled it around her hips.

She put the six- and eight-pound weights in the canvas bag and closed it, then took off her sneakers, ran the laces through the belt loops of the jeans, and tied them securely with square knots.

She found the lighthouse again. The boat had drifted surprisingly far away. The shore beyond was a low spine of black. The worm of apprehension gave another wriggle. She had never been an especially strong swimmer, but with the life vest, she would manage.

She opened the engine, then wedged the ten-pound weight against the throttle and corrected the course.

She threw the canvas bag overboard, into the wake. It disappeared beneath dark foam.

She clambered up onto the side of the boat, using a cleat as a handhold, and winced at the bolt of pain from her left hip. Mist drizzled onto her face. The boat was moving fast. The lighthouse was coming up quickly.

She took a deep breath, held it, and jumped.

She had thought the life vest would keep her above the surface.

But for a strangely long time, the world was all spinning bubbles and black, frigid water. Her heart skipped.

She bobbed back up like a cork. Shivering, gasping. Her clothes had sculpted to her body. The waterlogged shoes tied around her waist seemed bent on dragging her under. Whether the life vest could support her was an open question. She paddled, thrashing, taking in short, hard breaths. She got a mouthful of saltwater and, for some reason, swallowed instead of spitting. Her sinuses burned in protest.

She swallowed another mouthful and flashed back to crossing the Tumen, the second time, when her feet had floated. For a moment, she had lost contact with the bottom. If the current had been stronger, it might have taken her, swept her off her feet and turned her ingloriously upside down, filling her lungs, then deposited her bloated corpse somewhere on a bank downriver, like so much carrion.

The life vest was holding her up now. No need to panic. She stopped treading water, testing her hypothesis. Water came up to her chin, touched her mouth … and then dropped away as she bobbed over the swell.

She forced her breathing to slow, then felt to make sure she hadn't lost the fanny pack or the sneakers. Yes. They hadn't been ripped free as she skidded into the water. She was okay.

Everything was okay.

The boat was moving off at a good clip, a large, sleek silhouette racing toward the lighthouse and the buoys.

After taking another deep breath, she swam after it in the darkness, digging in with strong overhand strokes, finding a rhythm.

Twenty strokes. She rested, floating. Just beyond the lighthouse, the boat ran aground on something. Very undramatically, it stopped. She could see the bow protruding at a strange angle between buoys. Maybe it would sink, maybe not.

She swam again. Heart calmer now. Shoes around her waist heavy, dragging. But the water was not so bad, once you got used to it. She saw with daylight clarity where she needed to go. That stretch of beach, right there. She swam, rested, swam, rested. A sharp pain jabbed her side. A cramp. She waited, teeth gritted, the life vest buoying her up and over the swells.

She could hear her teeth chattering. The cramp loosened, and she swam again. Getting near shore now. Black water choppy. But she was making it.

Her foot touched something underwater. It rolled away immediately. But then there was another. Beach pebbles. And sand.

She climbed out of the water, dripping, shivering, teeth clacking away.

The water's surge and ebb was lower on her now, down to her waist, then her knees. A rough noise reached her ears. She turned. The boat was some distance up the shoreline. It was coming apart, waves tugging against rocks. Half of it was going back out into the bay. The rest looked as though it would stay where it was. The darkness made it hard to be sure.

She got all the way onto shore. Her hip throbbed again. While in the water, she had forgotten it.

Twenty feet away, she saw garbage cans. Farther up the sand, an outdoor shower.

And a path, leading up the beach and away.

She sank to her knees. For a count of thirty, she breathed, resting.

Then she untied the sneakers from around her waist, put them on, and made for the path.

CHAPTER TWELVE

LANGLEY, VA

Benjamin Bach had reached a fine, delicate state of exhaustion. He felt as fragile as an eggshell.

After swallowing another dose of pholcodine, he lowered himself onto the couch and checked his phone. No new message waited.

He frowned. Then checked the time. Almost twelve hours had passed since he sent the message with the subject line *Alas Babylon.*

Maybe his man had lost his nerve.

He checked again, in case a message had come in the past five seconds. Nothing.

Lying back, he set the phone on his chest. His heart beat light and fast in his ears—the metronome of his anxiety. He rubbed his eyes and looked around him without seeing, at the souvenirs and the framed picture of himself and his father and the rainbow.

His eyes closed. He could see his man losing his nerve. Turning himself in. Throwing Bach under the bus. It could happen.

In a way, it would be a relief. Let someone else take the responsibility, and let him die a normal, quiet death.

But no. Only he had the means, motive, and opportunity.

Maybe it wasn't necessary. Maybe the peace process, given enough time, would actually pay dividends.

But he knew how the Norks worked. He could see the yellow canary feathers poking out from the corners of the Supreme Leader's mouth with every promise he made.

He exhaled jaggedly. He was very tired, but sleep didn't come for a long time.

*   *   *

The doctor removed his glasses in a way that felt staged: an actor using a prop to create a pause during a monologue. He lifted his chin, donning an invisible mantle of authority. He was a big man, fiftyish, with a broad, honest face, and creases around the eyes that fell into place when he smiled.

During the examination, he had made smoothly disarming small talk about March Madness as he fed a tube up Benjamin Bach's left nostril, then the right. "Almost done," he had said, forcing the tube farther up. "So how do we feel about Michigan?"

Bach felt the tube curling inside his sinus, shaping itself to his skull.

Now the doc asked gravely, "Have you ever been exposed to any unusual environmental contaminants?"

After fourteen years with the Company, dissembling was second nature. Bach invented from whole cloth a history of summer work during college: contracting, construction, asbestos, fiberglass, Formica, God knew what else.

He had booked the appointment under the name Jim Brenner, an alias he sometimes used in Beijing. Jim Brenner had an entire backdrop—birth certificate, passport, Social Security number, tax history—and health records that exactly duplicated Bach's own. The doctor was up in Boston—good reputation, but far enough away that Bach would not likely run into someone he knew. If his worst fears proved true, he didn't want Langley hearing about it. He would not be forced into early retirement. He would maintain control.

If there was any skepticism about the summer-work story, it remained carefully veiled. "Well, you've got one hell of a drip. We'll do a CAT scan. And then, if we find what I expect, we'll take aggressive preventive measures—immediately. That means a sinuplasty. We go in and scrape the sinuses clean. Prevents brain and respiratory cancer from developing. I'll be honest, it's no picnic. But it beats the alternative."

* * *

As far as Langley knew, he caught a flu.

Three weeks later, he went back to Beijing.

A puddle jumper brought him to Yanji in Jilin Province—the closest a white face could get to the North Korean border without announcing itself as CIA or Christian missionary, neither of which was welcome. Climbing down from the Harbin Y-11, he felt pretty much okay. The scraping had been tough, but he was healing. The cough and drip were much improved, though not entirely gone. He had moved on. *Do-mode.*

He spent the next nine months living out of the same old suitcase, hopping between the same old fleabag hotels in Yanji, Beijing, and Vladivostok. Sometimes, he spent a week at the US Embassy in Seoul, or a month on a fishing boat or a Company freighter, sending and receiving radio transmissions from the Hermit Kingdom. North Koreans, desperate to feed starving families, proved open to collaboration despite the dire personal risk. He successfully cultivated army officers, comfort women, party officials, nuclear and ballistic technicians, operatives inside the Reconnaissance General Bureau. Paid with food or wan or forged ration books or the promise of relocation for themselves or their children, these assets helped find targets at which to aim the left-of-launch program.

And there were many successes. A large proportion of the DPRK's test missiles exploded on the launchpad, veered off course, disintegrated in midair, plunged into the Sea of Japan. Bach's technical team pushed the envelope relentlessly. To their arsenal of malware, lasers, signal jamming, and sabotage they added high-powered microwaves, frying target computer chips, turning North Korean missiles into so many tons of directionless junk.

But Pyongyang had successes of its own. The newly installed Supreme Leader had doubled down on the path forged by his father and grandfather, accelerating the nuclear and ballistic programs. According to the CIA's psychological profiling unit, he was only sticking with what had worked for him in the past. Projecting strength had vaulted him up the line of succession, ahead of two older brothers. Soon after assuming command, he had sent a stark and effective message by purging not only party members deemed disloyal, but also their children and aides, using theatrical methods such as a flamethrower and antiaircraft artillery. And over the years, aggression as a policy had served North Korea well in strong-arming international concessions. But the aggression had always been tempered by shrewdness and compromise. The father of the new Supreme Leader had spent two decades waiting in the wings, learning to read his enemies' tolerance for provocation, before taking power. The son, by contrast, had spent only two years. At best, he was an unknown quantity; at worst, a loose cannon with nuclear capability.

The new regime quickly launched a three-stage Taepodong/Unha rocket. They conducted a triumphant nuclear detonation. They tested a submarine-launched ballistic missile, and an initial failure was quickly followed by a successful launch. They flexed their own cybermuscles with the humiliating Sony hack, an embarrassment compounded by Sony's promptly pulling from theaters the movie that had raised the DPRK's ire. (The controversial film had come to DirecTV regardless. Bach had been unimpressed.)

The whole chess game was too close for comfort. Bach ground his teeth and wished for Luna Moth. Bringing light to the darkness on gossamer wings, giving the power to outmaneuver any cryptographer in the world. *Complete cybersecurity dominance.*

Then he learned through a back channel that the program had

been discontinued. The laws of quantum physics had refused to bend to the Pentagon's needs. A pipe dream after all, as the director of CERT had said. Back to the drawing board, the fleabag motels, the Company freighters.

Benjamin Bach was made station chief in Seoul. His devotion to the work was all-consuming. He had no close family still living. In all his years in the CIA, he had allowed himself only a single romantic dalliance. His first mentor in South Korea had been a woman named Esther Yong, eighteen years his senior. The sex had been clumsy. She had been too ill at ease in her own thick-shouldered frame. When she suggested that the affair complicated things, got in the way of work, he had readily agreed. Deep down, he had been relieved.

*   *   *

The year after the sinuplasty, he found himself back in Arlington, this time at the Hyatt. He was moving up in the world.

The ride to the Pentagon was provided now by a private security detail. Benjamin Bach was not the only one moving up. Woody Whitlock had been promoted, as predicted, to director for operations of J3. Nevertheless, he came to meet Bach at the River Entrance. Whitlock was still strikingly down-to-earth, friendly, and charismatic. But something had changed. The soft-spokenness that had distinguished him from most career military was gone. He spoke crisply, forcefully. Of course, it might have been just the promotion. In any case, Bach noticed, walking past the River E-ring offices, Woody Whitlock now inspired salutes instead of grins and handshakes.

In the subbasement conference room, they found the usual suspects from DIA, FBI, NSF, NIST, DHS, NASA, DARPA, and J3—and, to Bach's surprise, the same young man from the NSA and the same young woman from IARPA. This was his first inkling that perhaps Luna Moth had not been as decisively discontinued as advertised. Instead, it had gone black.

His second inkling came when he realized that the personnel around the table now included some very heavy hitters. There was the United States director of intelligence himself, and the directors and deputy directors of the FBI and CIA, NCS and NSA (the NSA director doubled as commander of United States Cyber Command), and NSA Directorate leaders including J2, Cryptography, and T, the Technical Directorate, as well as Company station chiefs from Moscow and Paris and Tel Aviv.

The director of intelligence, well-fed, graying at the temples, looked like an ordinary businessman. "If you're in this room," he began, "you have been deemed an integral part of America's defense. And you are about to be honored with the details of the greatest US intelligence coup of all time."

A drumbeat of excitement began in Bach's solar plexus. And all at once, he knew.

"You all recall a program called Luna Moth." *Beat.* "Officially discontinued." *Double beat.* "But unofficially, ladies and gentlemen, a resounding success."

The technical specifics would be made available to those who cared to try to comprehend them. Good luck with that. (Laughter rippled around the table.) But the upshot was that America's quickest and cleverest had banded together and vaulted humanity into a brave new future. Inside NASA's Advanced Supercomputer Facility at Ames Research Center, amid an array of wires, mirrors, lenses, and laser beams, the impossible had been made possible. Ions of ytterbium had been trapped, bumped into quantum states, entangled, assembled, and stabilized. To these men and women charged with safeguarding democracy, the development meant a dramatic new tool in their arsenal—but one that must be deployed with the utmost caution.

He alluded to Operation Double Cross during World War II. Every person in the room knew the story. During the early days of the war, MI5 had arrested and turned every Nazi spy inside England. As a result, the British had gained absolute control of the flow of information back to the Wehrmacht. To keep their secret, they had played a complex and dangerous game. Information had been mixed with disinformation to prevent the Nazis from realizing that their network had been compromised. Battles had been lost, lives sacrificed, saving up capital for the massive deception of D-day. The good of the many had outweighed the good of the few.

Similarly, Luna Moth would provide maximum value only so long as America's enemies remained unaware of it and, thus, took no measures to counter it—quantum-resistant cryptography was labor intensive but possible. Hence the official cancellation of the program, when researchers had begun to see their goal coming within reach. And hence their policy moving forward, modeled on the approach of Operation Double Cross. Every use of Luna Moth would be specifically approved by both the DI's office and the White House. Calculated losses would be not only accepted but invited. All too soon, America's enemies would duplicate Luna's achievement. Until then, the USA would maximize its advantage by focusing on quality of victories over quantity.

Through it all, the paunchy director of CERT smiled beatifically. Looking at him, you'd think he had been nothing less than instrumental in this accomplishment, urging on his troops through the inevitable patches of threadbare morale.

Fuck him. The achievement, Bach knew, was greater than any one person. And it was greater than politics. It was a true watershed moment, a paradigm shift as promised.

And it came not a moment too soon. North Korea's leaps in ballistic missile tech had been rivaled by its leaps in cyberpower. After the Sony hack, but more quietly, Bureau 121 had stolen eighty-one million dollars from the New York Federal Reserve, and hundreds of millions more from South Korean Bitcoin exchanges. They had hacked into a British television network to prevent the airing of a show about a kidnapped nuclear scientist. They had used the website of Poland's financial regulator to host a "watering hole" attack, installing malware onto systems belonging to the central banks of Brazil, Chile, Estonia, Mexico, Venezuela, and even the Bank of America.

Now Bach could enjoy free run of Pyongyang's servers. Like the proverbial kid in a candy store, but instead of Mike and Ikes, he could fill his pockets with nuclear infrastructure schematics and profiles of aerospace engineers. But of course, he would show restraint. To the outside world, and to the Hermit Kingdom's ruling regime, the game must seem to continue. Things would be missed accidentally-on-purpose. And so, when a true moment of crisis came, America would have a hole card to play.

*   *   *

Thrice yearly, Benjamin Bach became Jim Brenner and went to see the ear-nose-and-throat guy in Boston.

He paid for the comprehensive physicals and preventive scans out of his own pocket. First responders were entitled to free medical treatment through the Environmental and Occupational Health Services Institute. But while Benjamin Bach was a 9/11 first responder, Jim Brenner was not.

Scan after scan came up clean.

Until one didn't.

The doctor maintained steady eye contact as he delivered the news.

When he was done, he paused, letting the words sink in. Eye contact still direct. A small dollop of snot visible in one nostril, beside a silvering hair. After a few seconds, he leaned away, taking off his glasses—the pause in the monologue. "I'm honest, Jim. It's not always pretty, but it's the only way I know how to be. This is not good news."

When Bach had been a boy in the Bronx, a snow day seemed to go on forever. Summer vacations had encompassed eternities. Here, now, he was rediscovering that childhood temporal perspective. Perhaps five seconds had passed since he got the news, but it felt like forever.

"Chemo?" he managed.

"If we choose to go down that road … We'd start with surgery. Then chemo, yes. And radiation. And there are some very promising immunotherapies in trial. Keytruda, Opdivo. I'll make some referrals, if you like. I have a friend at Sloan. He's very good." Pause. The voice lowered. "But I won't bullshit you. We're looking at a tough slog. There's no denying that the treatment can be harsh. That's actually what kills most patients, not the cancer itself. And once you go that way, it's hard to turn back. If it's going to lead to the same place in the end …"

"Do I have other options?"

"Another option is palliative care. We focus on enhancing quality of life. For however much time remains."

"Which is …"

"I hate to put a number on something like that."

"If you had a gun to your head."

"I'd rather not."

Bach felt himself nodding. What was the etiquette here? Did you thank the doctor who had just told you that your body was riddled with cancer?

Outside the window, traffic droned past. The brakes of trucks wheezed. A siren rose and fell. The endless breath of life on earth, of mass transit and ambulances. It would continue merrily along, Bach suddenly realized, without him on the planet.

He closed his eyes. Blood-soaked children, melted badges. Cherry pickers floating aimlessly, shrouds of ash. He felt the itch in his lungs. He smelled smoke and melting steel and combusted jet fuel and pulverized concrete and scorched flesh and fingernails and bone and hair and pulverized Formica and asbestos and polystyrene foam.

He could picture it: the toxic smell becoming a toxic post-nasal drip, sliding down his throat and ruining his stomach, his liver, his kidneys, his bladder. Spreading, mutating, killing him, all this time, from the inside out. He sat here alive. But in fact, he had died almost two decades ago. He had died on 9/11. Like father, like son.

Emerging into the blindingly bright parking lot a few minutes later, he blinked stupidly. He donned sunglasses. Then he paused, keys in hand, beside his Mercedes.

The impression of the doctor as an actor remained. Bach felt not entirely convinced that this *wasn't* actually a play or a movie. The momentous news did not reconcile with the banality of tractor-trailers droning past on the nearby highway, with the smell of oil and frying food from a McDonald's down the road.

He got into the car. His reflection looked back from the rearview mirror. He took off the sunglasses. Heavy smudges underlined his eyes. Otherwise, he looked okay. Thin, maybe. And tired. But not *dying.*

Not *dying.*

*　　*　　*

He lay in his hotel room that night, staring at the unblemished cream-colored ceiling. He thought of jet planes arrowing across television screens. Massing oily black smoke. The world's biggest tire fire. People trapped on a roof. Opting to jump rather than burn. Holding hands. Had his father jumped? Somehow, the question had never occurred to him before. Somehow, he had avoided it.

He thought of the days following 9/11—days he usually didn't let himself think about. He had met other volunteers by the score. They had come from New Mexico, Tennessee, Canada, Ohio. Fire trucks designed to travel five miles at a stretch had driven seventy-two hours straight on interstates. He had met a young couple, social workers, who had postponed their marriage to drive up from Georgia. They all were in Do-mode. They all were locking their trauma away deep inside. How many of them, in the years since, had received diagnoses like the one he just got?

He had spent the second night at Stuyvesant High School. The school, half a mile north of the smoking pile now called Zone One, had been refitted as a staging area. A Red Cross nurse had given him two Tylenol PM. He had stolen three fitful hours of sleep on a thin mattress on a cot. The next morning, he had tried again to call his father. The phone line had popped and sputtered like grease on a hot grill.

When he made the walk down to Zone One on the third morning, it felt almost familiar. Muscles throbbing across his back, shoulders. Down the thighs and calves. Food stations everywhere, Michelin three-star restaurants doling out free sushi and filet mignon around the clock. He ate a California roll and drank a cup of coffee.

The situation was changing, federal and state agencies taking over. Security had appeared, chasing away those who did not belong. But the combination of the medical badge and the dust-encrusted two-canister mask gave Bach the right to stay.

He lugged more debris. He registered at Chelsea Piers along with everyone else seeking lost loved ones. He watched other first responders visit the Spirit of New York tour boats, docked in the Hudson and turned into massage and chiropractic centers. But he indulged in no such luxuries himself.

On the fourth day, President Bush addressed them over a bullhorn. Bach harbored mixed feelings about W. Nevertheless, he felt something inside him stir at the words. *We can't hear you,* someone shouted, and Bush answered, *But I can hear you,* and Bach felt hot tears spill down his cheeks.

The next morning, he couldn't leave his bed at Stuyvesant. Overtaxed muscles had turned leaden, useless. He lay on the cot until early afternoon. Finally, he got to his feet, wincing. He went outside. The street was crowded with people who had come over by ferry from Liberty State Park to deposit flowers, pictures, articles of clothing in a makeshift grave. But he had no keepsake of his father to leave.

That night, volunteers were sent home. Professionals took over. Leaving Zone One, Bach turned back for a final look. Smoke still plumed up like a floodlit gray feather. He felt something falling inside him. He expected that at some point it would hit bottom. But instead, it kept falling.

Palliative care. He would be spared surgery and chemo and radiation. But not pain and suffering and humiliation.

He remembered watching his grandmother die. Every Sunday, he and his father would visit her in Queens. They would park before her row house and climb the stairs. Benjamin would think of Spider-Man. Peter Parker lived in Queens. They would brace themselves. Dad's hand resting on his shoulder, supportive but also preventing escape. They would step through the front door, into smells of rubber gloves and medicine and dust and lemon-fresh Joy. Grandma would sit propped in her easy chair before a TV that played endlessly: sports, game shows, soaps, sitcoms, news, whatever. Each week, there was a little less of Grandma. And yet, she never died. Weeks turned to months, months to years. Grandma turned to ridges of bone supporting folds of gray skin. And yet, she never died. On a little table beside the couch, she kept her book and her reading glasses. During the first year, he would see a new book there every week. During the second year, a new book every month. During the last year, the same slim Agatha Christie sat gathering dust. By then Grandma couldn't speak. She sat grinding her teeth, counting down to her next pain pill. Wisps of ashy skin hanging from spines of bone. To this day, Benjamin Bach couldn't see a copy of *And Then There Were None* without shuddering.

One way or another, it would be an ugly death.

Take the initiative, he thought. Better to jump than to burn.

He thought of guns. The shooting range on the Farm. Morphine overdose. Carbon monoxide. The 5:37 express from Penn Station. The George Washington Bridge. The observation deck of the Freedom Tower. That would be only appropriate.

But then the fat little madman would have no one in his way.

The gross, fat, comical little psycho; the marshal, the Supreme Leader, as absurd a supervillain as Lex Luthor or any Bond nasty or cartoon megalomaniac. This gross little madman had the power to rain high-yield nuclear warheads down on Americans as they supped at their dining-room tables.

And whether Benjamin Bach jumped or burned, this overgrown child, this tantrum-throwing brat, would outlive him. The profiling unit insisted that the madman was, in fact, rational—that even the fat itself was a shrewd calculation, because by gaining weight the man increased the resemblance to his grandfather, who had commanded more respect than his father. But considering the stakes, was betting on the little fuck's rationality a gamble really worth taking?

When Bach was gone, who would seize the reins? Who would stand up to the fat little madmen of the world—and, closer to home, the ass-coverers, the naysayers, the beady-eyed women from NIST, and the spineless directors of CERT? Who would take the profilers' recommendations with a healthy pillar of salt?

He thought of windows of opportunity ... missiles plunging into seas ... planes plunging into buildings ... jumpers plunging from rooftops ... preemptive doctrines ... doors, windows, opening, closing ... nuclear arsenals around the world bristling, straining to be let loose ... one country aiming extinction at another ... melted badges, blood-soaked children ... chemo drips, radiation ... tripwires, thirty-eighth parallels ... Apache helicopters hovering before sinking suns ... F-15s making tight circles ... ruined ambulances, the remnants of firefighters' helmets ... safeguards, launch codes ... every system vulnerable, as Wyoming had proved ... every system built to be used ...

The idea was there already, coiled like a sleeping snake in the perfect center of his mind. The idea had been there for years, maybe for decades. Certainly since Luna Moth, which made it feasible.

Now the snake was uncoiling, stirring awake. Stretching.

One last good deed before he shuffled off this mortal coil.

His legacy.

* * *

His eyes opened. A sense of urgency nagged. Soon would come the decisive moment. Soon would come everything he had worked for. *Soon.*

He sat up. The quality of the night outside seemed unchanged. He felt oddly refreshed from what he sensed had been a very short nap. He felt strong, capable. Energized. No more doubt. No more fear. He was ready to see this through. Ready for the endgame. *Do-mode.*

Soon.

He checked his phone. His man's message had not come yet.

But soon.

He went back to the conference room to rejoin the game.

CHAPTER THIRTEEN

A handful of employees on the cafeteria's mezzanine spoke in low voices, with the occasional muted laugh. On the ground floor, McConnell and Dalia found a secluded table in a corner. He blew ripples across the surface of his coffee. She checked her phone. She had never listened to her daughter's voice mail. In Hebrew shot through with long-distance echoes: "Eema, I'm so sorry I missed your birthday. Don't think I wasn't thinking of you. Things have just been crazy here. Give me a call when you get a chance. In the meantime ..." Shuffling sounds, throat-clearing, and then an off-key version of "Happy Birthday," finishing with a ringing imperative: "*Yom hu'ledet sameach!*"

Dalia saved the voice mail.

She checked her email. The chair of Princeton's History Department wanted to coordinate next year's schedule. Amazon Rewards offered a credit-line increase. Her financial advisor in Tel Aviv wanted to arrange a conference. Her editor wondered when he might expect delivery of the Issus monograph. A spot in his schedule had opened up. No pressure.

She set down the phone. Her tired eyes locked on to a curl of steam rising from her coffee and, for a long moment, refused to disengage.

"I booked rooms in Bethesda." McConnell spoke diplomatically, sotto voce. "Say the word. I'll give you a ring the second anything develops."

She shook her head.

A few moments passed. "Sonny put in a call to the NRO." The National Reconnaissance Office in Chantilly. "They're lending us Rainbird." He saw the puzzled look on Dalia's face. "Cutting-edge spysat. Bypasses the Rayleigh criterion diffraction. Conventional wisdom says that from orbit you can't beat a ground resolution of about two inches. But Rainbird uses dozens of images, then chooses the best pixels from each and combines them. Of course, you need to know where to point it …"

He trailed off again. He had read her mood. And he already knew her opinion of dependence on overwhelming technological advantage.

"Maybe she hasn't seen the news," he ventured.

"Or maybe she's spooked." Dalia sipped her coffee. "Maybe she thinks it's bait."

"Could you blame her?"

Dalia gave no answer. She may have misjudged the woman's devotion to her family. *At the narrow passage,* the Bedouin said, *there is no brother and no friend.*

A titter of laughter came from the mezzanine, where one of the agents must have told a good joke. Dalia shifted, relieving the weight on her knee. She looked at McConnell. He was only a few years her junior. In ten years, she thought, he would have retired. He would find retirement surprisingly agreeable. He would pick up hobbies: painting, fishing. He would thrive. Burying his head in the sand, he would find, was acceptable after all. He would appreciate for the first time the little things in life. He would reconcile with his ex-wife. Together they would cherish their twilight years, helping their children raise a brood of grandchildren. He would die peacefully in his bed, a smile on his face.

That, she supposed, was what they called projection.

She gulped more coffee, then nodded. McConnell gathered the cups as she set the cane and pushed herself up.

Leaving the cafeteria, they ran into Shyam Radha. He had been sprinting to find them. He paused, hands on knees, catching his breath so he could deliver his news.

Dalia felt a keen straining inside her. *We've got her.*

EAST QUOGUE, NY

Song buried the life vest under sand and leaf litter a half mile in from the beach. She did her best to keep to the woods, but she also wanted to keep the road within reasonable distance, both to stay oriented and to maintain the option of a quick getaway.

For long stretches, she picked her way through dense foliage, over leaf mold and rocky sand. Then would come houses—cottages, mansions, estates. Then raw countryside again, babbling brooks, and deep virgin copses of parkland. Every half hour, she stopped to check herself for ticks.

She guessed she had been walking more than six hours. At first, she had been alone with the night wind and the trees and the animals. Then, as the sun rose, her shadow had joined her: a graceful, though limping, ballerina slowly contracting into a squat, hunchbacked dwarf.

Soon after dawn, she heard the racket of revving ATVs. Male laughter, a barking dog. She stopped and leaned against a tree. For much of the night, soaked to the bone, she had been chilly. Now, between the sun and the exertion, she was hot. The dampness of the limp sun hat was changing from seawater to sweat.

She pressed on, giving the ATVs a wide berth. Winding hiking paths, and beaches with sumac and dogwood and kinnikinnick, and always the road within earshot, growing noisier as the morning developed. Birds caroled happily. Squirrels chittered as they went about their morning errands.

Her leg hurt where the man had banged it against the bed frame.

She had thought the hip was just bruised, but maybe there was a hairline fracture.

That had been a lifetime ago. That never really happened.

Thinking of the man reminded her of the Adderall. She dug the Tupperware out of the fanny pack. She shook three tablets—proof that it had been real after all—into her palm. Down the hatch.

She walked on. Each step now sent shivers of pain radiating out from her hip. She had wanted to get beyond the search zone before she contrived a ride. But she was realizing now that she could not go much farther on foot.

She could still hear the road, just over the ridge of trees. Soon, she would need to take the chance.

Reaching a small rise, she paused again, then lowered herself to the ground. Her stiff body bent grudgingly. She would rest a few moments. Then she would risk the road.

She took off the damp shoes and set them in the sunshine to dry. She watched a single gull circling over blue-gray water. A fresh, pleasantly cool breeze teased her hair beneath the brim of the sun hat. She wondered how long she could sit here without being bothered.

She released a slow breath. Good heat baked up from the ground beneath her. The wind coming off the water was not too balmy, not too chilly. No mosquitoes yet—too early in the season. And no humidity worth mentioning. For this fleeting moment, she felt almost content.

She went into the Tupperware again, past the cash and gun and IDs, to her rations. She got out a granola bar, took a bite, and chewed mechanically. Had to keep the old engine fueled. She would need her energy. Today, and tonight, and tomorrow. And the day after, and the day after that. She would never truly be able to relax again.

She massaged her neck, then her aching feet. In a former life, she might have worried about calluses and bunions. What was the point of a hundred-dollar mani-pedi if you let yourself get bunions? But in the life before *that,* in her true life as Song Sun Young of Camps 14 and 15, she would have spared her vanity no thought whatever. Anything that had not killed her had not been worth her attention.

Who was to say which life was the true one? Yes, she had been born into Chosun. And something in her core would forever remain there, an orphan, small, sad, hungry, and frightened. A pitiful little *kochebi,* wandering swallow, who had never known her father, whose mother had died before her eyes. But she was also Mi-Hi Abrahams, PTA volunteer extraordinaire, mother of two.

Were some selves truer than others? Could more than one self be true?

She sat and listened to the forest rustling like an incantation and wondered.

Eventually, she released another slow breath. She couldn't sit here forever.

She pocketed the granola bar's wrapper and creaked to her feet. She put on her sneakers again and limped in the direction of the car sounds.

*   *   *

A group of day laborers hung out beside a convenience store, leaning against a cinder-block wall, spitting tobacco juice into the sand.

She walked past them, onto the gravelly shoulder of a narrow highway. She slowed, taking in the tactical features of the landscape. She saw plenty of potential cover for agents lying in ambush: buildings, trees, parking lots, crowded boat slips.

If they had tracked her, they would have made their move by now.

She wet her lips, then gave the brim of the sun hat a downward tug and kept moving.

She passed a Best Eastern Motel, then a place called Stone Creek Inn. Would they search every motel? Maybe not. Maybe she could rent a room and rest. Hide in plain sight. But her intuition told her to keep moving.

She crossed a footbridge above dun-colored water. Boats were moored underneath, all in a line. They would be quickly missed if stolen. She limped on. A dentist, a hardware store, a law office. Business hours starting soon. Monday morning. Dex would be getting ready for school, unless Mark was keeping him home. Probably, Mark was keeping him home.

People chatted on street corners. They bought coffee and Danishes. They walked dogs and pushed strollers. Couples ate breakfast at round tables beneath blue umbrellas. Flags licked in the breeze.

She felt acutely aware of the chance she was taking, showing herself in public. But she was mostly dry now. The wide-brimmed sun hat covered her face. She blended in because she willed herself to blend in. And so far, it was working. No one looked at her twice. In Chosun, at the Chongjin railway station, on the streets, and especially inside the camps, she had stayed alive by not being noticed. She had learned the small tricks of body language that made others' eyes keep moving without pause. She had made an art form of avoiding attention. When she came west, she had struggled to unlearn the habit. She had hated raising a finger to ask a waiter for a check. In doctors' offices and banks, anywhere they asked for personal information, she had died a little inside, responding lightly with a smile as she gave them the very means to track her.

A liquor store, shuttered. A bagel store with a line winding out onto the sidewalk. She crossed the street to maintain some distance. A Chinese restaurant and a butcher shop were both closed. She passed a newspaper rack, then stopped and backtracked.

A headline blared, *The Disappearance of Mi-Hi Abrahams: What We Know Now.*

Icy fingers grazed the length of her spine.

It has been two days since Mi-Hi Abrahams was abducted by terror suspect Yusuf Bashara.

A blurry screen capture followed. Her Volvo parked by a street corner at night. Song herself sitting behind the wheel. A threatening-looking man wearing a heavy black beard, caught in the act of emerging from a nearby doorway.

Since her disappearance, images of the woman—happy with

her husband and two small children, and held at gunpoint near her tony Upper East Side apartment just minutes before a violent confrontation outside Newark Airport—have haunted authorities and onlookers alike.

She was standing, goggling, mouth hanging open. Attracting attention. She could feel people on the other side of the street taking notice.

She broke the spell and made herself walk on.

A wave of unreality washed over her. For a few seconds, wheels spun in her mind, failing to find traction. It made no sense. Abducted by a terror suspect? Held at gunpoint near her tony Upper East Side apartment? What fuckery was this?

Then she ruthlessly forced the question from her mind. Later she would figure it out. Now she needed to focus. Avoid drawing attention. And get off the roads.

She turned down a wide avenue that intersected with the main street. Out of the corner of her eye, she had glimpsed an auto junkyard. Crumpled, ruined cars, cars half buried in sand, cars without windows, cars without tires. *Auto Salvage,* a sign proclaimed. SOLD AS IS. ALL SALES FINAL. Hand-lettered placards in windshields gave prices. The small cinder-block office was closed. She saw no indication of hours.

She approached a Mazda L-series that looked drivable. The placard read *$1,975.* The windshield was spiderwebbed with cracks. The car was old enough to predate transponder keys. Most of these cars were, which meant she had a shot at hot-wiring it.

She looked around. A plastic-bagged circular rotted in a driveway across the street. A crow on a high branch looked inscrutably back at her.

She tried the Mazda's driver's-side door. Locked.

Hunting on the sandy ground, she found a bent tongue of metal beside a rusted camshaft.

She would never get away with it. The salvage yard's owner would show up. Helicopters would appear overhead. Drones, satellites, dogs …

She slid the metal down outside the window and slipped the lock. Inside the Mazda, she located the hood release. Outside again, she lifted the hood. She tracked the red coil wire on the right side of the four-cylinder engine. Moving as if she had every right to be here, doing this, she used the metal's ragged edge to strip a half centimeter of insulation. She ran the wire to the battery, then slid behind the steering wheel again and popped the trunk, praying. Her prayer was answered in the form of a tire iron. She jammed the tapered end between the wheel and the steering column and gave it a hard wrench, unlocking the column. She found the starter solenoid and stripped two more wires, then paused briefly. So far, so good. She held her breath and touched the wires together.

Nothing. The battery was dead.

Her head felt suddenly stuffy, stupid with despair.

Someone was coming down the sidewalk. A couple walking a pug. They glanced in her direction. Maybe they had seen the newspaper. Some kind of Photoshop. But why? Who? How? To what purpose?

Later.

She smiled. The couple smiled back. They passed.

Her smile fell away. She sagged.

Now what?

She might try hitchhiking. But hitchhikers were noteworthy. Rare enough to stand out.

She might steal a car from a driveway. But cars stolen from driveways got reported.

She could see how this ended. She was circling the drain.

Her eyelid twitched.

She had missed the window when turning herself in would have meant anything.

One more try.

A 2003 Honda Civic: no windshield, no plates, one crunched taillight. She got beneath the hood.

She ran a wire to the battery, forced the steering lock, found the solenoid, stripped two more wires. This time, she didn't bother holding her breath. She crossed the wires.

Nothing.

Her face relaxed into soft lines. Her fingertips tingled as if an electric shock had come through the wires. Maybe it had.

Giving up hope was, in its way, a relief. She could stop running at last. They would capture her and probably execute her. But first, she would get a real meal, a real bed. She could not remember her last real meal or good sleep.

She would walk over to Main Street and buy herself some food—that was what she would do. That line had not wound from the bagel store for nothing. She would buy a toasted sesame-seed bagel with cream cheese, and a carton of sugary orange juice. She would sit on a stool by a window counter—it was the kind of place that would have a stool by a window counter—and enjoy her bagel and juice as she waited to be noticed and then arrested.

Of course, it meant death for her brother. It meant dishonor for her children. But she was only human. She had done all she could.

A few minutes passed. She slumped behind the Honda's steering wheel. No one else came down the sidewalk. No one showed up to open the locked office. The Adderall she had gulped before entering town started working. Layers of fatigue began peeling away. Beneath them, a second wind she had thought beyond her was gaining momentum.

She sighed. *Miles to go before I sleep.*

Wearily she opened the door of the Civic and climbed out of the car.

BROOKHAVEN, NY

The pilot turned and said, "Go!"

Jim McConnell shucked off his headset and safety belt, then yanked open the door. He jumped down. When he turned back to help Dalia, rotor wash lifted his comb-over like a roof shingle in a gale.

A Southampton Village Police cruiser waited to bring them to the beach. A prisoner screen separated them from their chauffeur. The driver concentrated hard on the road despite the complete absence of traffic.

After ten minutes, they turned at a sign reading PRIVATE PROPERTY. NO TRESPASSING. VIOLATORS WILL BE PROSECUTED. A chain had been unhooked. At the end of the road was a small parking lot. They pulled in beside two windowless vans, both bare of agency logos.

The cruiser's rear doors had no interior handles. They had to wait for their chauffeur to release them. Setting the cane carefully, Dalia stumped down a sandy path, past garbage cans and an outdoor shower, to the beach.

Her stomach was still unsettled from the helicopter ride. The organic tang of seashore made it roll queasily. She paused, letting her gut calm. Leaning against the cane, she shielded her eyes with one hand and looked out across the bay.

A barrel-chested man wearing an FBI windbreaker strode toward them. Police tape snapped loudly in the breeze. Two men wearing protective suits, rubber gloves, goggles, and helmets picked through a pile of wet wood on the rocky shore. A woman, also in an FBI windbreaker, took pictures. Far out above the water, a helicopter hung beneath the sun. Dalia glimpsed a frogman, surfacing briefly, getting his bearings before diving again.

"Bob Haynes," the barrel-chested man said. His eyes seemed too close together. "You're Charlie's guys?"

He crushed Dalia's hand with a trying-too-hard shake, then paid attention only to McConnell. "Underwater team's drawing a blank. But ERTU"—the FBI's Evidence Response Team Unit—"found this." He gestured down the sand, where a small vinyl bag sat like an abandoned puppy among long strands of algae. "Weight bag for the downrigger. Empty now. Possible the loads went to the bottom. But we're also one life vest short. Might have gone to the tide. But then, we'd expect to see it floating."

McConnell looked thoughtfully across the bay, toward a lone house on a stretch of beach.

Dalia faced the other way, down the beach. She blocked out the scent of seaside, the distant hovering helicopter. Opened her senses. Trying to feel the truth of what had happened here.

A dark and moonless night. The murder of a friend. A desperate theft of a boat, hazardous rocks.

It was certainly possible.

But it was too perfect. You could almost see the brushstrokes.

She moved sand with the toe of her shoe. Gravel, shells, tiny pieces of quartz, countless dips and valleys—the beach covered its secrets nearly as well as the water did.

She tested the relative weights of different possibilities. This, her instinct said, was not how Song Sun Young died. Song had stayed ahead of a trillion dollars' worth of equipment. She had escaped two high-security North Korean prisons before the age of twelve. Song had *juche* in spades. Song was master of her destiny. She didn't get herself killed in a stupid accident.

Dalia set her cane. Dry brush ran alongside the path. Scowling, she paced the distance: *step-clomp, step-clomp.* Something invisible startled into flight at her passage, rustling branches.

Here was a whitewashed fence. The beginnings of scrubby forest. Pine trees. A blue jay hopping, head cocked.

A trillion dollars' worth of equipment. ARGUS recorded one million terabytes of video per day. Operators could scan back over the entire thirty-six-square-mile overview at their leisure, cherry-picking a time and place after the fact, zooming in close enough to read a license plate. But ARGUS had been parked over Manhattan last night. The technology was worthless unless, as McConnell had said about Rainbird, you knew where to point it.

The path vanished over a low hill. She turned to look back down the beach, toward the talking men and the parking lot and the road beyond. Too close. Song, if she lived, would have wanted to gain more distance before rejoining civilization.

Dalia pressed on. The ground sloped up. Here were distinct prints, probably deer. The sun rose another degree in the sky. The day's heat was building. But a few hours ago, it had been dark. Cold, too, if you had just swum in the North Atlantic. Dark and cold and foreboding. And dispiriting, Dalia guessed, if you had the blood of a trusted friend on your hands. But Song would have been determined. And maybe not so dispirited after all. Maybe Dalia had misjudged her completely. Maybe she was utterly pitiless.

A glint caught her eye. The years when she could easily bend down were behind her. She stirred it with her foot. Just a flattened beer can.

The beach was giving way to woodlands now. The path was straggling, slowly disappearing. Up ahead, sand become actual dirt. Underbrush thickened. Dalia could not go much farther. She came to a stop.

But Song was young, fit. She would have kept going. Into the woods. Dalia wondered what was on the other side.

She closed her eyes. Listening, scenting, feeling. She opened her eyes and then, despite the effort, despite the scary shift of her center of gravity, she half-knelt, leaning heavily against the cane, ignoring the stab of pain from her knee.

Here were old leaves, half-mulched, from last autumn. Ants, a small cloud of gnats, a caterpillar. No prints, no sign of passage. But nothing that would have made passage impossible, either—not to a fit, determined young woman.

Master of her destiny.

Even as they had been laying a trap for the woman, she had been laying one for them.

Dalia straightened awkwardly, set the cane again, and went to rejoin McConnell.

CHAPTER FOURTEEN

EAST QUOGUE, NY

Song watched the café from across the street. A scrappy-looking girl with a long red ponytail pushed a broom across the sidewalk. Next door, a man leaned against a brick wall, reading a newspaper. Even from here, Song could see the headline. The man wore a double-breasted suit with a pocket square. Every time he turned a page, he gave his paper a smart crack to straighten the leaves.

Song looked up the street, then down. She saw a Capital One Bank, a self-proclaimed gourmet deli, and a restaurant called China Delight. A storefront labeled NEW HORIZONS KITCHEN AND BATH, a gift shop called Calico Garden, and a side yard with weathered boats stacked on a dry rack. One traffic light, one small church. Through a line of trees, blue water sparkled.

She looked back at the New Moon Café. A small hand-lettered sign in the window read HAMPTON JITNEY PICK UP HERE.

This was the sticks. It was entirely possible that no one was watching this tiny café. It was entirely possible that she could walk across the street and the man with the newspaper would not recognize her face. She could go inside, buy a ticket, and board the next bus without any trouble.

It was also possible that the man would place her, call the

police, or attempt a citizen's arrest. Or maybe the FBI was waiting just on the other side of that door. Or watching via satellite or drone or closed-circuit security camera. Maybe they had set up roadblocks on the highways. Maybe the man with the pocket square was their agent. But no. He was dressed too conspicuously. Wasn't he?

She fixed the brim of the hat—eyes in the sky would not find her with facial recognition, at least—and then drew a deep breath and let it out.

She crossed the street.

The overdressed man registered her presence without much interest. The girl pushing the broom smiled. Song smiled back and went into the white clapboard café. A bell chimed softly. She saw no cameras, but she kept her face angled down anyway.

The tables and booths were unoccupied. She heard activity from a back room: clattering, scraping, clunking. Through a cutaway, she saw a slice of kitchen: kettle fryer, reams of paper napkins on shelves, doors labeled EMPLOYEES ONLY and EMERGENCY EXIT—ALARM WILL SOUND.

A metal sideboard held Proctor Silex hot plates, syrup-encrusted caddies, trays of flatware, bleary plastic water glasses. The front counter had a cash register and a menu under glass. A wooden rack just inside the door held brochures for various local businesses. And more newspapers—but not with the same headline, thank God. These were weekly locals, covering high school sports heroes, zoning disputes, requests for gently used donations.

She found a jitney schedule. Westhampton Line South Fork. Monday. She had missed the eight fifteen. The next bus left at ten fifteen. She found a clock shaped like a porthole, hanging on the wall beside an old Coca-Cola sign. Half an hour.

The bell chimed again. The redheaded girl came in, leaned the broom against the wall behind an antique umbrella stand, and went behind the counter.

Something in the kitchen started sizzling. The smell of bacon wafted out. Song's stomach stirred, then grumbled loudly.

The girl laughed. "Table for one?"

Song paused; worked up a nice light laugh, and nodded.

SOUTHAMPTON, NY

Entering the spotless living room, Dalia became aware of her own unwashed clothing.

She glanced at McConnell, standing beside her, taking in the baby grand piano and the dried sea life on the walls. He had on the same sweater vest he had been wearing since Friday. Beneath it, his collar was noticeably dingy.

Dalia stood for a moment, feeling the room. Her quarry had been here. Seeing this same piano, same grandfather clock, same dried starfish and seahorses.

A few moments passed. Outside, the bay murmured and whispered. From the foyer near the front door the man standing guard gave a shallow cough. An edge of sunlight crept across the polished floor, touching the tips of Dalia's toes. She caught McConnell's eye and nodded.

They climbed the half-spiral staircase, Dalia gripping the banister hard. A gull outside gave a cracked caw. The first door they passed opened to a bed littered with stuffed animals. Song would have seen these same toys. She would have been reminded that Nina Brooks had a young daughter. As Song herself did. But that had not prevented her from shooting the woman, according to the medical examiner, from nearly point-blank range.

Dalia wanted to think the best of people. But she had misjudged Song. The woman cared about no one but herself.

Maybe.

They reached the master bedroom. Chalk outline, dried blood. Gray magnetic dust used to pick up fingerprints covered every smooth surface. Genetic material and prints recovered here had matched samples taken from Song's Lexington Avenue apartment.

Dalia saw no television or computer. They wanted to keep it simple here, these city dwellers. They wanted a break from the plugged-in world they inhabited in Manhattan. So it was possible that Song had gotten this far without seeing the news.

She looked out the window. Sparkling bay, circling gulls, floating lighthouse, and, farther away, suspended helicopter.

She thought about the interview DeArmond's men had conducted with Tristan Brooks in Manhattan. Brooks had last seen his wife on Sunday morning, when she went downtown to look at possible rental spaces for a fund-raiser next fall. Song must have called her friend. Doubtless told her a story. But Nina's phone was missing, so this, too, was only a theory.

One thing was sure: Song Sun Young had stood here. Looked out this same window. Seen this same lighthouse, these same hazard buoys.

Exhausted, frightened, disoriented, operating a boat she had never piloted before, on a dark and moonless night, the woman might easily have made a very human mistake, running aground and drowning. It would be a happy enough ending.

But the brushstrokes were too neat. And Song Sun Young had *juche* in spades. Song Sun Young was master of her destiny.

You give her too much credit, McConnell had said.

He joined her by the window. "What do you think?" he asked.

"I think ..." Dalia spoke slowly, feeling her way. "She stood here. She saw the lighthouse. The hazard buoys. She got an idea, staged a scene for our benefit. Throw off the pursuit."

He nodded. "She's got ten hours' head start."

"But she'd want to avoid traveling in any way we could trace. Not until she gained some distance. So maybe she's still on foot." Dalia noticed a wraithlike group of deer standing on the white sand. They boldly returned her gaze.

"Dogs?" he asked.

She nodded. "And checkpoints. And Coast Guard. And jitney stops, and train stations, and ferries. Get ARGUS out here. Scan every tollbooth camera on the Long Island Expressway. Police reports, too. If a car was stolen anytime in the past twelve hours, anywhere on Long Island, we should know. Hell, a bicycle. A skateboard."

McConnell was already dialing.

EAST QUOGUE, NY

The jitney pulled up outside. Song took a final sip of coffee, put down money, and left her booth.

Outside, the huge green, black, and silver motor coach hulked over the tiny storefronts. A moment passed before the doors gave an asthmatic wheeze and opened.

A driver descended, trim and compact in tie and nicely cut suit. He accepted Song's ticket, ripped it, and gave back a stub and an anemic smile.

She climbed four rubber-matted stairs. The bus was about half full. Heavily tinted windows screened out the bright morning sun. The air-conditioning was set too cold. Passengers wore earbuds, oxfords, and crop tops, sweaters draped over shoulders. A quick survey revealed no evidence of the incriminating newspaper, yet she hardly felt at ease.

She found a side door and, at the far end of the long coach, a rear exit. But those would require the driver to open them. She took a seat three rows in, as close as possible to the front, in case she had to make a quick exit. She took off the fanny pack and set it beside her to discourage company.

The engine idled. The driver loitered outside.

She exhaled.

A painfully thin man came aboard. His eyes grazed the fanny pack. He tossed Song a nasty look, then shuffled by.

Still they idled. Song gazed blankly through her window. She could see a stretch of sidewalk in front of the café, a parking meter, a fuzz of moss growing in a crack. Two college-age young men, laughing, broadcasting hail-fellow-well-met, appeared first as shadows. They passed. Someone on the bus was listening to music through headphones. She could pick out of a faint, tinny melody.

"Mommy, can I have a snack?"

Sitting behind Song, across the aisle. "We just had breakfast, Aiden."

"But I'm *hungry*."

"That's a no."

"But I'm—"

"Aiden Montgomery Portis, if you keep whining I will take you off this bus this instant."

The boy wound up, paused, and then burst into tears—not real tears, but the bratty, manufactured kind.

Instinct told her to show her face as little as possible, but she couldn't resist turning her head to give a commiserating smile. The mother smiled back. She was about Song's age, with tired lines around her eyes. Her blouse might be Eileen Fisher. The stain on the lapel might be orange juice.

Song faced the front again. Another person was coming aboard, torn ticket in hand. A teenage boy—rash of pimples beneath a long, greasy forelock. A distressed T-shirt bore the smiley-face Nirvana logo. He looked sullenly at Song, waiting for her to move her pack, then gave up and moved down the aisle.

And *still* the driver lingered. At this rate …

Two policemen walked beneath her window, less than three feet away. They were not paramilitary. They wore no tactical gear, no threatening black like in the city. These were friendly small-town cops, dressed in light, cheery blue. Your friendly neighborhood police officer, straight from a children's book that would also feature old-timey favorites such as your friendly neighborhood crossing guard and your friendly neighborhood barber.

The two policemen moved out of her line of sight. Maybe to chat with the driver, maybe to go on about their business.

Or maybe to board the bus.

She would be trapped.

She debated for only an instant, then stood, strapping the fanny pack around her waist. She descended two of the four rubber-matted steps and stopped, leaning forward, trying to see outside without being seen.

Shadows cast by three figures stretched into the center of the road, crossing the yellow lines. Voices were low, secretive, urgent.

She could feel the gun's weight in the fanny pack. But she would not shoot her way out of this. No, she would walk very calmly down these stairs. She had every right in the world to walk down these stairs. She would smile right into the faces of the cops. If it felt right, she might say something to the driver about holding on for a second before leaving. Just be a moment. She would walk back into the New Moon Café. Slightly pigeon-toed, suggesting some kind of female problem, something embarrassing—can't hold my wee-wee, or maybe a sodden tampon; don't make me explain. None of the three men would stop her. Surely, between the back doors labeled EMPLOYEES ONLY and EMERGENCY EXIT—ALARM WILL SOUND, she could find egress into an alley and slip away.

She felt the strange coolness creep over her again, as it had when the siren came on outside Newark. She could do this.

She descended the last two steps.

The cops stood next to the driver. All three looked at her. One policeman's trouser cuffs were slightly frayed. The other had a canker sore near the left corner of his mouth. She felt preternaturally alert.

"Do we have a minute?" she asked.

The driver frowned disapprovingly. "Behind schedule already." As if that were her fault.

The cops were studying her face. Too closely.

"Thirty seconds, okay?"

Without waiting for an answer, she struck off toward the café.

Her stride hitched as the bad hip throbbed.

That caught their attention.

She heard snaps opening on leather holsters.

"Miss?" one officer said mildly. "Hold on a second?"

CHAPTER FIFTEEN

Song ignored him.

"Miss." More imperatively now. "Halt."

She walked back into the New Moon Café. The bell on the door dinged. Heads turned. Over the past half hour, the place had filled up. Most of the booths were occupied now: by an aging hippie with long gray hair, a happy-looking middle-aged couple, a business-suited woman absorbed in her phone, a man who might be a trucker—although Song had seen no evidence of a truck—applying himself with concentration to a plate of gravy and biscuits.

The two college-age kids stood by the register, flirting with the redheaded girl. One leaned jauntily against the counter like an actor playing a college-age kid flirting with a girl. Through the cutaway, Song glimpsed the short-order cook, the first nonwhite face she had seen in this town besides her own. He wore a bleached chef's toque and was pushing something that crackled on the griddle.

She ignored nipping panic. To survive this, she must keep her head.

What would they expect her to do?

They would expect her to run.

So she would attack.

She put her back to the wall beside the door, beside curtains glowing with sweet sunshine. The push broom was here, leaning beside her. And the antique umbrella stand—art deco, brass with a solid marble base. The compact SIG Sauer was inside the pack, inside a Tupperware container, inside a baggie. It would take at least three seconds to deploy.

The door opened again. The bell dinged cheerily. The redhead looked around. Surprise made her mouth into a small flower.

Song used one foot to tip the broom down. The handle fell across the open doorway just as the first cop stepped in.

The cop tripped, sprawling into the khaki-clad backside of the flirting college boy, who spilled across the counter. A cup of toothpicks overturned and scattered everywhere. In a tangle of limbs, the cop followed them onto the tiled floor. The college boy managed to hold on to the counter, awkwardly keeping his feet.

Song watched herself pick up the empty umbrella stand. She watched herself wind up like a home run slugger, using both hands. If the second cop had followed right behind the first …

She swung the stand into the doorway and was rewarded with solid contact and the *whoof* of escaping breath. Still hyperalert; she smelled coffee, tobacco, a sour tinge of eggs. Beneath it was a trace of aftershave or maybe scented shaving cream—something leathery and masculine.

The first cop was trying to roll over. The second was buckling, down on one knee, struggling to refill his lungs or keep down his breakfast, or both. Neither had drawn his weapon before following her into the diner. A flash of disdain. *Amateurs.*

She had all the time in the world to unzip the pack, find the gun, and finish them. Instead, she dropped the umbrella stand. It rotated on the heavy base, oscillating like a dropped coin as she stepped daintily around the kneeling cop. She went back out through the front door. No one inside the café called after her.

The bus driver stared. She turned on her heel and walked away fast. No shots rang out. She took the first possible turn, down a path alongside a white picket fence. Red-white-and-blue bunting hung from rain gutters. She cut through a yard, past a doghouse, past an inflatable kiddie pool decorated with ducks wearing skirts, emerging onto a residential street, almost but not quite running.

Cars were parked on roads and in driveways. But soon her pursuers would establish a perimeter, if they hadn't already. Checkpoints, barricades, dogs. She had to stay off the roads.

She ducked into another yard. Pain radiated from her hip. But adrenaline made the pain distant, academic. She moved past a wraparound porch with rocking chairs and an old-fashioned swing. You could relax in a swing like that, she thought, and enjoy a tall, cool glass of lemonade. Yawn, stretch, and let your arm fall around your sweetheart's shoulder. Nothing to do but while away a pleasant early summer day. Maybe try for a kiss.

She paused to listen. She heard nothing except twittering birds, a faraway jet plane, and a distant television set, Wayne Brady on *Let's Make a Deal.*

She drew the gun, racked the slide. She crossed a backyard that became a rolling field. Weapon held down by her side, straight-armed. Tendrils of mist had yet to burn off beneath the morning sun. Her shoes picked up clots of damp, dewy earth, which meant she was leaving footprints. *Damn it.*

A dog gruffed somewhere off to her left. Her heart flipped like a trout inside her chest. She bore right.

She paced an embankment. A long hill sprawled down, and for a moment she could see three distinct towns, like sets accompanying a model railroad, straggling into the distance. She passed an old water tower, rusted scaffolding, flaking paint. Cigarette butts and plastic bags and beer cans littered the ground underneath. She passed a chain-link fence with a bold red sign insisting that this was private property.

She reached a brook and walked down the middle, getting her sneakers soaking wet again. Slipping on algae-covered rocks, she climbed back to shore.

A dirt road. The skeleton of an old tractor. How fast would a tractor move if she could start it? Not fast enough. She took the dirt road on foot, staying beneath cover wherever possible.

A helicopter passed, so far overhead she could barely hear it. She hid anyway, beneath a thick canopy of branches, until it was gone.

The dirt road narrowed to a path. The path became rough. She crackle-crunched through underbrush.

She was tired. She allowed herself sixty seconds of rest, then moved again.

Past another flat plain, a soccer field with goals. A low red-brick building stood in the distance. She heard the yelling laughter of small children. Monday morning. School day. A wave of self-pity surged, crested, tried to break over her. She kept moving.

She heard a thread of rising sirens. It faded quickly. Then she heard only birds again.

But she wasn't fooled by the pretty birdsong. She could feel the eyes above her. Prodding, seeking. Drones, satellites, helicopters. She could not stay undercover forever. She had to get inside.

How far had she come from the diner? A mile, at least. Maybe two. Maybe more. They couldn't knock on every door. Could they?

She angled across another stretch of backyards, seeking a house without an alarm system decal, with an empty driveway and shrubs or fence high enough to hide a clandestine entrance from prying eyes.

LANGLEY, VA

On-screen, ARGUS searched a thirty-six-square-mile area around the New Moon Café.

Surveillance camera feeds, helicopter feeds, Stingray, Rainbird, facial recognition, gait recognition, police scanners, tollbooth cameras, news updates—they all had nothing.

Footage relayed from checkpoints assembled around a perimeter twenty miles out in every direction—nothing.

On other feeds, DeArmond's people had taken control of the investigation. They grilled the local cops who had found the woman but then bungled it. They interviewed customers from the diner, the passengers and driver from the jitney—and learned nothing.

A helicopter followed dogs snuffling through countryside. But there was a lot of countryside within the perimeter. And a lot of countryside meant a lot of scents.

The dogs found nothing.

There were also a lot of houses inside the perimeter. Eventually, Dalia realized, they would have to knock on every door.

Once again, maneuverability trumped manpower. Song Sun Young had moved quickly, unpredictably, and left their overpowering force eating dust.

LAKE TOGUE, NY

The little town dozed beneath the summer sun. Rosemary Keefe drove slowly, partly to enjoy the weather, partly because her eyesight was almost gone, even with glasses. She turned onto a block lined with swaying elm and hickory and maple. Simple Cape Cods of a story and a half, modest but sturdy, white and yellow and wine colored. Low ceilings and central chimneys to hold in heat, steep gabled roofs to shed winter snowfall. A *Saturday Evening Post* town, Rosemary's husband had remarked when they moved out from the city nearly four decades ago.

Surrounding towns had long since been taken over by wealthy summer folk. But here in Lake Togue, houses remained humble, with nary a tennis court or swimming pool to be seen. Rosemary's own cozy cottage was fieldstone, with twin dormers like raised eyebrows above the front door. A small porch was lined with potted geraniums and begonias. The backyard was screened on three sides by tall, lovingly maintained hedges.

She parked in the empty driveway and used the top of her door to hoist herself out of the seat, then fetched her single grocery bag from the Jetta's trunk. She left the car unlocked. In Lake Togue, nobody locked cars, and few locked houses.

Her neighbor Dotty LaVerne, wearing paint-spattered overalls and a flowery sun hat, was spading the soil in her small garden. Rosemary raised a hand in greeting. Dotty raised a gloved one in return.

As Rosemary opened her unlocked front door, a helicopter passed overhead, rotors beating emptily. Just inside the foyer, her big brindle-coated dog turned in excited circles, tail thumping against the parquet floor. "Hello, Rocky. I missed you," Rosemary crooned. "My baby."

Rocky licked her hand, then spied something in the front yard behind her. He made a dash for freedom. Rosemary quickly pushed the door shut, stopping him cold.

She put away the groceries: mayo, iceberg lettuce, Pepperidge Farm fifteen-grain bread, and ShopRite cold cuts. She hung the car key on a rack in the kitchen, then went into the living room. After opening a window, she fell onto the couch. Even the effort of a brief shopping trip exhausted her these days.

Rocky found the open window, put his front paws on the sill, and balanced on his hind legs. His ears moved like radar dishes, scanning for squirrels and birds. Of course, he was such a slobbery, good-natured mutt that he wouldn't know what to do with one if he ever caught it.

Outside, a car passed. Someone down the block had the TV on, loud. Probably Don Bogut, who was deaf as a haddock. Fox News talking heads yelled about something or other. No doubt, Don watched them for the short skirts, not politics or world affairs. The yelling gave way to a commercial. *"Beactive Pressure Brace relieves sciatica. Order now and receive a Bealigned Knee Support Cushion at no extra charge!"*

A summer breeze graced the room with fresh air. A sprinkler hissed on somewhere nearby. Rocky left the windowsill, fell heavily across the throw rug, and began licking his not-so-privates.

Rosemary exhaled. Only late morning. Shopping already done. The entire day stretched out before her.

The crossword puzzle, she supposed. Then her exercises. Then walk Rocky. Then lunch. Then a nap. She tried not to turn on the television or have her first drink before five. Speaking of which, tonight she would open the Riesling.

She pushed off the couch, grimacing, and moved through the kitchen, almost tripping over the dog, who could be a little dangerous in close quarters. She opened the door to a garage so cluttered there had been no room for the Jetta for at least five years. "Stay," she commanded.

Rocky stood obediently in the doorway. Humming lightly beneath her breath Elvis' "It's Now or Never," Rosemary commenced searching, her only illumination a shaft of light coming from the open door behind her. Between a moldering bag of peat moss and a motorless lawnmower chassis, she found a slat crate, from which she withdrew a dusty bottle. Holding the label up to the shaft of light, she scowled. Yes, the Riesling from 'ninety-two—perfect.

A figure emerged from the shadows behind her. The bottle of Riesling shattered on the concrete floor.

A bolt of pain moved from her left biceps to her chest, then up the tendons of her neck. She put out one hand for support and found the garage wall, smooth and dry.

The intruder was staring. From the kitchen doorway, Rocky watched with tail wagging—the world's most hopeless watchdog. Rosemary blocked it all out. Her breath came in short, hard jabs. She closed her eyes. Now the burglar would have every chance to crack open her skull as she stood helpless, eyes shut and mouth agape, struggling to stave off the MI.

Already, though, she could feel the filaments of pain withdrawing down her throat, back up her arm. Not yet, then. With eyes still closed, she reached for her breast pocket. She pawed open the small plastic pillbox, fumbled two tablets into her mouth, and chewed, grimacing at the bitter taste.

At last she opened her eyes again, and faced the intruder.

The woman was around thirty, Asian, with dark eyes burning from deep hollows. She held a small silver pistol low near her right hip, like a thug in an old gangster movie. Incongruously, she wore an embroidered fanny pack.

"How many inside?" the woman asked.

Rosemary hesitated. "Just me." And after a moment: "And Rocky."

At the sound of his name, Rocky gave a friendly bark.

The gun gestured, like a gun in a Jimmy Cagney flick. Rosemary turned, mind churning. She couldn't remember the last burglary in this neighborhood. She couldn't remember there ever being a burglary in this neighborhood.

Together they moved back into the kitchen. Rocky sniffed the intruder's crotch, presumptuously but without hostility. The gun gestured again, this time toward an empty chair by the gingham-checked table. Rosemary lowered herself.

The woman came very close to Rosemary and spoke directly into her ear. "Don't make a sound. Don't move. Or you'll regret it."

She shot Rosemary a final warning glance, then moved silently into the living room. Rocky followed, tail wagging.

Rosemary looked at the portable phone sitting in its charger, almost within reach. She leaned forward to peer into the living room without leaving her chair. The intruder was closing the window, then drawing curtains. Inspecting framed photographs, then moving on to the base of the staircase, momentarily out of sight. Rocky followed close behind.

Rosemary looked back at the phone. She strained to listen. The woman must be searching the house. Was that the creaking of a riser on the staircase?

In the next instant, the woman was back, having made a circuit of only downstairs. Had Rosemary reached for the phone, she would have been caught red-handed.

The woman moved to the kitchen window, looked cautiously

out into the backyard. Rocky sat on his haunches, head cocked, tail switching back and forth. At length, the woman turned and regarded her captive flatly. "Where's the man?"

"What man?" Rosemary asked.

"In the photograph."

The photograph on the étagère, she meant: young versions of Rosemary and Ralph, standing on an altar wearing white and black—like a salt-and-pepper set, he used to say. The wedding had been held at morning mass, with an all-day feast and reception after. The bride and groom had together sawed through a log, with the traditional double-handled saw. They danced the tarantella, accepted weepy kisses and blessings from old ladies. At twilight, they ran through a shower of rose petals, climbed laughing into a waiting car, and caught a flight to Hawaii. The honeymoon had been a gift from Rosemary's parents. Her father had owned a hardware store; her mother worked the register. They were not wealthy people—just thoroughly decent sorts, rest their souls, who wanted to give their only daughter a honeymoon gift worth remembering. And in that, they succeeded. As the DC-9 neared the Big Island, Rosemary had taken hold of her new husband's hand, looked out the window of the descending jet, and thought, *Paradise.*

Remembering it now, she felt a faint glow of pleasure. The white sand had looked impossibly pristine, the turquoise waters impossibly clear. And the handsome man sitting beside her, green eyes shining even after the long, tiring flight, had been now and forevermore hers. In the hotel that night, he had planted kisses in the hollow of his bride's throat. He had put his hands on her breasts and paused for a moment to savor her breathlessness. He had laid her gently back on the bed …

"My husband." Rosemary raised her chin defiantly. "He's passed."

"What's your name?"

"What's *yours*?"

"Expecting any visitors today?"

Rosemary shook her head.

"Caretaker? Housekeeper? Landlord?"

"I said no."

The intruder looked at her impassively. For a moment, Rosemary had the feeling the gun might snap up, no warning, and shoot her once, right between the eyes. *Take that, you dirty rat!* After which Rocky would surely reward the criminal by walking over and giving her a warm, wet lick.

Instead, the woman said, "Sit tight."

On her way out of the kitchen she took the phone.

* * *

Song hooked aside a corner of curtain. Another lovely summer day. Across the street, a little boy on a tricycle accompanied his mother down the sidewalk. The neighbor had put the spade away and gone inside. Out of sight but within earshot, a Mister Softee truck played its endless jingle.

Letting go of the curtain, she envisioned the layout of the surrounding streets and yards. She might need to get out in a hurry.

If they came, they would use multiple incursion teams. They would cover every side of the house and would enter simultaneously through front and back doors, maybe the garage, too. They would use battering rams and Halligans. Maybe tear gas. Maybe concussion grenades ... maybe snipers.

She made a more thorough search of the first floor, with the dog following eagerly behind. The walls were decorated with crosses and saints. The living room contained a TV and tchotchke-lined shelves. The small dining room featured a sideboard and buffet table. A ghost of old urine haunted the tiny bathroom. The sink backsplash was frescoed with mildew, and the dish of canned dog food on the bathroom floor looked crusty. The old woman had told the truth. This house didn't see a lot of visitors. No one cleaned; no one looked after the woman and the dog.

The bathroom window was too small to climb through, but it would be easy enough to get a grenade through. Or gas.

Behind that drywall would be an outside wall of solid stone. But behind *this* one—she touched the wallboard experimentally—was the garage. No stone, just gypsum drywall and maybe some thin veneered paneling. Exert enough force and she could break through between the studs. That might be her best emergency escape route.

The dog came into the bathroom, nuzzling her thigh. Song scratched him behind one ear. His tail thumped. She eased out of the room, pulling the door behind her and shutting him in.

Back in the living room, she set phone and gun on the TV. Then she paused, listening. From the kitchen came the laboring hum of the refrigerator. The old woman remained eerily silent. In the garage, she had looked to be on the verge of a heart attack. Maybe Mother Nature had done Song's dirty work for her.

She moved to the kitchen doorway. The woman slumped in the chair, glaring back at her, very much alive.

Song retreated again to the living room.

She could not let down her guard while the old woman lived.

She had no other options. She needed rest.

But it had to be quiet.

Silently, she unhooked a curtain drawstring from its eye. Winding the cord around her right hand, she returned to the kitchen.

The woman's rheumy eyes tracked Song as she took down a water glass from a cabinet. She crossed to the sink. Out of her captive's line of sight, she set the glass noiselessly onto the countertop.

In the last instant, the old woman sensed something. She started to turn. But too slow. Song dropped the cord neatly around the throat, drew it tight, and threw her weight back.

The woman staggered to her feet. The chair skidded with a chalkboard squeal and tipped over. In the bathroom, the dog started barking.

The woman was surprisingly powerful. Before Song knew

it, they had done a lumbering dance across the kitchen floor. The flimsy back door shuddered as they slammed against it. The old woman's glasses came loose, dangled for a moment from one ear, and fell to the tile floor.

Song held on tight. In the glass door of the microwave oven, she saw a nightmarish profile: eyes bulging, cheeks flushing, mouth gaping, trying to get in enough air to scream. A thin whistle, nothing more, came from the old woman's lungs.

Tangled together, they fell onto the floor. Song kept pulling, her hands turning bloodless white as the woman's face went blue. Still she pulled. Now she could hear whimpering interspersed with the dog's barks. Song's own hoarse panting seemed strangely loud.

Abruptly, the woman stiffened. The bulging eye in profile two inches away glazed over. Her struggles ceased.

Song kept up the pressure for another full minute, just to be sure.

At last, she released the cord. Sweating, the muscles of her forearms aflame, she unwound the drawstring and massaged her hands until blood flow returned. She didn't have the strength to stand up yet, so she sat on the floor beside the old woman.

The dog had fallen quiet. No neighbors showed up. No phone rang. No gas grenade came through a window.

Song made herself stand. Her hip throbbed. She looked at the dead woman on the floor. She couldn't just leave her here.

Grabbing the body by the armpits, Song dragged it to the hall closet. In death, the old woman seemed to have doubled her weight.

The closet smelled strongly of mothballs. It was jammed with coats and jackets, umbrellas, and unmatched gloves. Song shoved aside a laundry basket filled with shoes and folded the heavy body beneath the coats, then leaned against the door until the lock clicked.

She went back to the living room and got the gun, then paused, looking at the television set. She might find a news report that made some sense of the article she had glimpsed in East Quogue.

Later.

She went upstairs. The second floor was tiny: one bedroom,

one closet, one minuscule guest room. The master bed was a queen, the frilly quilt thick with dog hair. More crosses and a Mother Mary hung on the walls. A framed scriptural quote above a dresser: *There is no authority except from God. Do what is good, and you will receive his approval.*

Song's brow crimped. Back home, of course, religion was forbidden. But she had studied Christianity at Heaven Lake. She had wanted to pass as an upper-class South Korean, which meant passing as Christian—an artifact from days when the church was the center of political resistance against Japan. She had not been able to see the appeal. How could you make yourself believe a fairy tale, no matter how comforting?

On the other hand, what besides a fairy tale could you call the stories she had once half believed about the Supreme Leader's magnificence?

At length, her gaze moved on. Curtains were open. A sparrow hopped along a tree limb outside. She closed the curtains, then lowered herself onto the creaky mattress. An Android smartphone sat within reach on a night table. She blew dust off the display, tried the power switch. Either the phone was broken or the battery was dead.

She returned the phone to the nightstand, then listened. Except for the distant thrum of the refrigerator, the house was quiet. Even the Mister Softee jingle outside had moved on.

She would not allow herself to doze, but she would rest, relax, recharge.

Her sneakers were still wet. But she had to be ready to move fast, so they stayed on.

She did the math. An alert would have gone out the instant she fled the café. They would have calculated the fastest she could travel. Say it would take them a quarter hour to set up roadblocks. So twenty miles, give or take, in any direction. Once the perimeter was established, they would squeeze. That involved mustering a lot of manpower. A circle forty miles in diameter encompassed a lot of doors to knock on. But it was only a matter of time.

Sometime today, more likely than not. She remembered the helicopter flying overhead.

She heard her own breathing become deep and even. *Don't sleep.*

She might take the Jetta in the driveway. She had seen a key on a rack in the kitchen. Try to bull her way through a checkpoint. A slim chance was better than none.

She yawned. *Don't sleep,* she warned again.

The slumber was deep, dark velvet. She did not dream.

CHAPTER SIXTEEN

LANGLEY, VA

Watching the screen, Bach smiled grimly. Song Sun Young was like a weed that could survive anywhere.

But still no message from Minot.

The mind wanted to run worst-case scenarios. His man had lost his nerve. Or been caught in the act. Or, worst of all, turned himself in.

Bach massaged his temples. He drew and released a long, even breath. His man would come through. And the woman would stay free long enough to justify continued use of Luna.

He slipped away to his office, composed another intel report for the deputy director of operations, then lay down on the couch. Holding the phone against his chest in case a message came in, he closed his eyes.

He sank quickly into dimness populated by flickering shadows.

*　　*　　*

Woody Whitlock drank with concentration.

Even as Benjamin Bach had turned teetotaler—his postdiagnosis regime replaced alcohol, sugar, and salt with cardio, mindfulness, and yoga—Woody Whitlock, feeling the pressures of his job, had leaned in the other direction. He was drinking single-malt scotch. Bach had a seltzer with lime and bitters.

At the far end of the bar, an attractive thirtysomething woman in a white halter top was flirting with a man in a tight blue shirt. Closer to hand, a skinny, morose-looking man flipped through the laminated pictures of chicken wings and pot stickers while the bartender broke up a block of ice in a cooler.

Whitlock wore a faint, preoccupied frown. Bach tried to gauge his friend's line of thought. They had just spent eight solid hours reviewing silo technology that was woefully out of date even by the relaxed standards of the Ninety-First Missile Wing. And, of course, funding to bring it up to snuff was nowhere in sight. Everybody wanted to invest in the fastest, best new aircraft and the fastest, best new naval vessels. Modernizing land-based relics from the Reagan era just wasn't good box office. And so Global Strike Command, responsible for the Air Force component of US nuclear armament, was stuck using thirty-year-old technology.

Or maybe Whitlock was thinking about the fat little madman. Just this afternoon, Pyongyang had announced a successful test of an H-bomb that could be miniaturized and attached to a Hwasong-15 ICBM. If even half of it was true, it was distressing. Even more distressingly, the work had apparently been accomplished at a site somewhere off the CIA's radar. Luna Moth was valuable only if it could be brought to bear.

After letting Whitlock get some whiskey inside him, Bach said, "Talk to me, Goose." In his experience, everyone from the Air Force responded to the quote. They all wanted to be in *Top Gun.*

Whitlock smiled without amusement and moved his broad shoulders carelessly. His all-American good looks seemed a little frayed tonight. "I'm thinking …"

Bach waited.

"Hate to say it."

"Say it."

"Maybe you ought to go back."

"Back?"

"Amatulli doesn't inspire confidence."

Gina Amatulli, the officer warming Bach's seat in Seoul while he focused his attention here in Washington.

"Not Gina's fault." Bach toyed absently with his swizzle stick. "Blame Bureau One-Twenty-One. They're sneaky."

Whitlock snorted. "She thinks strictly inside the box. Not like you, Ben."

It was not entirely untrue. But Whitlock's generous assessment of Bach was born also of personal affection. Over the past eight months, they had grown close. Getting close to Whitlock had been the main reason Bach proposed his GSC cybersecurity task force in the first place. To run it, he had created a restricted-access compartment administered under his own authority. He reported his findings to no one, and no record of the task force existed on any agency server.

He and Woody Whitlock worked late, sometimes until midnight, poring over GSC and NMCC systems. They visited sites around the country, often on weekends, doing snap inspections. They blew off steam in the Pentagon Athletic Center's weight room and Olympic-size pool. They broke bread together. Once, Whitlock's wife and daughter had joined them. Afterward, Whitlock had reported that his wife wanted to set Bach up with a friend of hers, to which Bach graciously begged off, but not without expressing gratitude.

To unwind after marathon sessions they sometimes came here, to this Doubletree far enough from Pentagon City to afford some privacy. One night last month, sitting on these very two barstools, Bach had finally shared his diagnosis. He had spoken of his father, of the old man's pride in his restaurant. He had described his own experience at Ground Zero—medieval, biblical. By the end of that night, the bond between them was ironclad. In Woody Whitlock's eyes, Benjamin Bach was nothing less than a genuine American hero.

Bach had sworn Whitlock to secrecy. Terminally ill CIA officers and top-tier TS/SCIOP-ESI clearance did not go hand in hand. Whitlock had nodded solemnly, promising to take Bach's secret to the grave.

Bach paused, still trying to read his friend's mood, before continuing.

Whitlock was depressed. They all were. There was no longer any denying, or even downplaying, the threat posed by the Hermit Kingdom. In recent months, awareness had spread from the subbasement labyrinth of the NMCC to op-ed pages and cable news pundits. Every American now knew about the thousands of North Korean artillery pieces lining the world's most heavily armed border, about the TELs, mobile launchers that would frustrate efforts to eradicate the nuke program by force, about the fat little madman's stockpile of chemical and biological weapons.

Anxiety tingled Bach's scalp and the back of his neck. He might never get a better opening, and he was living on borrowed time. Eight months had passed since the doctor refused to give him a timeline for the cancer's progression. He had undertaken no treatment except the change in diet and exercise.

"Not Gina's fault," he said again. "It's the Gordian knot. Even if they promise complete denuclearization, there's no way to hold them to it. A single underground facility, a single TEL hidden in a cave ..."

At the other end of the bar, the woman in the white halter top whistled through her teeth at something the chubby man had said.

This was it. The deep dive. Bach reminded himself that he had nothing left to lose. "But Alexander *solved* the Gordian knot. By thinking, as you say, outside the box—sliced it in half with one stroke of his sword."

Whitlock gave a not entirely sober grunt.

Bach's eyes held soft focus on the sweating glass of seltzer before him. "It could be done." He spoke calmly and evenly. "All at once, full-out. Yongbyon, Pyongsan, Pakchon, and Cheonma-San. Yongjo-ri, Sunchon, Taechon, and Punggye-ri." He rapped the bar hard enough to make his glass shake. "*Bam.* All at once."

"Fire and fury." Whitlock's tone was ironic.

Pyongyang would manage one final destructive spasm, of course—the fat little madman's last temper tantrum. South Korea would soak up the brunt of it. But then it would be over. The first strike of American Tomahawk missiles would knock out the sea-based leg of the North Korean defense triad. Hit Uiju and Changjin, and they would have no working H5 bombers left with which to retaliate by air. That left the TELs. And that was where an accurate intelligence picture—such as that afforded by Luna Moth—became priceless.

Of course, that afternoon's revelation of sites unknown to Luna complicated things. But the Norks would still be limited to whatever they managed in their first desperate counterpunch. Then, at last, the nepotistic regime, the nuclear production infrastructure, the devices and warheads themselves, the associated delivery vehicles, the mining and enrichment facilities—all would be gone. And at last, Americans would be able to sleep soundly at night. Or relatively so.

"Dream a little dream," said Whitlock.

Bach scooted his stool a tiny inch closer to his friend. "Everybody and his uncle wants Luna computer time. But under the right circumstances, I go to the front of the line. I'm still Seoul station chief. I'm still in charge of left-of-launch."

Whitlock looked at him shrewdly. Eyes glassy, slightly parted lips connected with a silver cord of saliva. If the man didn't take it easy with the whiskey, his days in J3 were numbered.

"I'm not just talking about using Luna to find targets." Bach kept his tone moderately light. "Tomahawks go when they receive a short burst of computer code. They don't care who sent it. They don't care if it's authorized or not. They're machines." *Every system vulnerable, as Wyoming had proved. Every system built to be used.* "You see where I'm going?"

"Enlighten me." But Whitlock did see, it seemed. At least, he was beginning to.

"The EAM." The Emergency Action Message sent from

STRATCOM, authorizing a nuclear strike. "That's impossible to fake. Even with Luna." The EAM contained the Sealed Authenticator System Code, a random key generated by a machine that stamped only two copies. It was never seen by human eyes until the key holder was broken. One copy, the so-called biscuit, was carried in a satchel by an aide who never left the president's side. The other was sent to NMCC, which Whitlock was in charge of. But NMCC cryptovaults were double-locked. No one person could gain access, not even Woody Whitlock. "But come into the process *after* the EAM. *After* the keys would have been turned in the silos …"

Understanding dawned. Access the launch system inside STRATCOM's secure internal network, and you could fire every land-based nuke, regardless of DEFCON, regardless of the SAS code, regardless of foot-draggers and naysayers and ass-coverers.

"Internal network uses AES encryption." The look on Whitlock's face now was hooded. "Gold standard. And it changes every day."

"You guys drill constantly. Does each drill use a dedicated algorithm?"

Whitlock shook his head.

"So picture two guys like us, having a conversation like this. Someone like you agrees to get a version of the encryption, and someone like me agrees to have Luna Moth waiting on standby to crack it." He was thinking already of Song Sun Young, the sleeping RGB agent in New York City. The master of her destiny. Song's activation would justify using the quantum computer. Bach, who had unfettered access to Pyongyang's servers, could pose as RGB and activate the agent himself.

"We could do it, Woody. Two guys like you and me. One bold stroke. That's all she takes." He heard himself sounding too eager. He shaved off the edge, then repeated more mildly, "That's all she takes."

Whitlock raised his glass and lowered it without drinking, staring unseeing into the middle distance. After a moment, a weird smile appeared on his lips. He quickly wiped it away.

He favored Bach with a gimlet eye. "Buddy," he said, "you're scaring me."

His tone was light, but his expression was crafty. Bach tried again to gauge the man's thinking. Was he getting on board? Or was he scanning, parsing, judging?

Whitlock's mouth twitched. And suddenly, Bach realized that his friend was straining to affect casualness every bit as much as he himself was. Antennas were extended, rotating to pick up a signal.

Retreat!

Bach made a loose gesture. "I'm *trying* to scare you. You see how it could go down. Just like this. Eventually, someone else will have this conversation. Then we'll *really* be fucked. Everybody with access to Luna needs to be watched. Closely."

Woody Whitlock gave Benjamin Bach a long, measured gaze. Then he sighed and nodded. He raised his drink and polished it off.

* * *

DeArmond was shaking him.

Sitting up, Bach put his feet flat on the floor. Outside the window, the sun had lowered noticeably. Monday was winding down. Wordlessly he gave his place on the couch to DeArmond.

When he checked his phone in the men's room, he found no message waiting. He leaned against the sink's edge. In the mirror, the divots beneath his deep-set eyes had become chasms. His skin looked nearly translucent. Fine lines webbed the eyes; deeper ones bracketed the mouth.

He remembered his high school cross-country coach. Run through the cramps, the man counseled. Run through the pain, through the fear, through the fatigue. Nothing mattered except taking that next step. *Do-mode.*

He turned slightly, considering his reflection from another angle. Between the new health regime and the cancer, all the fat had melted away. His face was all sinew and skin and bone. A man pared down to the essentials. Only pure resolve, pure strength, remained.

He saw his father's face there. And also, now that every ounce of excess fat had been trimmed away, his grandmother's, near the end. And also, for the first time, his grandfather's. Dad's dad had been a boxer in World War II—so gifted a fighter, according to family lore, that Bob Hope and the USO had excused him from combat, tapping him instead to entertain less-fortunate troops who would serve as cannon fodder. Razzle Dazzle Bach, they had called him. The Battling Tail Gunner. He'd had no education beyond fifth grade. But in America, land of opportunity, he had always found work. First boxing and then, as he aged past his prime, modest but honest labor—construction or house painting or loading and unloading at docks and warehouses. He had given his wife six children before the heart attack took him.

Bach had never met the man. But he had seen pictures in Grandma's row house in Queens. He had seen the fire in the eyes— the same fire he now saw in his own.

Razzle Dazzle.

He splashed water on his face and straightened, nodded once, and went back to the conference room.

CHAPTER SEVENTEEN

LAKE TOGUE, NY

Song blinked awake, reprimanding herself. She could not allow such weakness, or she would never survive.

The light coming through the window had taken on a tinge of gold. She sat up. Her mind sluggishly engaged. Monday evening—dinnertime back home. Of course, not a regular Monday. The Monday after Mom went missing. But still, a Monday. Still, you had to eat.

Even after days of deprivation, she had no appetite. The buttermilk pancakes from the café breakfast sat like concrete in her stomach.

In Chosun, families were old hands at dealing with betrayals from loved ones. Your own mother, daughter, father, son, spouse might denounce you or steal your food. They were only doing what they had to do to survive. You could not blame them for surviving.

But Mark came from a different world. Softer, gentler, more spoiled. What did he know about survival?

What had he told the kids? What was *he* thinking?

Her gaze moved to the Android phone.

She opened the nightstand drawer. Beneath Super Glue and rubber bands and old coupons, she found a power supply that fit the phone. She plugged it in and switched it on.

One percent power. But charging. The device automatically

found a neighbor's unsecured Wi-Fi network. She opened a web browser, bracing herself against what she might see.

The same headline blared: an AP dispatch picked up by multiple outlets. THE DISAPPEARANCE OF MI-HI ABRAHAMS: WHAT WE KNOW NOW.

It has been two days since Mi-Hi Abrahams was abducted by terror suspect Yusuf Bashara …

Hypertext led to a video. She clicked, then watched in disbelief. It was the video that the screen capture had come from. Her Volvo, pulled over onto a nighttime street corner. She was driving. A suspicious-looking man with a black beard emerged from a doorway and entered the car. Brandishing a gun, he searched the Volvo's interior. The car pulled away and vanished offscreen.

Song shook her head in bafflement. It had never happened. Yet here it was.

Her eyes watered. She wiped them absently and read on. *Less than one hour after the abduction, a violent confrontation with Bashara sent two federal agents to Newark Beth Israel Hospital, where they remain today. Both are expected to make full recoveries.*

These must be the two federal agents she had gunned down outside Newark Airport. How had this become "a violent confrontation with Bashara"?

Mi-Hi's husband, Mark Abrahams, delivered a dramatic plea on Sunday night to both his wife and Yusuf Bashara. But so far, police efforts have failed to uncover even a clue to the woman's whereabouts.

An embedded video followed the text: Mark, frozen and blurry, sitting on the couch in their Lexington Avenue living room. Song felt something tilt and slide in the pit of her stomach. Her children were sitting beside her husband. Dex looked stunned, as he did when he didn't get enough sleep. Baby Jia was distracted by something offscreen.

You don't need to watch it.

But she watched anyway.

First came a photograph from Martha's Vineyard, her in a

yellow sundress, Mark with a protective arm slung around her shoulder. Some segment producer had selected this picture to give tragic context to her disappearance. *The way they were.* Then Mark sitting on the couch with the kids, addressing the camera:

"*Mi-Hi. If you can see me or hear me, please know we are looking for you. We will find you. You will be okay. And to Yusuf Bashara: Turn yourself in. If you don't, there's no telling what might happen. The authorities promise me that every effort to be fair will be made if you turn yourself in. We are going to get you one ...*"

She floated away, not hearing the rest.

For a timeless moment, bewilderment reigned. How had they gotten footage of a man who didn't exist entering her car? What the fuck was going on?

Then clarity came.

Of course the video had been manufactured. Digital trickery, sleight of hand. It was a message from whoever had dispatched the vans to follow her in the first place. For the first time, Song got a sense of this presence. Someone, somewhere out there, was onto her. Following her. Watching her. Behind all the satellites and surveillance drones, behind the cameras and emergency-sprinkler inspection and the bad *nunji,* and now behind the video—all the same someone. She sensed this presence as a blurry, larger-than-life phantom. Genderless, ageless, ethereal. An intelligence, a life force. The counterbalance to all the faceless but powerful someones back in the RGB, back in Pyongyang.

The message of the video was, *we can provide a story that will give you an out.* The terrorist from Central Casting was the story element that would let Song off the hook. She had been kidnapped. She had not been in control of the situation. Once everything was worked out, she could go back to her life.

This someone was going a step further. *We have the means to make this story real.* Witness the video. The stock footage, or whatever it was, of the stock terrorist. *Come turn yourself in, and we'll write the end of the story together.*

Song knew the power of a story. Stories could get you sent to labor camps or to the executioner's chamber. Stories had the power of life and death.

But, of course, the way to con someone was to offer the illusion of getting away with something. That was how all scams worked. You let the mark notice the bent corner of a card, so they thought they were getting away with a cheat. Then when they weren't looking, you unbent the corner and bent another card. Or a wealthy Nigerian prince appealed for your help in moving a vast illicit fortune out of his home country—"*I must solicit your strictest confidence in this transaction ...*"—only to con you out of a "processing fee," by whatever name. The someone realized that Song wanted more than anything a return to normality, to her home life. Hence the appeal to Song's need, to her greed. *Come work with us and you'll get everything you want—your family, your husband, your children, your life, your freedom!*

A trick. A con. It was hard to cheat a cheater.

She watched the video again. Relishing, she realized, the brief glimpse of the kids. Relishing the glimpse of Mark. It had been only two days. It felt like forever.

How would the someone explain the fact that Song had left the apartment of her own free will, bearing luggage, and taken the car from the garage, and picked up this man on a street corner? How would they explain *that*?

It didn't matter. The bait—for that was all it amounted to— would remain untouched. She would not give herself over to this someone's machinations.

She could never touch that life again. No matter what.

*   *   *

She turned off the phone and laid her head back against the pillow.

She remembered the first time she met Mark. They had sat together over crudités, and her future husband had looked at her with frank, undisguised sexual interest. His leg had casually brushed hers when he leaned forward to pick up his drink. He had smiled knowingly.

Song had read about men like him in magazines. She had seen actors portray them in movies. But she had never before encountered one in person. Where she came from, there were no men like this. *Hookups,* as Americans called them, were unheard of. In Chosun, one could not check into a regular hotel without the appropriate travel permit. Hotels would not accept unmarried couples. Just a century ago, middle-class Korean women had not been allowed to leave the family home, except at special times when the streets had been emptied of men.

Mark's brand of flirting had been uniquely American. That gunfighter-with-belt-slung-low quality, that deep-rooted, unexamined assumption of entitlement. A cowboy, through and through. Except that, instead of spurs and six-guns, he equipped himself with merino suits and encyclopedic legal precedents.

Even with all her training, she had struggled to play his game. At Heaven Lake, she had learned seduction from a kidnapped South Korean woman named Jeong Mi-Hwa. (The name, meaning "beautiful flower," had been the basis for Song's chosen alias, Mi-Hi.) The tutor had been a product of her own upbringing, and so the lessons had been shot through with South Korean values. In *areh dongae,* culture was very much geared toward twosomes. Couples coordinated outfits right down to their underwear; they worked out together, using each other as counterweights. Valentine's Day encompassed three separate holidays, with girls giving their boyfriends chocolates on February 14, then boys giving their girlfriends candies one month later, and then, a month after that, on April 14, Black Day, single people eating black noodles and lamenting their loneliness.

Americans put less emphasis on coupledom—that cowboy mentality again. Men overly eager for domestic bliss were perceived as soft. Hence Mark Abrahams' undisguised aggression and vaguely predatory male gaze.

Song, fumbling, had improvised. She bit her lip; she touched her hair. A shy pose with an undertone of eroticism. She knew that many American men fetishized East Asian women. She operated on instinct, batting her lashes, gazing submissively down.

It worked. She reeled him in even as Eliza Crystal shot her sideways looks. Eliza had harbored her own designs on Mark Abrahams, having invited her friend to the dinner party only as her wingwoman. The friendship with Eliza had not survived that night. But it had served its purpose: providing access to Mark Abrahams.

Song had engineered an encounter with Eliza inside MoMA's sculpture garden six months earlier. She had struck up a conversation about a piece that seemed to defy gravity, a cylinder floating impossibly atop a pyramid. Chatting, they had discovered common loves in Picasso and Matisse. The friendship had evolved naturally, from meals to yoga classes, from movies to Netflix binges. All for this moment: the casual brush of the leg, the knowing smile.

Song had genuinely enjoyed the courtship with Mark. He was handsome, rich, tall—two full heads taller than the tallest Young Pioneer in Chosun, where an entire generation had grown up stunted by the Arduous March. He knew opera. He knew restaurants. He squired her through a real-life fairy tale.

She remembered a six-course meal at a restaurant in Gramercy Park. The salad had contained pears, celery, red lettuce and cheese, and something she couldn't identify—some distant cousin of the artichoke. This had been early spring. Back home in Chosun, people suffered a lack of food at the end of every winter. Pyongyang responded by ramping up rhetoric about American dogs who starved them with unjust sanctions, about the imminence of Seoul being turned to a lake of fire. But you could not eat rhetoric.

If you pause while eating, set down your silverware on the plate. She had learned American manners at Heaven Lake, from a woman named Seungwon. How Seungwon had learned American manners, Song didn't know. Maybe from Emily Post.

In America, utensils should never touch the tablecloth. Not even handles. If you're pausing for just a moment, set them down any way, as long as they're completely on the plate. If it's a longer pause—if your companion has said something particularly fascinating and

you're too absorbed to keep eating—put the flatware on the right
side of the plate, so it crosses into the middle.

Whatever the source, Seungwon had been surprisingly on target. American manners were very different from Korean, where slurping noodles, chewing with mouth open, and eating with both hands at once, brandishing two utensils, were not considered rude.

The napkin goes into your lap the moment you sit down. Sitting up
straight, elbows into the body. No elbows on the table. When you use
the napkin, you'll be delicate. A little dab around the lips, another if
necessary. The napkin shouldn't get dirty at all. When you're finished
with the meal, place it lightly by the side of the plate. No twisting, no
folding; just set it down loosely. And never on your chair.

One winter night, inside a horse-drawn carriage on Fifty-Ninth Street, surrounded by holiday shoppers and carolers and holly and lights reflected on snowdrifts, the fairy tale had reached its natural climax: Mark Abrahams asking for her hand in marriage.

And she had enjoyed the marriage as much as the courtship. He was kind. He was considerate, steady, faithful. A good father, a devoted husband, a passionate lover.

But she had always held some part of herself in reserve. Because someday, she had realized even then, the fairy tale would end.

Now that day had come.

She should get going. She must risk the roadblock. She must move on.

To her new life.

Whatever, and however short, that might prove to be.

*　　*　　*

She woke up thinking about the cell phone. What if she used it?

They could place it only to the nearest tower, and maybe not even that. Cell phones, she knew, used an algorithm to choose a tower, based not on proximity but on signal strength, tariffs, and existing mobile traffic. So she could call and they might not be able to pinpoint her location, and then she would be able to say a few crucial words to Mark, to make sure he and the kids understood that no matter what else she had been, she had been, first and above all else, in her truest heart, a wife and mother. There had been lies, yes. But it had not *all* been lies. The part that mattered most had not been a lie.

A stupid risk. She must not even consider it. They would triangulate her or install some tracking software onto the phone.

But she wanted to call—so compellingly that something inside her seemed to crack when she thought about it.

She wiped at her cheek and walled the idea neatly off from her mind. She closed her eyes again and set her head back against the pillow.

They would be here soon. No time for more rest. Open your eyes, dummy. You've rested long enough. Get moving, already. You're asking for it.

She turned onto her other side, punching the pillow.

LANGLEY, VA

Dalia sat at the conference table, watching Sam work his way through a bag of barbecue potato chips. The door to the conference room opened, and DeArmond came in, yawning. Bach, standing before the monitor with hands on hips, did not turn.

McConnell caught Dalia's eye and mimed raising a cup of coffee.

They found their same table in the cafeteria's ground-floor corner. Caffeine cut through the mist inside Dalia's head. She felt as if she were surfacing from a long sleep. For the first time, she noticed the view outside the floor-to-ceiling windows: a sweet summer sunset, budding buckthorn and sycamore, dogwood and maple and fresh-cut grass. A small gray swallow perching on a low branch seemed to look directly back at her.

As she surfaced, so did a thought that had been nudging around the edges of her mind. It involved her dream of thundering hoofbeats, a frozen pond, bloody ice. The dream, she guessed, had been inspired by the Battle of Austerlitz. One of the most decisive engagements of the Napoleonic Wars, widely considered Napoleon's greatest victory. Faced with superior forces in the allied Russian and Austrian armies, *le petit caporal* had deliberately weakened his right flank, abandoning the high ground and encouraging attack by the enemy. The resulting heavy focus on his right side had weakened the enemy's center. A fierce counterattack had routed them. And then, as men and horses fled across the Satschan frozen ponds, a bombardment from Napoleon's artillery shattered the ice, plunging the fleeing army into icy water.

She remembered the dream's feeling of dread, of something dangerous right underfoot, all around. She had been trying to tell herself something. But her conscious mind had not heeded the message.

Now her thoughts moved to another icy battle. During the Winter War of 1939, at Suomussalmi the Finns had dealt a crushing blow to a much larger and far better equipped unit of the Red Army. Eleven thousand Finnish infantry had defeated fifty thousand Russians supported by a tank brigade. The Finns had accomplished this unlikely feat through intimate knowledge of the terrain. They used skis and sleds where the Soviet heavy armor foundered on tank treads. And through morale—for the Finns, the battle had been existential; for the Red Army soldiers, it was merely political. Most importantly, the Finns had worn white uniforms. The Red Army had stubbornly—and disastrously—clung to its standard dun. Against the ivory snowdrifts, they had stood out like clay pigeons. Suomussalmi proved the value of camouflage.

And that was why she thought of it now. *Camouflage.* Blending in, hiding in plain sight.

Something dangerous right underfoot, all around.

The thought came almost within reach ... but then skittered away before she could grasp it.

Jim McConnell stared dully into his cup. Behind his bifocals, he seemed very far away.

Dalia sighed and drank more coffee. She looked outside again, into the deepening summer gloaming, seeking the swallow on the low branch. But the bird was gone.

PART THREE

CHAPTER EIGHTEEN

Bach's phone vibrated.

Incoming message. He checked the display.

The subject line was *Alas Babylon*.

His hand began to shake. He turned in his chair to face the shaded window, so that his expression would not betray him.

This was it. Here, now, finally. He felt excited, but also scared. Those words did not begin to touch the immensity of his feelings. Just as "surreal" had not begun to describe downtown Manhattan in the hours following the attack. He felt electrified, exhilarated, euphoric. And also terrified, tiny, trapped. Overpowered, overwrought, overcome. Galactic, transcendent. The hand was shaking harder. He had to leave this room now, or he would give himself away.

He muttered an excuse, stepped past Sam, and walked to his office.

He closed and locked the door, then read the message. A seemingly nonsensical string of hexadecimal characters. Today's algorithm for GSC's internal network.

Just past 20:00 hours—four hours until the encryption changed. More than enough time.

His mouth twitched. He could feel himself cringing now that

the moment of truth was at hand. But that was okay. The reaction was understandable. Anybody would cringe. Many millions of innocent souls would perish by his hand in the next few minutes. Men, women, and children. Thankfully, he had rehearsed the next stage so many times that his body executed the necessary motions now without needing his mind to sanction them.

He didn't even need to power up his desktop. He could do it from his phone. On its way to Pyongyang, the encrypted algorithm would travel through four separate servers on four separate continents.

Once he pressed SEND, there would be some small delay before the same algorithm registered on Sam's radar as a message sent to Song Sun Young.

He pressed SEND.

In a few minutes, Sam would come and get him, eyes shining, declaring that the RGB had sent new instructions to its agent at last. Sam would request permission to forward the new encryption to Fort Meade. And then Luna Moth would accomplish, in a matter of seconds, something that no other computer in the world could accomplish before midnight came and the encryption changed.

And very soon after, it would be done.

Survivors of the initial blasts would face overlapping circles of burn, force, and radiation trauma. Winds would carry fallout. And, of course, the fat little madman, if he lived through it, would throw his final tantrum—one last blindly infantile destructive spasm. Twenty-five million people lived in Seoul, just thirty-five miles from the DMZ. Likely targets also included Kunsan and Pyeongtaek, hosts to the bulk of US airpower on the Korean peninsula. And Incheon and Busan, and Ulsan and Masan, and Mokpo and Pohang and Gwangyang. And the Yukosuka naval base in Japan. And Yokota Air Base, and Marine Corps Air Station Iwakuni. And Sasebo and Atsugi and Okinawa. And, quite possibly, Pyongyang itself. The madman had shown many times his willingness to sacrifice his own people. And if a secret base unknown to Luna contained an ICBM capable of reaching Los Angeles or Washington or New York City, so be it.

Because compared to possible alternatives, this remained the most contained and humane outcome.

He felt weary. The burden would have been inhumanly heavy even to a healthy man, which he was not.

He collapsed more than reclined on the bonded leather couch, closed his eyes, and heaved a long, papery sigh.

* * *

MINOT AIR FORCE BASE, ND

Benjamin Bach followed the second lieutenant down a corridor of industrial gray. The man had the pallid, hollow-cheeked look common among personnel at Minot, less than fifty miles from the Canadian border. Even now, on the trailing edge of spring, a biting wind howled across the low flatland outside.

Inside a gray, functional room, Bach gave a dry smile of thanks. Once alone, he settled behind a gray, functional desk. He paused for a moment, gazing abstractedly through a gray, functional window. The slice of visible sky was bright blue, belying the fingers of cold feeling their way in around worn casements. Minot Air Force Base was nearly as notorious for its crumbling infrastructure as for its awful weather.

He opened his briefcase. Took out the dossier. Squared it on the desk. But he did not turn back the cover. He had already gone over the case of Captain Guy Keller enough times to know the salient details.

Like Bach, Keller had been born in the Bronx. He had been schooled at Fordham, managing a 4.0 GPA. Upon graduation, he had joined USAF. According to his application interview, he opted for Air Force because it offered the best deal—a free ride all the way through grad school.

Bach fancied that he understood Keller. After all, they had in common not only the Bronx, but also the determination to leave the

Bronx behind. Yet, while Bach had pulled himself up from SUNY to NYU to Columbia, from Langley to China and Korea, to station chief and now to head of the GSC task force, becoming his best possible self, Keller had at some point taken a wrong turn. Giving in to his demons, he had reverted to his roots, to the underhanded street kid he had almost managed to move beyond.

Assignment to Minot may have triggered the devolution. Bach didn't know who Keller had pissed off at the academy, but for an Air Force Academy graduate, Minot was the ultimate embarrassment. The Ninety-First Missile Wing was for the dregs: the malcontents, the moaners, the troublemakers. "Why not Mi-not?" they said with a philosophical shrug. Because what else could they say? They had been shipped out into the middle of nowhere, to Bumfuck, North Dakota, to crew obsolete equipment while earning the derision of their peers. The weather was shit, frozen half the year. The isolation was profound.

Captain Guy Keller's regular routine involved waking up at 4 a.m. for his daily briefing, then freezing his ass off as he drove three-plus hours through terrain so monotonous, it lacked even hills. By the time he went through changeover at his silo, he had been awake for eight hours already. But he was just warming up. He would spend the next twenty-four hours locked behind blast doors, manning equipment outdated during the Cold War. Sitting, waiting, stealing the occasional catnap. When something did happen, it was always a jackrabbit, a false alarm. And a good thing—the Ninety-First Missile Wing silos were so far out in the hinterlands, it took the Tactical Response Force twenty minutes to show up when summoned.

And after his shift, going into his thirtieth consecutive hour on duty, Keller drove three-plus hours back to base only to find an understaffed facility, commissary closed half the week, wait at the clinic pharmacy ninety minutes on a good day. Adding to the indignity, he always seemed to pick the short straw in scheduling. For his first six months at Minot, Captain Keller had been steadily

8-0: eight active-duty shifts, zero standby. That was as tough as it got. He would have been lucky to grab a few hours' shut-eye before the whole grim sequence started up all over again.

No one would fault Captain Guy Keller for feeling some disenchantment. Plenty of people with ultimately fond memories of the military harbored some mixed feelings while they were in the middle of it. But Keller had made several critical mistakes. The first had been to shoot his mouth off inside the canteen after a few Rolling Rocks. Keller had given up his First Amendment rights when he swore to protect everyone else's, relinquishing the privilege of pounding a six-pack and blowing off steam about his crap job.

Someone had overheard. And so Guy Keller got himself put on a list. And when Bach started his task force, probing for weak spots in the wake of Cheyenne, that list had crossed his desk. Yet he could never have anticipated what he would find upon closer investigation: that the complaints were only the tip of the iceberg.

Over the past five months, Keller, using dummy email accounts, had contacted embassies belonging to Russia, China, Venezuela, and Iran. He must have thought himself smart. He had not given his name; he had used a virtual private network to cover his IP address; he had avoided making any direct offers. But he had said enough to hang himself. He had described his position as missileer at Minot AFB, commanding a flight of ten Minuteman III LGM-30Gs. He had hazarded theoretical questions: Did the Air Force pay people like him enough to keep them loyal? What would his lifestyle be like after discharge? How would that lifestyle stack up against an offer of, say, five million dollars from a foreign agent?

The Russian and Chinese consulates had not replied. They must have considered the offer either a hoax or a dangle from the CIA—too good to be true. Iran had requested sample intelligence, to prove Keller's bona fides, that was beyond Keller's ability to provide. But Venezuela had set up a meeting that would take place during Keller's next leave. Reading the correspondence,

Bach had felt an arctic chill. How many similar dramas played out unbeknownst to Global Strike Command? If he had not come sniffing around ...

Ah, but he had. And because he ran his task force as a restricted-access compartment, reporting to no one and keeping no records, the determination of Captain Guy Keller's fate would be his and his alone.

He squared the dossier on the desk again. The task force had originally been a means of getting closer to Woody Whitlock. Here, however, was the next best thing. Any second now, his last best chance would come walking through the door. And none too soon. America's latest commander-in-chief was proving himself incapable of handling the fat little madman—taking the enemy at his word, handing over concessions and international respectability in exchange for hollow promises.

Bach would help the man understand, one Bronx boy to another, what was at stake. Keller was looking at more than just getting cashiered. More than just a general or other-than-honorable discharge. He was looking at a straight-up general court-martial. Unless ...

Here Bach would trail off. Let Keller participate. Give him some ownership. Then, when the time came, he would be more likely to follow through. Psych 101. Bach had applied similar techniques every day at Seoul Station.

Unless? Keller would prod at last.

A sample of GSC's internal network encryption, Bach would answer, was all it would take to set things right.

The door opened.

Captain Guy Keller entered the office warily. He was six feet four, with a heavy gabled brow, piercing blue eyes, and the pale complexion universal among those posted at Minot. He looked confused—not sure why he had been sent here, not sure whether he should salute the man in civilian clothing seated behind the drab desk—but also defiant.

Bach half smiled. He gestured toward the chair across the desk and placed one hand significantly on the dossier.

"Captain," he invited. "Have a seat."

*   *   *

Frantic knocking. Bach struggled up. He had locked the door, then passed out without unlocking it. He reached it, twisted the knob.

Sam's eyes were shining, just as Bach had pictured it. "RGB sent a new message. New encryption. Fort Meade ...?"

Bach nodded. He felt a prickling on the nape of his neck, a tingling of anticipation in his chest. The pleasure of putting the last piece into a thousand-piece jigsaw puzzle, seeing the picture finally come together just so.

He followed Sam back to the conference room, slowly, as if moving underwater, through a dream.

CHAPTER NINETEEN

"Ho, now," Sam breathed.

Bach was starting to tremble inside. This was it. At last …

But the window Sam maximized did not contain decrypted data. It contained a Stingray feed that was monitoring Mark Abrahams' cell phone. *Unknown caller*, second ring.

They watched on a thermal, top-down, as Mark Abrahams staggered from his living room, where he had been collapsed with his children before an episode of *PAW Patrol.*

"Hello," he answered dully.

Silence.

A red dot appeared on the ARGUS map. "Cell tower," Sam said. "Lake Togue, sixteen miles from Southampton."

Mark Abrahams said softly, "Where are you?" his voice as clear as if he stood in the conference room with them.

"I can't tell you that."

Song.

Her voice broke. "And I can't stay on the line. I just wanted to say I'm sorry. I love you, Mark. I miss you, and I'm sorry. Whatever else you hear—"

Mark cut in. "Is he listening right now? Don't hang up. They'll trace …"

"Geolocation," Sonny growled. "Goddamn it, get geolocation."

"Trying." Sam's fingers drummed across the keyboard. DeArmond was dialing his phone.

"Tell the kids I love them. Whatever you hear, whatever *they* hear, they have to know that. And you have to know: I love you all."

"Mi, I don't understand. I don't understand any of this."

"I have to go. I love you. Mark, I'm sorry."

"Don't ha—"

The connection died.

"Mi?" Abrahams' voice turned cold, dangerously controlled. "Mi."

"Got her," Sam said. "*Got* her, goddamn it."

A second dot was on the map: the cell phone that had placed the call.

The second dot was moving.

The door to the conference room opened. Dalia entered, followed by McConnell, who carried a tray of coffee in Styrofoam cups.

Her eyes moved to the wall-mounted monitor and the two dots, one moving, on the satellite map. Comprehension dawned.

Bach nodded. "She couldn't stop herself—family trumps tradecraft after all. Well, better late than never." His voice sounded rusty. He cleared his throat.

Dalia moved nearer the monitor. McConnell set down the tray and followed close behind, hand poised by her elbow.

"Lake Togue," Sam said triumphantly. "We've got her. Goddamn it, this time we've *got* her."

LAKE TOGUE, NY

She climbed into the old woman's Jetta and keyed the ignition.

The bag she had tossed onto the passenger seat contained a loaf of fifteen-grain bread, two cans of sardines, a liter of water, her cash and IDs, and the SIG Sauer.

She backed out of the driveway. Streetlights had come on, giving the tree-lined avenue a vaguely sinister cast. She drove to the end of the block, through shadows obscuring other shadows, and then paused.

If her ruse had worked, they would drop the roadblocks, concentrating all their manpower to pursue the signal. Or was that wishful thinking?

Either way, checkpoints would be thickest heading back toward the city. So she turned north. *Stay positive,* she thought. One way or another, she would get through. To Connecticut. Then Massachusetts. Or maybe Maine. Or maybe New Hampshire. *Don't tread on me.* Or maybe west. Into the wild blue yonder. She would go whichever way the wind took her, so long as it was far away from here.

She kept to the speed limit.

Whether Mark believed her was beyond her control. At least, she had tried.

The town receded in the mirror. She met a rattling old farm truck in the other lane, one headlight dead. Beyond the soft shoulder to her right, a pond sparkled. The stars glinted like crushed glass.

She had tried. She had gotten to apologize, to acknowledge, however lamely. He had heard the words directly from her. What he would do with them, she didn't know. But she had spoken them. It was something.

The road worsened. The Jetta rattled and banged through potholes. She crested a wooded ridge, passed a farmhouse, a pale smudge against darkness. A doghouse in a dirt yard. The sweet smell of alfalfa hanging in the air.

When she first heard the percussive *whut-whut,* she thought it came from the Jetta. Maybe a pothole knocked the exhaust pipe loose above the muffler. But the beat didn't speed up when she gunned the engine. Frowning, she craned her neck to look through the sunroof. Stars, a thin rind of moon …

There: a sharp glint. The angle changed, and the searchlight dazzled her eyes. Then it moved on, heading back the way she had come—toward the house, if she judged the angle correctly.

She had hoped for more time. But no. Within minutes, they would find her.

She had to change cars.

No. First she had to gain more distance.

She was screwed either way.

On some level, it would be a relief. Her guilt would be expiated. She had carried too many secrets for too many years. Time to pay the piper.

It is the beating of his hideous heart!

She thought of the cloner and high-frequency antenna she had hidden in the hall closet back home. Incriminating as hell, should Mark have found them. For that matter, she had tempted fate for a full year by keeping the Kate Spade bag, filled with disguises and passports and cash, in the bedroom closet. Tempting fate. On some level, she must have wanted to be caught. Only then could she begin to atone. *Only after having acknowledged sins and reflected deeply upon them can a prisoner begin anew.*

She opened the bag and moved the gun onto the passenger seat.

She killed the headlights and drove through darkness.

Another ridge. And beyond it, barely half a mile out, a checkpoint. She knew it subconsciously even before her eyes assembled the pieces: police prowlers, orange-and-yellow barriers, glaring floodlights, and the familiar anonymous vans.

She could still hear the helicopter behind her. She could not turn back.

Circling the drain again. Finished. For real this time.

It had been worth a shot.

Her hands tightened on the wheel. *Not done yet, goddamn it.*

*   *   *

Dalia watched the monitor. The helicopter wheeled, broadcasting a vertiginous bird's-eye view as the searchlight found a copse of pines. Twelve men wearing helmets and gas masks, camo, and tactical body armor formed a tight circle and converged.

Team leaders exchanged signals, and silver tubes fired in unison. CS grenades billowed gas through pine boughs. Snipers posted on neighboring rooftops shouldered rifles equipped with infrared scopes.

Flashbang grenades followed the CS into the trees. Muffled concussions blew needles and branches into a funnel. Team members brandishing M4 rifles advanced smoothly across backyards. Dalia's anticipation was so intense it verged on nausea.

The circle closed. Men entered the stand of pines ... and came out, not with Song Sun Young, but pulling a yelping brindle-coated dog by the collar.

Dalia blinked.

By the time the all clear was given, spreading hazes of tear gas had dissipated into the night. A report was relayed to DeArmond. The phone had been recovered from a fanny pack affixed to the dog's collar. The animal was no doubt smarting from the tear gas, but otherwise none the worse for the wear.

Another report came from a quarter mile away, where another incursion team had simultaneously entered the address the phone was registered to. They had also led with CS and flashbang grenades. The locked front door had been battered down with a ram. Inside, they had found one old woman, recently deceased, multiple ligature marks at the level of the hyoid bone, stuffed unceremoniously into a hall closet.

*   *   *

The floodlit roadblock was bright as day. She saw reflective traffic barriers, local prowl cars, unmarked SUVs, turtle-shell helmets, Kevlar vests, and at least eight M4 carbines trained on the Jetta.

Song shifted to a lower gear. The engine revved as it caught. The Jetta slowed.

On the left side of the roadblock, spike strips extended onto the soft shoulder, but not all the way to the tree line.

She accelerated again, leaning down as low as possible. Shifting up again. For a moment, she sailed toward the checkpoint unimpeded. Then a spotlight found her, beaming directly into her eyes. She flinched, looking away. Tracers of light smeared her vision.

She had just scrunched lower when the windshield starred, one-two-three. A beat later, she heard the distant *pop-pop-pop* of gunfire. It sounded nowhere nearby, not even in this same reality.

With her view compromised by the dashboard and the smeary glaring spotlight, she plowed into an orange-and-yellow barrier.

The world rocked. A wall of white slammed into her face. Blood poured from her nose. The engine screamed in a high, climbing whine. The car was caught on something. She felt the wheels spinning, crunching, but not tearing free. Holes opened in the passenger door, and light poured through.

She hit the gas. Again. Her stomach rolled as, with a great heaving sway, the Jetta tried to clamber over something. To no avail. She risked a peek above the deflating airbag. She couldn't see what she had hung up on. But she saw a man in tactical gear standing five feet away, taking careful aim. She grabbed for the gun on the passenger seat. But it was gone, somewhere on the floor, beneath the seat.

She blinked furiously. Her eyelids were sticky. The substance sticking them together, she realized, was blood. *Her* blood.

She swiped a forearm across her eyes, then slammed the transmission into reverse. With a grinding wrench, the Jetta reared backward. A bright flower unfolded somewhere to her right, puncturing the night. She felt the shock wave, then heard the sound in delay.

Slewing backward, finding drive again, then plowing forward. This time, she hit a police cruiser low and hard, nosing it out of the way and gaining the road beyond as a miasma of smoke or gas or both spread behind her.

She glanced in the sideview mirror. Cracked glass, hanging by a thread, her crooked reflection looking right back at her. For some reason, she was grinning.

She aimed down the potholed road, flooring it.

She spat blood onto the floor. The car was riding lopsided, grinding along on rims, sparks flying behind her. But she was through the roadblock.

Two smoking holes in the dashboard. Two matching holes in the passenger's door. Three more holes starred the windshield. She realized dreamily that each hole corresponded to a bullet that had entered the interior of the car. And each bullet corresponded to someone holding a gun, who had tried to kill her.

She forced her eyes back to the road. Dark farmland rocketed past. The wheel vibrated crazily. Sparks danced in the rearview mirror. The engine whined, straining.

And then the searchlight: the helicopter giving chase, falling into place behind her like a giant, lumbering insect.

LANGLEY, VA

On-screen, the searchlight illuminated the roadblock—a crumple-hooded police cruiser and a crushed construction barricade. It swept on, quickly finding the racing Jetta, pinning it and keeping it pinned.

A gout of sparks poured from the right side. An orange glow might have indicated a fire starting inside the car. DeArmond was barking orders. Extend the perimeter; set up another roadblock; get boots and dogs into the woods in case she fled on foot; get backup air support.

Bach leaned against the table, trembling again. What was taking Luna so long? For the love of—

Ping.

"Fort Meade," Sam observed.

Bach's hands closed into fists. His thoughts must be written all over his face. But happily, no one was looking at him. They were watching the monitor. The helicopter kept the Jetta pinned. The vehicle was losing speed now as the exposed rims ground flat. Any moment now, Song would ditch the car and run for it. She would not get far.

Sam opened a new window and put the decrypted data up on the screen. Scanning the algorithm, he grunted softly. "Not sure what we're looking at here …"

Bach paused long enough to make it look good. *Don't cringe.* But he could feel his mouth pulling. *Don't let your voice shake. Five seconds more and it's done. It's done. Done.* He tried to steel himself by picturing his father. And the fat little Bond villain, the cartoon megalomaniac. And the melted badges, the ruined ambulances, the blood-soaked children. But what he pictured, strangely, was a small flower that had grown from a crack in the sidewalk near his childhood home. He had been three, maybe four years old. He had found the flower while riding his Big Wheel. A pretty yellow flower. So tender, so fragile, in the face of so much city filth and traffic. That it had grown at all was a miracle.

Dalia Artzi had sensed something. She had turned from the screen. She was watching him. He lowered the steel door in his mind. Negative air pressure. Do-mode.

He felt as if he had somehow stepped through a movie screen or onto a stage. Like when the doctor had given him his diagnosis. Except that now *he* was the one preparing to deliver the scripted line. Taking the dramatic pause. Biting his lower lip thoughtfully: the theatrical gesture.

His head pulsed with hot blood. *Do it!* Now, before his face betrayed him …

Affecting mild introspection, he said, "Send it to Shelby. See what she makes of it."

Shelby Choo was part of their team in Seoul. She knew Bureau 121 as well as anyone—it made perfect sense to request her input on this mysterious burst of code.

But the address Shelby Choo had always used now funneled the data not to Seoul, but back to Minot.

Sam nodded and clicked SEND.

Bach sagged as if poleaxed. He reached out a hand to steady himself against the conference table, but his fingertips slipped from the black beveled edge. The fluorescents in the ceiling seemed to buzz louder. He heard Dalia calling out, the quality of alarm in her voice, but the words unintelligible.

He collapsed into a sweet, humming semiconscious blur, soft and welcoming as a womb.

At last.

It was done.

Razzle Dazzle.

CHAPTER TWENTY

Seventy-five feet underground, behind twelve tons of reinforced steel-and-concrete blast doors, Deputy Commander Todd Li poked halfheartedly at his grilled chicken and mixed vegetables. He shot an envious look at the Lima Flight commander, who had brought his own meal. Some kind of rice bowl with avocados and black beans. Li kept meaning to pack a cooler himself. But this month, he was 7-0. Back on base, he barely had time to give his pecker two shakes after taking a piss. How on earth did the flight commander find time to make rice and prepare a bowl?

Li gave his rubbery chicken a final poke, then set down his fork and pushed the tray away. After signaling the commander, he unstrapped and left his seat. Inside the tiny head, he relieved himself. Then he gave it a good shake. In the bunker, unlike on base, there was nothing but time, waiting endlessly for an emergency that never came.

He washed his hands, working up a good lather, and dried off with paper towels. He went back to his chair—mounted on tracks so it could slide smoothly back and forth between shelved binders and knee-level lockboxes and eye-level consoles featuring phones, keyboards, sensors, monitors, and keypads.

He buckled himself back in: standard procedure in case the bunker took a direct hit. After a moment, with a sigh, he pulled the tray to him again.

As he lifted the fork, Lima Flight commander said in a subdued voice, "I have calibration alarms."

Indicator after indicator, alpha zero-two through alpha one-one, was turning red.

Li stared in disbelief. "Did we have DLC message transmit?"

"Negative. We …" Lima Flight commander paused to moisten his lips. "We have positive launch indications throughout the flight."

The flight consisted of ten Minuteman-III LGM-30Gs. Each missile stood sixty feet tall, weighed eighty thousand pounds, and packed twenty times the explosive power of the warhead dropped on Hiroshima. Five flights, aggregating to fifty missiles, made up a squadron.

If the sensors were to be believed, their entire flight had just launched.

"It's a drill?" Li asked.

Lima Flight commander shook his head.

For an instant more, Deputy Commander Li stared at the indicators. Then he grabbed the secure line, overturning the tray and scattering mixed vegetables across the console.

NORTH OF LAKE TOGUE, NY

A burst of automatic-weapon fire from the helicopter punched new holes in the roof. She swerved off the road, bumping over the shoulder, through a ditch, into forest. The car was done, anyway. Smoke rose from the mangled remains of the two right tires, from the undercarriage, from beneath the hood.

She threw open the door. A canopy of branches and leaves momentarily blocked her from the copter's line of sight. It was the best chance she would get.

But she paused. She needed the gun. She searched through broken glass in the well beneath her seat. Then the passenger seat. The acrid, sour smell of burnt rubber filled her nostrils. The world seemed to spin around her. From the distance came the sound of sirens, rising and falling. And closer in, the rotors, pounding the night, thrashing it.

She found the gun. Her fingers closed around the grip.

She left the car. In the strange light trickling through the canopy, she saw the forest floor slicked with something wet, which might be gasoline or might be blood.

She took a few aimless, staggering steps. Her free hand went to her face, searching for a wound. Was she dying?

No. Her legs still carried her. She was hurt. The airbag had broken her nose, but she wasn't dying.

The sirens grew louder. She moved away from the Jetta. *Now what?*

Another burst of gunfire. Leaves stirred, shushed, puffed. An intercom crackled. The voice was calm and measured. "Freeze. Put your hands on your head. You are under arrest."

Through the shushing leaves, she saw a glowing light. A lit window. Surprisingly close. Between her and it was a backyard: a swing set, a sprinkler, a Nerf football, a back porch.

She moved toward it as the sirens drew closer and her head whirled like a centrifuge.

CHEYENNE MOUNTAIN, CO

The signals traveled from SBIRS, the Space-Based Infrared System, to NORAD, the North American Aerospace Defense Command, six hundred feet inside the granite heart of the mountain.

"Ten heat plumes registering at Minot Air Force Base." The captain's voice was steady. "We've got ten launches from Minot AFB."

The four-star general who served as CINC-NORAD commander-in-chief crossed to the display in two long strides. "Valid launch?"

"Yes, sir. Jesus wept, valid launch."

"Incoming call from Minot," the warrant officer reported.

The general's facial muscles tightened. He paused for two seconds, then said, "Confirm with PAVE PAWS and SBX." PAVE was a military identification code. PAWS stood for Phased Array Warning System. SBX was Sea-Based X-band radar, mounted on floating rigs off the Alaskan coast. "Get C2BMC"—Command, Control, Battle Management and Communications—"and NMCC. Get First Heli in the air." The Hueys of USAF First Helicopter Squadron, based at Andrews, were tasked with carrying key members of the US government to the National Emergency Command Post at Mount Weather, to Site R at Raven Rock, to the airborne command centers of Night Watch and Looking Glass.

He rubbed his hands together, as if trying to wipe away an invisible stain. "And get the Gold Phone."

LANGLEY, VA

Benjamin Bach had never felt so tired. Over the past few days, of course, he had built up one hell of a sleep debt. But this fatigue went deeper.

He had finished what he had to finish. Now he could let go. Like those old married couples who died within an hour of each other.

His sleep would be long, he thought. And, God willing, peaceful.

In his mind's eye, he saw Esther Yong, his last lover. Despite the awkwardness of the affair, he had taken pleasure in it. The touch of skin on skin. He wondered where she was now. He hoped not Seoul.

He thought of his first lover, Mary Elizabeth Bianchi. She had walked around the Bronx barefoot. Fearless. And stupid. Every time they kissed, her mouth had tasted of warm beer and Juicy Fruit.

He thought of Dad, beaming with pride, giving him the tour of Windows on the World. Shoulders thrown back, trying to stop himself from smiling too much. *The best view in the history of great views.*

He thought of the pretty yellow flower growing in the sidewalk. Tar bunched up on either end. Broken glass and glinting quartz inside the tar. The flower struggling up anyway. Fragile yet tough. Tough. Fearless. Determined. Stupid.

The run of his thoughts bounced against the present—the missiles would be in the air now—and then banked back into the past. He remembered Grandma's funeral. Dad helping him with his tie beforehand. That had been pre–Windows on the World. Back then, Dad hadn't had much experience with ties. He had tried again and again, and again. The tie had ended up too short, too long, too short again. Benjamin Bach had braced himself. When Dad got frustrated, he yelled. But something had been different that day. Something had been missing. Dad had stayed calm.

At last, he'd gotten the tie just right. He gave it one final tug and then leaned back and looked at his son. Looked directly into his son's eyes. Warmth and kindness spilling out of him like golden honey, filling his son's brain, body, and soul. *It happens to everybody eventually,* Dad said, *so in a way it isn't so bad. But it's still sad when it does happen, because then that person isn't with you anymore. They're with God in heaven. That's where Grandma is. With Mom.*

Driving home from the funeral that afternoon, Dad had stopped at a traffic light. Moments passed. The light turned green, but Dad didn't go. He was looking out his window, up at the sky, head tilted, as if trying to tune in some kind of signal. Trying to tune in Grandma, young Benjamin Bach thought, up there in heaven with Mom and God.

Esther Yong's abdomen had featured a scar in the shape of a fishhook. He once asked her about it. An appendectomy? A C-section? She had said she would tell him when she knew him better. But she never had.

In the faded photograph of his grandfather, the eyes had burned. Even in sepia, even bleached with age, you could see the fire.

Razzle Dazzle Bach, the Battling Tail Gunner.

A hazy corkscrew led down. He spun along, not trying to slow his descent.

He thought of the dusty gray garbage bags hulking on curbsides in lower Manhattan. They had contained powdered Formica and asbestos and polystyrene foam. And human skin and bones and eyes and lungs and fingernails. He had breathed it for twelve full hours before receiving the old-fashioned two-canister mask.

The dust had taken two decades to finish its work, but all that time, his fate had been settled.

He didn't want to think about that. He wanted to think about the yellow flower, the touch of a woman, skin on skin. Sweet.

Peace.

The corkscrew steepened, leading into deeper darkness, and he rode down, down, and released a shuddering breath, without looking back.

*   *   *

Dalia began chest compressions. At some point, an EMT took her shoulder, drawing her away.

She let McConnell help her stand. The director of the CIA appeared in the conference room doorway. He was handsome, with a full head of silver hair swept back from an aristocratic brow. He paused for a moment, lifting his chin, absorbing the scene, then came forward and took a knee beside his fallen officer.

The EMT, now cutting away Bach's shirt, blocked Dalia's view of his torso. But she could see his face. Skin like cellophane, eyes half-lidded. For the first time, he struck her as handsome. He reminded her of someone. After a moment, she had it. He looked like Alexander the Great, as sculptured by Lysippus.

Her gaze moved back to the on-screen helicopter feed. The searchlight had tracked Song Sun Young into a forest. She had abandoned the car. She was surrounded. Trapped. Finished.

But Dalia's chest felt tight, and as she watched, other windows on-screen began opening, the monitor filling with tense, strained faces.

Sam was hailing the director. "Ten unauthorized launches," he was saying. "Six minutes ago, at Minot. Flight path consistent with North Korea or Vladivostok. POTUS in transit to the Presidential Emergency Operations Center."

Ten unauthorized launches.

Dalia looked at Bach again. That tranquility on his face. But beneath it, evoking Alexander, something cold. Brutal.

The director was leaving Bach, joining the teleconference. Sam patched him in. Acronyms were flying. From the White House Situation Room, the vice president asked about DAL. From Cheyenne, a brigadier general explained that Minutemen maintained no uplink/downlink communication after launch. Already midcourse, the missiles were beyond comm reach. From J3, a square-jawed man in dress blues, handsome as a groom in a wedding catalog, suggested BMDS, Ballistic Missile Defense.

Dalia felt dizzy. They used acronyms and tech-speak to gain distance, it seemed, to make themselves feel in control. To protect themselves from the ghastly truth. In this case, if she understood correctly, the truth that ten nuclear missiles were flying toward North Korea.

She looked again at Bach. Remembering her feeling that something was being kept camouflaged. Some hazard right underfoot, all around. Her unconscious mind trying to tell her something. But she had not been able to hear.

And now this. Ten missiles flying toward the Korean Peninsula.

Somehow, Bach had done this.

"Worth a shot," CINC-NORAD was saying from Cheyenne. "GBI—Godspeed."

CHAPTER TWENTY-ONE

NORTH OF LAKE TOGUE, NY

The doorbell rang.

Sarah Carmichael looked up from her magazine. Her husband, watching TV, seemed as surprised by the bell as she was. "You expecting someone?" he asked.

She shook her head, set down her copy of *People,* and went to see who it was.

She didn't recognize the young lady standing on their doorstep. Pale and shaken. Wearing clownish makeup—or was that blood? Grimacing a smile. Clutching her midsection in a way that seemed suspicious. If Sarah had seen a woman standing that way in a store, she would have thought the woman was shoplifting.

And that sound … She had thought the helicopter rotors were coming from the television. But no. And behind them were sirens, far away but getting closer. Before Sarah could put the pieces together, the woman said, "I hit a deer."

"Oh, my goodness."

"May I use your phone?"

"I …"

But the woman had already pushed past her.

SEVEN HUNDRED MILES ABOVE THE BERING SEA

Forty Raytheon Exoatmospheric Kill Vehicles rose like soaring sparks. As the Taurus launchers spent their solid fuel, gouts of flame faltered and died, and the boost vehicles began the long, dreamy tumble back to earth.

The Minutemen III held course. Decoy balloons deployed: dozens of Mylar inflatables streaking forward at twenty times the speed of sound, without friction or gravity to slow them, presenting the Kill Vehicles with a tempting target.

NMCC, lacking time to calculate a proper mission plan, had opted for quantity over quality. The forty interceptors represented the entire complement of GBIs based in Alaska, roughly halfway between the contiguous United States and North Korea. Thanks to a jury-rigged C2BMC patch between PAVE PAWS, SBIRS, and SBX, they were not flying entirely blind.

A shining silver net drew tighter, closing.

Minutemen and decoys alike exploded in showers of tumbling sparks. The ground-based interceptor system used a hit-to-kill approach, destroying targets with raw kinetic energy without detonating their payloads. W78 thermonuclear warheads tumbled back toward the frigid Bering Sea.

In the blink of an eye, eight Minutemen went down.

But two continued, driven by gimballed inertial guidance systems toward series of coordinates: latitude and longitude in degrees, minutes, and seconds, north-south and east-west.

In fourteen minutes, they would reach those coordinates.

NORTH OF LAKE TOGUE, NY

Song moved through a living room, past a man of about sixty watching the evening news from an easy chair, and into a bathroom.

"This is your last warning. Freeze and put your hands on your head. We are authorized to use deadly force."

She wet a hand towel in the sink, then pressed it across her nose and mouth, moving back into the living room just in time to catch a shadow chasing across the wall: a man crossing outside the window, backlit by a searchlight.

Glass splintered, tinkling. A huge windy gust swept through the first floor of the house—gas.

The gas spread quickly. She let her knees buckle, holding her breath beneath the wet towel. Hiding the gun in the hollow beneath her. Playing up her weakness, her soft helpless underbelly, inviting assault. Make them reveal their position, their numbers.

Two men wearing tactical gear and gas masks appeared from nowhere. She remembered the long-ago border guard beside the Tumen, five feet wide and ten feet tall. These giants were his brothers.

The sixtyish man was choking, gasping, falling from his chair. The incursion team moved past him without concern, weapons raised, approaching Song.

They could have shot her.

They didn't.

She fired. One ducked behind the sofa. The other returned fire. A dullness took her left leg, turned it to dead weight.

She ducked into the bathroom again, put her back to the wall beside the door. Pulse thudding hard in her temples. The gas beginning to dissipate already. With multiple windows broken, cross-ventilation would quickly disperse it.

The wall behind her buckled—a battering ram.

She snapped off a covering shot into the wall, encouraging the man or men out there to keep their distance. She fired again, again, again.

On the shooting range at Heaven Lake, she had always felt quiet competence. She had been a good shot. The neat, orderly holes in the paper targets had testified to her competence. Here, by contrast, there was no order. There was only chaos. Burnt powder, tear gas, and the slaughterhouse smell of blood hung in the air.

She left the bathroom. In the living room, a man lay facedown, twitching. Had she hit him? Was it the one who had been watching TV? She couldn't tell. Her head thudded horribly—echoes of gunshots, her own thundering heartbeat.

She was taking fire from a broken window. One, two, three shots, whizzing so close that her hair stirred. She felt cool, almost numb. Calmly she returned fire. She moved toward a kitchen, snapping off another round as she went.

She stepped into the kitchen. A man in SWAT gear lay crumpled against a wall. She saw no wounds. Another man was looking at the injured one. He had taken off his mask, perhaps to speak to his friend. He turned to face Song and she shot him between the eyes.

She shouldered open a back door and gulped clean air. She had lost the bag somewhere. Back in the car. The towel was gone, too. She ran toward the same woods she had just left. Trying to remember how many shots she had fired. She saw the carcass of the Jetta and veered away.

Her eyes were watering. Her ears were ringing. Her left thigh was soaked with blood. The flesh was purplish and swollen, the blood dark. The leg folded out from under her. She face-planted into a bed of half-composted leaves.

Shot. The thought was sludgy. She poked gently at her thigh. The wound was without feeling, but everything around it was aflame.

She tried to stand. Couldn't. Instead, she dragged herself up onto elbows and knee and hauled herself forward.

She could not stifle a cry, but she kept going. Now she had lost the gun, too. Twigs and dirt and blood smeared her face. Fresh splinters of pain shot from hip to torso. Her lips crimped into a jagged line.

Forward again. She heard thunder, breaking waves. The thunder was in her head. Barking dogs, helicopter rotors—those were real. Boots and paws blundering through woodland, twigs crackling.

She planted her elbows and hitched forward again. The air was full of smoke. She could not draw a breath, could not fill her lungs.

She collapsed. The smell of earth, rich and fertile, filled her nostrils. The smell of graves, of life, of death.

She thought of her mother, face bulging and purple, eyes horror-struck. Reaching out a hand to her daughter, wanting human contact in her moment of extremis. But Song had been too horror-struck herself to take the hand. And now that she was in a similar position, there was no one to reach out to. There was only hot darkness, waves of dizziness, smells of blood and encroaching death.

Death. The wages of sin. But she did not believe in sin. Or in fate. She believed in playing the hand you were dealt. Nothing else.

Breaking waves. Barking dogs. Crackling branches. Pounding rotors. A rising tide of darkness.

The tide went over her head. Then it lowered and she saw them all around her. Men with guns. Anonymous white shirts and blue jeans. Tactical gear and polished boots. Flashlights and crackling radios and the helicopter hovering overhead. A loudspeaker spitting static. Dogs straining against leashes. A closing circle.

She put her head down. Dark spirals filled her vision.

She closed her eyes. She released a breath.

Finished, at last.

It was a relief.

LANGLEY, VA

"Eight takedowns."

Dalia felt a collective, tangible lifting of spirits. Better than expected. The ground-based interceptors, previously untested against ICBMs, worked after all.

But it was not enough.

For several seconds, silence reigned in the conference room. On-screen, two Minutemen continued toward their targets. The time code on the live feed ticked past 20:31.

Then the brigadier general barked, "*Monterey,* you're up."

THE SEA OF JAPAN

Aboard the USS *Monterey,* the captain rubbed his chin. His wife made gentle fun of him when he rubbed his chin. *Ahoy, ye matey,* she said. During his last leave, he had grown a beard, which only encouraged her ribbing. Then when she caught him stroking his graying whiskers, she had laughed out loud and said, "You look like Ahab. Does that make me your white whale?"

Now his wife was five thousand miles away, and he was regulation clean-shaven. If God was with him, his wife would learn what had happened here today, only on some peaceful night far in the future, when he told her the story in a low voice and then swore her to secrecy.

Still rubbing his chin, he watched the two incoming missiles on the radar screen.

Just six months ago, he would have felt despair. The AEGIS system had not been designed to handle ICBMs. But Block III Alphas had bigger boosters, higher and faster, than their predecessor. According to Raytheon, they could intercept the target exothermically, during midcourse flight, so that the debris fell harmlessly into the sea.

Of course, Raytheon was in the business of selling missiles. Last year, the US government had paid them over twenty-five billion dollars. They would not talk themselves out of a sale.

He felt, rather than heard, the MK-41 vertical launching systems thunk into ready position. He asked mildly, "Online?"

"Online." The weapons officer matched his mildness. "System enabled."

"Target range?"

"One thousand miles."

"Special-auto."

The computer took over.

A few seconds of deceptive silence followed. Then the entire six-hundred-foot length of the *Monterey* shuddered as the first Block III launched.

"One away." The weapons officer sounded almost bored.

Another shudder. "Two away clean."

The captain's gaze traveled around the bridge, across intent faces illuminated by glowing screens. C2BMC, with an assist from Johns Hopkins Applied Physics Lab, had patched together AEGIS, AN/TYP-2, SBX, SBIRS, and PAVE PAWS tracking data to give the USS *Monterey* a composite picture of the two missiles' trajectories. But ballistic missile interception plans were notoriously tricky even with forewarning of targets, speed, and launch sites. An unexpected shot in a reverse direction, even with an abundance of off-board assistance …

Another shudder. And another. "Three away. Four away."

That was all the Block IIIs.

It would be their last chance. The Terminal High-Altitude Area Defense system based in Seongju under the control of the Thirty-Fifth Air Defense Artillery Brigade was intended only to intercept Hwasong-12s targeting US military interests in Busan and Kunsan. Its effective range was 125 miles. If the THAAD batteries had moved close enough to effectively protect Seoul, they would also have moved within range of North Korean artillery.

The captain watched a monitor. Four pillars of gray smoke climbed. He remembered to breathe.

*   *   *

Four streaking meteors rose from the Sea of Japan where, thirteen hours ahead of the District of Columbia, chalky dawn had given way to blue morning.

Two Minutemen coasted through space.

The first Block III Alpha found its target, destroying the warhead with less than 130 megajoules of energy, creating an inferno of sparks and twisted metal without detonating the payload.

The wreckage tumbled down into the atmosphere, then into the cold water below.

The other three SM-3s missed, and continued out into the colder abyss of space.

The single remaining Minuteman III coasted toward its target, less than four minutes away.

LANGLEY, VA

Dalia watched on a real-time satellite map as the Minuteman III continued on its way.

Unstoppable now.

She set her jaw.

She would remember this day, she thought, on her deathbed.

Her eyes ticked from one window to the next. Sam was typing desperately, apparently running at top speed through North Korean websites and servers, trying to hamstring a counterattack. But he need miss only a single mobile launcher.

On a link to the fortified bunker beneath the East Wing of the White House, the commander-in-chief of the United States had appeared. He was dictating a message to a White House fellow, reporting an accidental launch of LGM-30Gs. The cause of the launch had been determined and neutralized. Targets were contained within the borders of the Democratic People's Republic of Korea. Armed forces were not being placed on alert. There was no intention of hostility. There had been no declaration of war. The message would not go to North Korea, Dalia guessed. Pyongyang lacked early detection capability. By informing them of the launch, the president would risk triggering retaliation. Instead, it would go to Beijing and Moscow, who, with their satellites and Arctic sensors, had surely already detected the incoming Minutemen.

She looked at the helicopter feed from Lake Togue again. A clean-up operation now. Police tape, windbreaks, forensic teams, big lights on scaffolding. Song Sun Young had been carried on a stretcher into a medical van.

"Let me talk to her," Dalia said suddenly.

The director, McConnell, Sonny, Sam, and DeArmond turned toward her as one.

CHAPTER TWENTY-TWO

In a conference room next door, Dalia settled into the chair, faced the laptop, and nodded. Sam touched a key, then leaned quickly out of frame. But the agent on the other side hadn't logged on yet. The connection remained dark.

Dalia took the moment to get her thoughts in order. She reminded herself to consider the woman who would soon sit before her, not as a North Korean, not as an enemy, not as a foreign agent. But only as a woman who, like Dalia, knew the horror of labor camps. Who, like Dalia, loved her two children.

The laptop's screen flickered.

Song Sun Young appeared on-screen. Face swollen, hair bedraggled, dried blood framing the upper lip. Dark eyes fatigued, and clouded from whatever painkillers they had given her. One eye was bloodshot. Broken blood vessels laced the nose. Yet still, she gave an impression of wiry strength, of coiled springs and calm readiness.

A small window containing Dalia's own face appeared in a lower corner of the screen. "She's all yours," said someone on the other end.

A moment passed as they regarded each other.

Song moved slightly. She was reclining on a cot inside the van. She unveiled an ironic smile. "The someone, at last," she said.

Dalia let a moment pass before answering. "I've met your children."

A twitch of annoyance, as if at a mosquito, briefly marred the face. Then the ironic smile returned.

"Lovely children." Dalia lowered her voice. She leaned in closer, as if sharing a secret. "The boy takes after his father. But the girl takes after you."

Something changed in the set of Song's face. She looked at Dalia impassively, but with something veiled underneath.

"I love my children, too," Dalia said. "More than America. More than Israel, my homeland."

Silence.

"I am more than my homeland. My life has been devoted to *tikkun olam.* Repairing the world. Regardless of race, religion, national borders."

Song looked at her through hooded eyes.

"You are also more than your homeland." Dalia raised her chin. "Song Sun Young," she said, "a missile is about to strike Korea."

The hooded eyes shone with cold fire.

"This is not an act of war. It's the act of a rogue agent. A desperate man. Now contained. If Pyongyang retaliates with full force ..."

The eyes flickered.

Dalia repeated it slowly, as if the words contained a riddle. "If Pyongyang retaliates with full force ..."

She spread her hands plaintively.

PYONGSAN, NORTH KOREA

Even this early, the marketplace was crowded. Kahn Gun moved between stalls, scowling. He saw no rice, no corn, and only shriveled, sad-looking jujube. In Pyongyang, he'd heard, they were eating well. They had dried squid and meat, rice, and lotus root. But here in Pyongsan, there was never enough. Things were not quite as bad as during the worst of the Arduous March, but they were getting close.

A clutch of Workers' Party special police pushed aggressively through the throng, jeering, looking for trouble. Kahn Gun, recognizing the better part of valor, left the market empty-handed.

He took the long way home, hoping to find seeding grass or weeds in the countryside to take the edge off his hunger. It was an imperfect solution. His own growling belly might be calmed by a few bites of weeds or bark. But his young daughter had a tender stomach and could not keep down such rough fare.

He searched in vain. Every edible thing growing up between dusty stones had already been picked. Except for acacias painted white to assert government ownership, which he dare not touch, trees had been thoroughly denuded of bark.

He would need to go into his carefully hoarded supply of soup once he got home. The thin broth of dried turnip leaves was all they had left. Or maybe … The neighbor was a friend. But Kahn Gun had found a jar of kimchi buried in the backyard.

His gaze tracked a shooting star hurtling in his direction.

The morning sun birthed a twin.

A thrill moved down his lean body—dread mixed with excitement.

The second sun moved to join the first. Boiling furiously, climbing into the heavens.

A boom roared, reverberating. Reflexively he covered his head. The earth shuddered, groaning on some fundamental fault line.

Then came heat. He ducked into a crouch, covering his face.

He peeked between his fingers, darkly fascinated.

A mushroom of fire was rising, spreading, slow and regal, wearing a skirt of dust and debris. He saw a flying bird disappear in a flash. Then the government-owned acacias turned to ash.

Keen winds pummeled him. His eyelashes singed. Every hair on his body stood on end, then disintegrated. His clothes caught fire. Then his skin. The wind lifted him off his feet. He was flying.

And pebbles, dirt, trees, railroad ties—the world flew with him.

The sky was red, blue, purple, orange, emerald. Every color he had ever seen, and many more. Reality itself cracked open—a red, gaping wound. The sight was beautiful and terrible, stunning and grotesque.

He could not close his eyes. His eyelids were gone.

Then the colors faded and combined.

First to white.

And then, mercifully, to black.

CHAPTER TWENTY-THREE

JARRETTSVILLE, MD

McConnell drove slowly, scowling through his bifocals. He was about to speak, no doubt to ask Dalia to consult the map again, when the Range Rover's GPS interrupted him. "Your destination is coming up on your right. You have reached your destination."

The property was screened by box hedges set far back from the road. Tuesday's rising sun backlit a grand center-hall Colonial. There was no fence, no garage, no window sticker advertising an alarm company, nothing suggesting unusual security. Curtains on the first floor glowed softly. Potted plants hung from the underside of a porch roof.

McConnell parked beside a Ford Ranger with smoked windows. A bird somewhere clucked bossily. Dalia caught a vague hint of poplar, an undertone of spruce.

A lantern-shaped fixture blazed by the front door. A single straggling white moth circled it. Dalia chose the brass knocker over the doorbell and gave it two brisk thumps.

Moments passed. She had the feeling of being watched, although she saw no camera or spyhole. McConnell waited beside her, humming absently under his breath. She didn't think he was aware of doing it.

Multiple locks worked: deadbolt, rim latch. Someone audibly programmed a four-digit code into a keypad, and the door swung open. A man with a shaved head gestured them in. Dalia's eye was drawn to a weapon in a side holster, almost concealed beneath tailored Hugo Boss. Her nose twitched, registering a complete lack of cooking or cleaning odors. Judging from the echoey acoustics, the sprawling house beyond the foyer was big but sparsely furnished.

The living room had a maritime theme: oils of ferryboats, Chinese junks, outrigger canoes, and topsail schooners. A large screen above a fireplace displayed an idyllic beachscape with palm trees and seagulls. The curtained windows let in only the barest gleam of sun.

In the kitchen, a heavyset man wearing a holstered weapon stood to meet them. He used a key to unlock a door, then moved downstairs into shadow. Dalia held the railing carefully, cane in her free hand, and descended with McConnell behind her.

The basement windows had been bricked over. A separate exit had been sealed with steel. Yet the space did not feel like a prison. The lighting was dim but kind, the air pleasantly scented, touched with honeysuckle.

Song Sun Young reclined on a black love seat. Her left leg had been bandaged and splinted. She took her time acknowledging her visitors. Arrogant. Or maybe the painkillers had slowed her. Maybe some of each.

McConnell opened his mouth, but Dalia cued him with a glance to remain silent. She set the cane and moved forward alone, leaving Jim McConnell and the heavyset man in the gloom near the base of the stairs.

"The someone," Song pronounced caustically.

"What does that mean?" Dalia asked.

No reply.

Dalia lowered herself onto a chair beside the couch. She caught subtler odors: decontaminants and antiseptics, latex and fresh laundry. The smells of hospitals.

Several moments passed. Dalia leaned in, speaking quietly, so the men couldn't catch the words. "We've done something good together," she murmured. "Let it be the start of something. Not the end."

Half of Song's face was hidden in shadow. The other half was swollen, battered—but perfectly composed, like a doll's.

"Nobody wants war." Dalia paused. "But at the same time, nobody dare look weak. See how this played out. We estimate the DPRK lost six thousand last night ..."

She had meant to present that fact more gently, but there it was. Perhaps the bald number, stated so nakedly, was her own effort to gain distance, to reduce the human cost to a statistic, to make herself feel some vestige of control.

"And there will be more losses in days and weeks to come. A radioactive plume blows downwind from ground zero. Fortunately, winds are light and trending east. There's no reflective cloud layer. It could have been much worse. But it is, by any measure, a terrible catastrophe. A profound crime against humanity."

Song said nothing.

"And yet," Dalia continued, "Pyongyang heeded your warning that retaliation would result in mutual destruction. They believed your message that the launch was accidental. They must have realized that the American government had gotten to you, but they listened anyway." She paused again. "I find that reassuring."

No response.

"Rather than retaliate, today they fight to save face. Instead of reporting a missile strike, they announced an accidental detonation, set off when they dismantled a testing site as promised during the Singapore summit."

No reaction.

"And the rest of the world conspires to maintain the illusion. Even China and Russia, who must have tracked the missiles, help to cover the truth. Because nobody wants Armageddon."

No reaction.

"You and I, working together, might sustain a unique back channel. We might make sure this never happens again."

No reaction.

Dalia leaned even closer. "Jews have a concept called *teshuvah*." Her voice barely above a whisper now. "The person who makes a mistake and then works hard to make amends, to repair the harm they have caused, is holier than the person who has never sinned at all."

No reaction.

But Dalia thought she caught something in the woman's eye: a small, hot spark, which was quickly hidden.

*   *   *

For several minutes after they left, Song sat motionless on the love seat. At last, she stirred. Moving cunningly in case of hidden cameras, she dipped her fingertips behind a cushion of the couch. She brought her hand to her mouth, as if covering a cough, and slipped two pills onto her tongue.

She swallowed. The pills left a bitter aftertaste. She found two more, covering a yawn as she put them in her mouth.

She swallowed again.

She would never go back to prison.

She would rather die.

She was the master of her destiny.

She had hidden ten of the pills since last night, stoically bearing the pain they were meant to take away. No one had noticed. Americans were too distracted by the ready availability of food and tobacco and alcohol and entertainment and sex, perfume and makeup and hair dye, lavish clothes of cotton and linen and silk, without a stitch of vinylon to be seen. They were too caught up in their limitless freedom.

Ten pills, she thought, would do the trick. She was considerably weakened. To call her stomach empty would be an understatement. And after swallowing the first two, last night, before realizing that she should hoard them, she had floated away on a bed of soft, sugary clouds. Even as she sent the message to the RGB, using the code phrase proving her identity, she had been floating, swaddled in light, watching from somewhere outside her own battered body.

She swallowed two more. Then told herself to be patient. Vomiting them back up would defeat her purpose.

She wished she could talk to Mark just once more. The kids. Her eyes teared up at the thought. She thrust the idea away viciously. Don't draw attention, fool; you'll ruin it.

Her family was dead to her. They had never been real, anyway.

Breathing was becoming a chore. Like when she had hidden in the coal train, escaping from Camp 14, with her brother huddled close against her. A great weight pressing down on them both. Black dust in her lungs, itching. She had willed herself not to cough, not to give them away. They would escape. They would survive. By sheer force of will. Or they would die trying.

She had pulled her brother close. Pressed her ear against his chest. Listening to the tick-tock of his respiration, using it to calm her own.

Her brother was far away now, beyond her reach. But the memory was here. *Tick-tock.* Yes.

She was okay.

She could do this.

Four pills remained.

When she reached between the cushions again, her hand seemed to go down forever. Maybe the six she had already swallowed would do the job. But she wanted to be certain. She wanted to take all ten. Feeling around with fingertips as blunt and heavy as anvils, she brought two more pills up at last, reminding herself in the final instant to cover the motion. Hidden cameras. They would pump her stomach if they realized …

She casually rubbed her mouth again, and the pills fell in. Then she closed her eyes. She felt sleepy. Behind her eyelids she saw guttering candles, buzzing flies, rats splayed open on shovel blades.

The man she had killed by the Tumen. Someone's son, she had thought. A husband, a father.

Dex taking his insolent bow after his piano recital. Baby Jia wriggling around in Song's lap, her tiny Cupid's-bow mouth pursed.

Two pills were still in her mouth, sour as vinegar. She swallowed. Almost there now.

After a hard life, she deserved a good rest. But she did not believe in *deserve*. There was only playing the hand you were dealt. Nothing else.

She found the last two pills. When she tried to lift them, her hand had grown terribly heavy. But somehow, she managed. When she tried to open her mouth, she lacked the coordination to get the tablets onto her tongue. And then to swallow. But somehow, she managed. That was what it should say on her tombstone, she thought wryly. *Somehow, she managed.*

Goodbye, Mark.

She swallowed. She smelled a trace of flowers now, fragrant honeysuckle.

Goodbye, Man Soo. Goodbye, Baby Jia. Goodbye, little Dex.

She should have left a note.

Too late.

She leaned back, settled her head comfortably against the armrest, and dreamed.

CHAPTER TWENTY-FOUR

PRINCETON, NJ

Dalia Artzi was back home by noon. They passed the Princeton Battlefield, an open, hilly plain where, on January 3, 1777, George Washington had capped off a spectacular rally that began nine days earlier with the crossing of the Delaware River. Deftly applying the core tenets of maneuver warfare—moving faster than the enemy thought possible, striking a blow and then withdrawing unexpectedly, decentralizing command, adapting to difficult terrain—he had provided his troops with a much-needed boost in morale. And not a moment too soon. In late December 1776, the early successes of the American Revolution were already a quickly fading memory. General William Howe, having received bountiful reinforcements, controlled over thirty thousand troops in America, the largest British expeditionary force in history. In contrast, Washington's Continental Army and its attendant militias numbered fewer than ten thousand. They had been ill trained and poorly equipped, racked by hunger and disease. For General Washington, the flash of military brilliance had been exceptional. The man possessed many undeniable strengths, but as a tactician, he had been mediocre at best. Yet he had come through when it mattered.

The Range Rover passed a small white pattern-book cottage,

once home to Albert Einstein, then turned right onto Prospect Avenue with its mansion-like eating clubs—Princeton's version of fraternities and sororities. Preparations for the night's festivities were already gearing up as boys with linebacker shoulders unloaded kegs from 4Runners and Tundras.

Beyond "the Street," as it was known, houses came in a jumble of styles: midcentury moderns with lots of glass and flat rooflines, a few regal Queen Annes, and a handful of teardowns waiting to happen if only aggressive real estate developers could gild the right palm.

Drawing up before Dalia's duplex, McConnell eased to a stop. He looked at her through his smudged lenses. She nodded curtly and found her cane.

"Dalia," he said. "Thank you."

She grunted.

Inside, her desk looked just as it had on Friday afternoon. A slanting pile of books: Clausewitz, Keegan, du Picq, von Moltke, Dragomirov. Her laptop, waiting for her to get back to the banks of the River Pinarus in November 333 BC.

Bee-beep—McConnell giving a double blip on his horn as he drove away.

She sighed, and leaned more heavily against the cane. For a moment, she felt her mind slip, slip … and then catch, like a transmission clicking into drive.

She would bathe. Eat. Rest. Brew tea.

And then get down to work. The monograph about Issus now seemed timelier than ever. Song Sun Young had repeatedly trumped superior manpower with exemplary maneuverability. Dalia had, in the end, managed to apply some of Alexander's genius herself, defining the battlefield of her choosing—one not of mutual nuclear annihilation, but of behind-the-scenes strategizing. The need to remind future policymakers of ancient lessons was imperative.

Before moving to draw a bath, however, she lingered a few moments in the study, considering souvenirs she had seen many times before. A fragment of German 5.9-inch howitzer shell from Ypres. A minié ball from the Muleshoe at Spotsylvania. A bullet casing from an isolated cottage in nearby Hopewell, New Jersey.

For someone who called herself a pacifist, her ex-husband had said, she certainly liked to immerse herself in war.

The better to avoid it. If she had not heeded McConnell's call, how many more would be dead today? Strike, counterstrike. Thousands, millions. She could all too easily imagine a thermonuclear conflict spreading beyond North Korea and the United States—to India, Pakistan, China, Taiwan, Russia, the Persian Gulf. Hundreds of millions dead. Even billions.

All sparked by a single man.

Using insight provided by Woody Whitlock, the square-jawed head of J3, they had reconstructed Bach's actions. The terminally ill CIA officer had used a top secret Pentagon supercomputer to seize the reins of America's nuclear arsenal. He had personally activated Song Sun Young, exploiting her as a pawn to justify using that arsenal. He had justified the justification by accessing another CIA compartment, which had scrutinized key American financial infrastructure that might be vulnerable to manipulation by foreign agents, and coming up with the name William Walsh.

Too much power, Dalia thought, concentrated into too few hands, invited arrogance such as Bach's. Of course, the root word of *arrogance* was *arrogate,* as in to arrogate control.

Yet part of her—although she hated to admit it—couldn't help but wonder whether perhaps history would show that Bach had been right. He had wanted to accept the short-term pain to reap the long-term benefit. Every child understood the wisdom of tearing off a Band-Aid all at once. By stopping him, Dalia might unwittingly have contributed to a greater disaster down the road. Pyongyang's nepotistic regime remained in power. Its promises of disarmament rang hollow. This had been the most recent Battle of Korea, but very likely not the last.

Her *kibbutznik* side retorted: North Korea would not be the only rogue nation to achieve nuclear capability. One's enemies could not all be stamped into rubble and ash. Brute force was not the solution. They must instead learn to coexist.

She collapsed into her desk chair.

Maspeek. Enough.

But her mind ticked stubbornly ahead.

She could not bury her head in the sand, because her grandchildren woke up every day knowing that people wanted them dead. Wiped off the face of the earth, pushed into the sea. And if they should forget, their enemies were all too happy to remind them. Loudly, shamelessly. With rallies and effigies and troop movements … and ovens and lampshades and mass graves … and Hwasong-15s and miniaturized thermonuclear warheads … and daggers and stones and checkpoint bombings and SCUD missiles and Zyklon-B. Her grandchildren could not board a bus without scanning every face, looking for the one that didn't meet their eyes in return. Stiffening at every stop as each new potential killer came aboard. Taking every stranger's measure, maybe edging toward the window, knowing that those in the aisle seats would absorb the brunt of the blast.

But someday soon, those blasts would become atomic. Then window seats would offer scant protection. In Beersheba, half the population would be killed outright by a single nuclear detonation. A double strike on Tel Aviv, home to Dalia's children and grandchildren, would vaporize a quarter of a million instantly. And that would be only the first wave of dead. She had once worked up a simulation with RAND. She remembered the mood in the office—wisecracking, bluff. The horror had been far too great to consider straight-faced.

But neither could they become too comfortable in their own righteousness. Dalia rejected the doctrine of *ein breira,* "no alternative"—the viewpoint that Israel, surrounded by antagonists who sought its annihilation, had no choice but to strike first and fatally. Because preemptive doctrines *created* "situations" like the one haunting them from Gaza and the West Bank. Having second-class citizens created "situations." Israel's string of tactical victories had led to a strategic dead end.

And an Israeli response to a nuclear attack would deliver two hundred fusion weapons with yields ranging from twenty kilotons to one megaton. Dense population centers and the reflective effects of basin cities surrounded by mountains rendered Iran's sixty-nine million people especially susceptible to nuclear holocaust. Earthquake-sensitized populations were apt to rush outdoors after blast damage from a detonation, increasing their exposure to radiation. Half the dead would be children under the age of eighteen.

The twenty-five million citizens of North Korea were also innocents, victims who had already suffered horribly.

Dalia—and Bach, and the Pentagon, and Tel Aviv, and Pyongyang, and Moscow, and Beijing—could not simply dehumanize the enemy, thus justifying the preemptive wiping clean of the slate. The North Koreans were not animals, no matter how brutal their behavior might sometimes seem. In fact, Pyongyang's shrewd pose of unpredictability had paid handsome profits. Cultivating a volatile image had enabled them to cross one red line after another without provoking a serious international response—and then, when the time came, to seek legitimacy by coming to the world stage from a place of relative power.

One could not crush the enemy.

But neither could one bury one's head in the sand.

It had to be the middle way: skilled diplomacy and real statesmanship—neither crushing the enemy nor kowtowing to his every demand.

But that path was dark and shadowed and tangled by weeds. Hard to find and even harder to stick to.

Sparrows perched outside commenced a session of name-calling. *Cheap, cheap.* And the retort: *Whoo-mee? Whoo-mee?*

There was cause for hope, Dalia told herself. Humanity had reached the twenty-first century without seeing mushroom clouds over Washington, Moscow, Beijing, or Jerusalem. Proof that the species nurtured at least a spark of sanity. The trick would be to fan that spark into a flame. Forsaking nationalism, uniting humanity into a single global community with no borders and, thus, no enemy tribes to fight.

That was her kibbutznik self talking, of course. Her mother, who had survived Auschwitz, would have answered with a snort of derision, *Az Got volt gelebt oif der erd, volt men im alleh fenster oisgeshlogen.* If God lived on Earth, all his windows would be broken.

Dalia kneaded one eye. So tired …

An incoming SMS message dinged on her phone.

Her daughter. An image was attached.

She opened it and scowled in confusion. A Rorschach test. Swirling black and white lines. She saw snow in those lines. Tangled roots, whinnying horses. A frozen lake, a hasty retreat. Atomic fallout. Radioactive dust and ash incorporated with the products of a pyrocumulus cloud. More than six thousand dead.

Then something clicked, and the Rorschach image resolved into an ultrasound.

Another text appeared:

> I wanted to talk to you, but I've been trying for days and can't get through. Meet your new granddaughter. !!!Happy birthday, Savta Dalia!!!

As a slow smile began to spread, the phone rang in her hand. Not her daughter.

McConnell.

EPILOGUE

MANHATTAN, NY

The Range Rover pulled over before the green awning. Before grabbing her cane, Dalia took the lay of the land. The sinking sun had acquired a hint of copper. But the city that never slept showed no indication of slowing down. A doorman was signing for a package, then stealing a sip of coffee before rushing to hold the door for a woman and her miniature poodle. Two deliverymen were balancing a huge box, waiting their turn to enter the lobby. A man cradling a phone against one shoulder adjusted an enamel cuff link as he hailed a cab.

McConnell turned to look at her, one brow raised.

Dalia sighed, then nodded.

She planted her cane on the sidewalk, then followed it with her foot. As she approached the awning, the words she had rehearsed during the drive from Princeton moved restively through her mind.

I come as the bearer of bad news.

She was moving slowly, buying time. Not eager to have this conversation.

"Dalia Artzi," she told the doorman, "for Mark Abrahams."

She waited as he buzzed.

But you deserve to know, she would say.

Your wife is dead.

The doorman listened to his phone, nodded, and waved her on. Dalia proceeded through the lobby, past urns of hydrangea and peony and dahlia, Tiffany-shaded wall lamps, hand-carved marble, ornate molding elaborately wrought. How had this luxury struck someone who came of age amid the deprivations and degradations of the Hermit Kingdom?

However much Song had hated America, she had, in the end, loved her children more. That much, at least, Dalia had gotten right.

There's more, she would tell Mark Abrahams.

It's a lot to get your mind around. And the details must remain classified. If anyone asks, I never told you this. But you should know: Your wife's true name was Song Sun Young. She was sent here from North Korea, as an agent to work on their behalf.

The best lies, of course, hewed as closely as possible to truth. But the most creative ones strayed far afield.

The jihadist named Yusuf Bashara discovered your wife's true identity. We suspect ties between Pyongyang and Tehran. He blackmailed her. Apparently, he wanted her as a collaborator. But she escaped. She came to the FBI, but not before receiving a wound that ultimately proved fatal.

Mark Abrahams would believe it. Because, although the details were false, the emotional essence was true. Song Sun Young had, in the end, redeemed herself.

Your wife was a victim. She was caught in a political crossfire, but she died a true hero.

Dalia reached the elevator. Her heart broke into a trot. Her stomach felt sour. She pressed the call button.

She prevented Bashara from claiming countless innocent lives. In return, she gave her own.

The elevator door opened.

Dalia didn't move. She was dreading this. The eyes of the children—that was what would get her.

But her life had been devoted to *tikkun olam.* Repairing the world.

Song Sun Young had earned this.

When it was done, Dalia could go home. Call her daughter at last. And celebrate her new, yet-unborn grandchild.

There was cause for hope, she thought again. There would always be thaws and freezes, tensions and rapprochements. But so long as people like Dalia and Song existed on both sides, hope would never be lost.

The thought brought a faint and fleeting smile.

A last hesitation. Then she set the cane and moved forward.

END

ACKNOWLEDGMENTS

Thanks to my agent, Richard Curtis, for his many contributions to this book. And to Lieutenant Commander Rob Watts, US Navy. And to Mandi Moolekamp and Noah Green, and Christopher Brennan. Very special thanks to Michael Libertazzo. And to Fred Moolekamp, who was extraordinarily generous with his time and his patience, his ideas, and his knowledge.